DAYZEE DAZZLE

AND THE

KILDARE KILLERS

Other Books by Edward Allen Karr

SERIES: Thrills N Kills in the Hills
(Racy, Comical Horror in Beverly Hills)
Dayzee Dazzle and her Manic Mansion – Book Two
Dayzee Dazzle and the On-Set Onslaught – Book Three
Dayzee Dazzle and the Cadaver Collectors – Book Four
* * * * *

SERIES: Socrates Lewis Stories
(Psychological/Religious Fiction)
Crosswinds – Book One
Crossovers – Book Two
* * * * *

SERIES: Fringes Of Infinity
(Contemporary Fantasy Fiction)
Lin Finity and her Mayhem Rising – Book One
Lin Finity in Holding On – A Novella
Lin Finity and the Words Unspoken – Book Two
Lin Finity and the Islands of Time – Book Three
Lin Finity and the Flights to Forever – Book Four
Tayo Tersoo and the Hunter of Souls – Book Five
* * * * *

SERIES: A World So Close
(Middle-grade Fantasy Adventure & Coming of Age)
Jayden Blue and the Gift to Imagine – A Prequel
Jayden Blue and the Sword in his Shadow – Book One
Jayden Blue and the Call of the Wings – Book Two
Jayden Blue and the Lair of the Iron Lions – Book Three
Jayden Blue and the Journey to Val ka'Yoom – Book Four
Jayden Blue and the Forest of Night Fallen – Book Five
Jayden Blue and the Wait of the Sun – Book Six
* * * * *

DAYZEE DAZZLE

AND THE

KILDARE KILLERS

Thrills N Kills in the Hills
Book One

Edward Allen Karr

LAKESIDE
LETTERS, LLC

Lakeside Letters, LLC
30628 Detroit Road, #247
Westlake, OH 44145

This is a work of fiction. Names, characters, businesses, events, and incidents are the products of the author's imagination. Any resemblance to actual persons, living or dead, or actual events is purely coincidental. Certain long-standing institutions are mentioned, but the characters are imaginary. The opinions expressed are those of the characters and should not be confused with those of the author.

Dayzee Dazzle and the Kildare Killers
Thrills N Kills in the Hills Book One
©2021 Edward Sechkar.   All rights reserved.

No part of this book may be reproduced in any form, stored in any retrieval system, or transmitted in any form by any means—electronic, mechanical, photocopy, recording, or otherwise—without prior written permission of the copyright holder, except as provided by United States of America copyright law. For permission requests, submit a written request to the publisher at the address shown.

First Edition, 2021
www.LakesideLetters.com

Cover design by JD Smith Design
Editing by Preferred Proofreading, LLC

ISBN-13: 978-1-950886-19-7

"Yep, we'll just put the burnt mess in some plastic bags at the curb," said Sophia with a smirk.

Marilyn laughed and said, "After it all cools down."

"Right, Sis. We can't leave smoking body parts at the curb."

"Are you sure nobody will notice all that in the trash?" said Marilyn.

"Such a sweet kid," Dayzee said while grinning and shaking her head. "It's Beverly Hills, remember?"

From Chapter 15 – That Limo Ride

Table of Contents

Chapter 1 – Dayzee Dazzle

"Dammit, Dayzee, this is just too weird. Do I really need to be here?"

Jiff Roberts stood just inside the closed door of the plush room in a hotel on Wilshire Boulevard. Bright mid-day sunshine filtered in through the white curtains, which blew around from the light breeze.

"Oh yeah, Jiff. I want a special photo for your next creation."

She'd let her photographer in after she'd nudged the other man onto his back on the bed. The door had closed itself, Dayzee had latched it, and Jiff stood with his camera, staring at the bed. Just seconds before opening the door for Jiff, she'd yanked the other man's jeans down around his knees, but his white shirt was still buttoned most of the way up.

"He looks like he's out cold. If it wasn't for that,"—Jiff pointed toward the man's obvious excitement—"I'd think he was dead."

Dayzee sighed after turning to look at the man on the bed, then she offered a weary grin to Jiff.

"No, he's absolutely fine. This is just what happens with all of them. He's not dead, but he's sure dying to give it to me."

"You want me to photograph that?" He pointed again. "Come on, Dayzee, that's not my kind of—"

"No, silly. Wait till I climb up there and get busy."

She led Jiff a few steps closer toward the bed and let go of his arm. She continued walking, her tall heels clicking on the polished wood floor as she slipped her blouse down over her shoulders and let it drop.

Wearing only a short skirt and a bra, she lifted one knee up onto the bed and turned to look at Jiff.

"This might be a good shot too. Take a few, Jiff."

He shook his head, aimed his camera, and snapped a few photos. She turned back to the man on the bed and climbed all the way up. After throwing one leg over him and kneeling above him, she looked down on a man who appeared to be sleeping peacefully but was paralyzed by the potion she'd given him.

"You can take all the photos you want, Jiff, but when it really counts, I'll let you know. I want you to catch me at just the right time, alright?"

"Sure. Exactly what right time is that?"

"It's something you have to see to believe," she said with a grin. "You'll see."

"Sure, Dayzee. Whatever you say. It's just . . . I mean, I don't feel like—"

"Hush now, Jiff."

She took in a deep breath, expanding her chest then letting the air out slowly, smiling as she thought of the countless times she'd done it before.

"You know I need this. You're the only one that knows about me and this fun little game."

She looked down and saw the man ready for her.

"Real soon, I won't be so tired anymore."

She turned to Jiff and winked.

"Okay, time to rock and roll."

"No one rocks like you, Dayzee."

She rolled her skirt up and bunched it around her waist, showing the lean, fit body everyone thought she got from the gym. As she slowly dropped down, she found the one part of the immobilized man that still proved he wasn't dead.

"Ah . . . that's good. You can open your eyes now, lucky boy."

The man beneath her snapped his eyes open and stared up at her without saying a word.

"Aren't you thrilled now that I chose you? You're performing a service for me more valuable than you'll ever know."

"Why are you telling him all that crap, Dayzee? Are you sure he even wants to be here like this?"

"Oh, Jiff, you have no idea what he feels right now, but I do."

She began to bounce up and down on him, her strong legs flexing and looking soft and solid at the same time.

"Right now, he wouldn't leave if he could. He feels it working its way through him."

"That stuff, you mean?"

"Yeah, that stuff. All he wants is to give it back to me, and he will."

"You can't get it to work any way except—"

"There's no other way, Jiff. Only like this. He wants that more than anything, and I *need* that more than anything."

Jiff moved around the room, aiming and shooting from different angles.

"I want all of these for my personal collection, but the final one, that's the one you'll paint. Got it?"

"Yeah, Dayzee. Yeah, of course. But these are all pretty good. Any one of them would—"

"You don't know what's coming, Jiff. I've never told you, and no one has ever seen it. I wouldn't have known either, except the first time, I happened to look in a mirror at just the right time."

He dropped the camera down and said, "I have no idea what you're talking about."

"You will, silly boy. You will."

The only sound in the quiet Beverly Hills hotel room was the camera clicking and the deep breaths of the helpless man as Dayzee rose and fell repeatedly.

The man still stared at her, and she saw the confusion in his eyes, so she said, "In case you're wondering, I spiked your drink at the Prism. You wouldn't have volunteered for it, but now, you can't imagine wanting anything else. Isn't that right?"

He managed to nod his head so slightly that Jiff never saw it, but Dayzee did.

"You want only to give me what I need, isn't that right?"

The man nodded again, and Dayzee ripped his shirt open, sending buttons clattering and bouncing across the floor to each side.

"You feel it inside you, working its way through you. It's just about there now."

His eyes were locked on hers. She rose almost entirely off of him and fell back to rest on him. She'd pulled her skirt up tighter around her waist, revealing the strong legs that she knew helped keep her a star on the silver screen. She turned to her left again.

"Maybe you'll like this view better, Jiff," she said. "I do like getting you riled up."

She stared back at her cameraman with a faint smile as she reached up with both hands and brushed back her long blond hair. Then, she grabbed the thin straps of her bra, and she pulled them down along her arms until she'd almost exposed herself. She let the cloth hang up, and she held it there.

"When was the last time you saw these?"

"Last time I painted you," he said with a laugh. "You can't seem to stay dressed for that, can you?"

"The camera likes me naked. Besides, you never complain."

"Damn right, I don't."

"Yeah, you've seen them before, but you've never seen them bouncing like this, have you?"

Jiff stared in silence before softly saying, "God, no."

She continued a steady up and down, raising and lowering her hips on the helpless man and bouncing herself around for both of the men.

"I'm glad you're watching. I bet you're getting pretty excited yourself, aren't you?

"Hell yeah, Dayzee. I'm only human."

"Oh yeah, I sometimes forget."

"Huh?"

"Nothing. I'm giving you your inspiration. You can title the painting *Eternal Beauty*, or something like that."

"You know I love painting you, and I always will. But like this? Now?"

At the sound of Jiff's voice quaking, she got a sly smile.

"You're lucky I'm letting you see this. No one else ever has."

She let go of the straps, and the sheer garment slid down over her breasts, got snagged for only a moment in two places, then dropped down around her waist. She gave Jiff a wink as she pulled her arms free.

After shaking her hair back, Dayzee turned to look down and dug her manicured fingernails into the man's chest, just enough to draw out a couple of sticky beads of his blood. He gasped but didn't speak. He only looked up into her eyes.

"You wouldn't want to move even if you could, would you, sweetheart?"

She saw some veins bulging across his forehead and his temples, and thin trails of sweat began to slide down from up in his thick black hair.

"Let me know if you like this," she said, then she shook from side to side, swaying her full breasts.

"Ooh . . . I felt that! You did like it. Good boy."

She continued to twist each way, bouncing them and shaking them around.

"Oh yeah, that's even better in there now. You're being so good for me!"

She turned back to Jiff and said, "You like them, too, don't you?"

"You know I do, Dayzee. They're magnificent."

He shook his head at the sight and looked back up into her eyes.

"You paint with your hands, but the beauty of your art, that comes from your lust, doesn't it? That's why your paintings are so stunning?"

"Well, yeah, but—"

"Your desires go right into what you paint?"

"Yeah, but I never knew that until the first time I painted you."

"When you're painting me later, remember all of this. Remember the sight of all my skin, my hair thrown back, and my breasts swaying while I ride this lucky boy. And, when the memories get you . . . um . . . excited, *then* start the painting. That's your gift. Your feelings go right into your creations."

Jiff lowered his camera again and gazed at Dayzee.

"I know you like being in front of a camera, and I like painting you, I really do, but—"

"Then, you'll paint, silly boy, or would you rather take the next drink?"

"No. No, I don't want to. I mean—"

"Just a sip, tough guy, and you'll be on your back, too, just like this one. You'd love it."

"No, I don't think—"

"I'll pencil you in on the schedule for my next dose, alright?"

"Please, no."

Dayzee kept riding and smiled at Jiff.

"You don't know what you're missing."

"Yeah, well, I don't want to know. Do you have to hurt him, too, Dayzee? What's the point of that?"

"Do I really have to explain it to you right now?"

"Well, I wish you would. I don't want to watch you torturing some guy."

"A little bit of pain just sweetens it up for me."

"But you're . . . he's—"

"Here's the deal, Jiff: that stuff will heal him too. He'll sleep like a baby and be just fine when he wakes up."

"Seriously?"

"Oh, yeah."

She dug her nails deep into the man's chest, causing a low groan and more bleeding. She raised her right hand and sucked the blood off of her index finger while she turned to see Jiff staring.

"The camera, Jiff. Don't stop."

"Okay. Okay, I'm getting some good shots. How often do you have to do this?"

"It's getting more urgent—every other day does it—but I don't get as agitated from it as I used to. Still, it's like being reborn."

"It was different before?"

"Oh, God yeah. I'd be a horny monster right after doing it."

"How long can you keep doing that? You're going to live forever?"

"I don't know about forever. A long time, I hope."

"Well, whatever it's doing, you look damn hot tonight."

"Thanks, Jiff. Make sure your art shows that."

"When you first told me about this . . . this thing you do, you said once a month was good enough?"

The man lying beneath Dayzee groaned when she dragged all of her nails down his chest, leaving eight sloppy, bloody scratches.

"So what if it's every two days now? Can't argue with the results."

"No, of course not. You're drop-dead gorgeous, but—"

"But what?"

"Are you sure he's going to be okay?"

"I'm sure. They always are."

"I don't understand. How can that—"

"It's just the way it works, Jiff. I could do a lot worse to him, and he'd still be fine. I could probably kill him."

She laid her palms flat on his bloody chest and continued her steady motions.

"Not that I'd ever want to."

Without stopping, she turned back to look at her artist. She glanced down away from his eyes.

"Oh, look at you. It's obvious you like what you see. How about this?"

She sat up straight and rested down on the man. With both hands, she drew red lines across her breasts and the smooth skin of her chest above them, pushing her gold chains from side to side. She dipped a finger into the man's blood and dabbed it onto two prominent features.

She looked down from Jiff's eyes again and said, "Yeah . . . that gets your attention. I guess I have both of you just where I want you."

"God, you sure do, but—"

"I need you to be really turned on when you remember all of this. This painting is going up on the wall above my bed. Make sure it's a good one."

Jiff continued to gaze at Dayzee's blood-streaked breasts with a smile.

"He's being really good for me," she said as she scratched the man again and continued to bounce on him in the quiet room. "This guy won't fade no matter how long I do this."

Silence ruled the room as Dayzee kept taking the nameless man and played with his blood and the punctured skin of his chest.

"I'm taking my time with this one," she said to Jiff, "just because I want to."

"He hasn't blinked in a while, Dayzee. Is he still alive?"

"Of course, he is. He's kind of hypnotized by what he's feeling."

"And what is he feeling? The stuff, you mean?"

"Oh yeah, he's feeling it bubbling and boiling through him. He's getting real close now."

She held his face with both hands, decorating him with his own blood, and looked into his unblinking eyes gazing into her own. When she turned his head to one side, his eyes stayed fixed on hers.

"Yeah, he's alive, but he's past the point of even remembering how to speak. I love when that happens!"

She continued to rise and fall on the motionless man.

"All you need to know is that he's even more excited for me than before. I could show you, if—"

"Uh . . . no thanks."

"Anyway, he's sure getting close now. I can feel it. You getting some good shots?"

"God yeah, Dayzee. I think I've taken enough. Any of these would make a—"

"No, these have just been for fun. He's right on the edge of giving me what I need. That's the time for you to take the photo you'll paint from."

She looked back down at the man's torn and sticky chest just as a fountain of red sprayed up from his shoulder, a quick explosion that left a few drops clinging to the textured plaster ceiling and the rest raining down on Dayzee like a tossed glass of wine. Then, they heard the gunshot.

Jiff dropped to his hands and knees and covered his head. Dayzee never slowed down.

"What the fuck, Dayzee? Who's shooting at us?"

"Ah, here he comes," she said as she laid her palms flat on his chest and jiggled her hips up and down. "Oh, that's good. Such a good boy."

"Dayzee! Someone's shooting at us!"

She turned to Jiff with eyes burning like tiny little hot white suns. Despite the gunshot, Jiff stood back up, froze on the spot, and stared at her eyes, both so bright they blocked his sight of anything else and forced him to squint.

He held one hand up to block the light and said, "Dayzee. That's . . . I mean, that's—"

She breathed out heavily and said, "Dazzling?"

"Yeah! Oh, shit . . . that's why your name is—"

"Dazzle." She panted a few times. "Now you know."

"Yeah, Dayzee Dazzle. I had no idea. You mean that's . . . that's why—"

Her breathing evened out, and she said, "Take the photos now, Jiff. Now, while this wonderful boy is giving me all that life!"

She kept staring with her eyes blazing as Jiff took several more photos, standing still as if he'd forgotten all about the risk.

"Mm . . . oh, he's being extra good for me, just like I need," she said with a smile as she patted his cheek.

Just after she'd pulled her hand away, another bullet raced through his head, sending a sloppy pattern of blood and gore onto the pillow. Another crack of a gunshot followed quickly after.

"You need to get out of here! Never mind that!"

"Almost done. I want all of it. I *need* all of it."

"He just got shot! He got shot in his goddamn head, Dayzee!"

"Don't worry. He wasn't a good man at all. And he still hasn't lost it. That potion is to die for."

"Yeah, I guess so! He's going to heal from that? That stuff is that powerful?"

"I don't know, Jiff," she said with her eye lights reflecting off of the man's blood. "Can't say one ever got shot before!"

She closed her eyes and slowed her motions, but the smile never left her.

"Dayzee! Someone's shooting at you!"

She continued her slow up and down motions and said, "Or, you. Maybe they're shooting at *you*."

"What? Why would—"

"If you got the photos I wanted, pack your stuff and go if you're scared."

"Aren't you? How can you keep—"

She turned to him with opened eyes still burning brightly.

"Oh, I can't stop once I get started. But you go ahead and run. You're no good to me full of bullet holes."

Jiff held his camera in one hand while the other protected his face. After jerking open the door, he took one look back and saw Dayzee rubbing her bare breasts on the dead man's chest, smearing it all around and getting her even more excited. Her hips continued to rise and fall. She turned to smile at Jiff, two blazing eyes flaring at him.

"I know I'm acting crazy, Jiff. I'm not really like this. It's that damn potion."

"You're going to get shot! Get down off of there!"

"I'm glad the shooter's a lousy aim. Alright, I got all I wanted from this one."

She slid off of him and lay by his side, where she rolled him onto his side to block two more shots zipping through clean new holes in the window screen. The bullets found his back with dull thuds and little red geysers.

She rolled down off of the bed, leaving the spent man to take two more shots on his own, and she crawled toward the door. She and Jiff had just stepped into the hall, pulled the door shut, and moved off to each side as two bullets ripped through the door.

"Dayzee, who's trying to kill you?"

Dayzee pulled her tight skirt down and slipped her bra back up into place. She looked down with a grin at the blood she'd smeared all over herself.

"I have no idea, Jiff. But now that the rush is gone, I feel terrible for that poor young man!"

"It wasn't your fault, Dayzee. You didn't kill him."

"It's still upsetting. This sure isn't the best way to live."

"What do you mean?"

"I've been doing this a while, but I know there has to be more to life, that's all I'm saying. I'm going to need a drink or three, but now you know why I chose that name."

"God, that's a perfect name for you. Your eyes do that every time?"

"Mm-hmm. Yep. They sure dazzle, don't they?"

"I saw it, but I still can't hardly believe it. So, who wants you dead?"

"Oh my God, Jiff, I haven't exactly been a saint. Blame it on Beverly Hills."

"What are you going to do?"

"Try to stay alive, obviously! Other than that, I don't know, but I sure know who I'm going to call. If someone's trying to kill me, I need the Kildare Killers by my side."

"Sounds like a dangerous bunch, Dayzee."

"Yeah, they can be deadly as hell, Jiff. Mostly, though, they're just obscenely gorgeous!"

Chapter 2 – The Kildare Killers

"Refill, ma'am?"

Marilyn looked up from her magazine and shook back her blond hair with a smile and her bright blue eyes sparkling.

"Yes, thank you."

The girl serving her in the quaint coffee shop in Kildare poured more hot water and left a full basket of teabags before retreating. At the sound of the tiny bells on the door jangling, Marilyn looked up to see Sophia strutting through the doorway wearing the new black boots she said she'd buy.

"Very stylish, Sissy. Don't you ever get tired of black, though?"

"Oh, Sis, don't I look good in black?"

"You sure do. You're really good at showing off everything too."

"I like short tops and even shorter skirts, Sis. Clothes should be like a chain link fence: I'm properly covered but not really obstructing the view!"

Marilyn laughed and watched her twin sister fling back her straight black hair, giving a better view of her smiling red lips.

"Well said! You look hot in black, Sissy. You know you do. All the time, though?"

"I'm not as bad as you, at least. You insist on everyone calling you 'Marilyn,' and hardly anyone even knows your real name anymore."

"Well, Sis, no one here would be able to pronounce it anyway."

"That's true. Same with mine. Still, though, everyone thinks that's your real name."

"Don't you believe in reincarnation?"

"Oh, don't even start that again. I've been hearing that from you since we got here. They told us to blend in, remember? We had to study the culture and pick a style we thought we'd be comfortable with. Just because you picked Marilyn doesn't mean you *are* Marilyn."

"Well, for a while you thought you wanted to be Elvis, but Elvis never had a chest like that," she said with a grin while looking down at Sophia's cleavage showing above her low-cut sweater.

"Not until the jelly donuts caught up with him!"

"Yes, you're right! I'm glad you gave up that Elvis bit. You're a seductress, so Sophia is a perfect fit for you."

"Thanks, Sis."

Just as Sophia waived for the server, Marilyn's phone rang in her purse. She slipped it out and gave it a look, smiled, and set it to speaker.

"Dayzee! I was just thinking about you! How are you?"

"Oh, life's more interesting than I can tell you over the phone. I need your help. Your sister's too."

"Why? What's going on?"

"Someone's trying to kill me. I barely got away without getting shot."

"Okay, we knew this would happen eventually, didn't we? What did we tell you about married men and—"

"No time for a lecture, Mare."

"Fine. Where are you? We'll jet over there as quick as we can."

"I'm still in L.A. When you know your schedule, text me. I'll meet you at our fave hangout—the Prism. Get here quick, alright?"

"Don't worry, Dayzee. The Kildare Killers are on their way."

"Ooh, I like the sound of that! I feel better already. Tell your ravishing sister I said hi."

"I'm right here, Dayzee. Can't wait to see you again."

"Hi, Fia! Okay, see you girls soon."

Marilyn ended the call, put her phone away, and took a sip of her tea. Sophia had received her coffee, and before taking a drink, she held up the cup, and Marilyn clinked hers against it.

"Well, here we go again, Sis, but that's part of our job, right? When any one of us needs help—and we always do at some point—we have each other's backs, no matter what it takes."

"Yes, this time it's Dayzee. It'll be nice to see L.A. again anyway. We get our biggest thrills there, don't we?"

"Oh yeah, Sis. And our biggest kills too."

"You're funny, Sissy. You know we've never killed anyone there."

"Not yet," she said with a smile before her big blue eyes smiled at her sister through the steam rising from the coffee she sipped.

*   *   *

After finishing their drinks, Sophia made a call. Several minutes later, they exited the shop and climbed into their limo for a short drive to the airport. Marilyn tapped on the acrylic separating them from the driver. He turned only enough to show that he was listening. He couldn't see, but she gave him a playful smile anyway.

"Make it snappy, mister. Don't make me turn up the heat on you."

"Oh, Sis, you wouldn't. He doesn't deserve that."

Marilyn turned to face her sister.

"No, of course not. I'm not that kind of girl anymore. He'd like it, though."

"Yep, he sure would. But then, who'd get us to the airport?"

"I could probably drive this thing if I had to."

"Oh, sure. You haven't driven yourself anywhere in years. It's nothing but limos for you, Ms. Marilyn."

Marilyn laughed and glanced out her side window before turning back to Sophia.

"You might be right about that. Okay, I'll just let the man drive."

Sophia gave her a look with her eyebrows raised.

"For now."

*   *   *

Their private jet was fueled and ready to go, so they boarded and took their seats.

"Where's my butler?" Marilyn said with an impatient frown. "I need a drink."

"Sis, he's not your butler. He's a flight attendant. I swear . . ."

Marilyn's butler took their drink orders, turned away, and began the walk to the galley.

Sophia turned to watch the man walking away to fetch their drinks and prepare for takeoff and said, "You weren't really going to burn up the driver, were you, Sis?"

"No, I guess not, but I've never come close to feeling that good since that one time."

"Back when we first got to Kildare, that was the best, right? Do you even remember that?"

Marilyn's face lit up with big smile.

"Of course, I remember! We'd just arrived here as eighteen-year-old twin sisters."

"Well . . . Earth years, you mean," Sophia said with a smirk.

"Yes, of course, and right away, I found out how weak earthmen are. I really didn't know that would happen."

"Bad for him but good for you?"

"It was really good for me. I don't regret it much, but that's only because I didn't know that would happen."

Sophia lost her smile and looked into her sister's eyes.

"It really did bother you to kill him like that, didn't it?"

"Yes, but you should have seen his face when I was done with him. What did you see that first time for you?"

"What did I see?" said Sophia. "That he looked insanely happy!"

"Dead but happy. That's how I left him. Isn't that how you left yours too?"

"Yep, he was happy like you wouldn't believe, and then he was just dead. He's still dead."

"So," said Marilyn, "we both killed, and we both made them happy. We're quite a team."

"The Kildare Killers . . . that's us. I'm glad Dayzee gave us that name right before she left for Hollywood."

"Yes, I remember, Sissy. I still wish she hadn't run off to be a star like that."

"Well, so did we, Sis. Maybe we should think about moving there permanently too."

The jet had taxied out and began its screaming dash down the runway. It angled up sharply, pinning the sisters back into their seats, then it began a more gradual climb on its way to the U.S.

"Alright, things have settled down. Tell me again, Sis," said Sophia, "about the first time. I never get tired of that story."

"Okay, because I never get tired of telling it. I'd just studied a whole bunch about human culture and decided Marilyn was a good fit for me. At first, I didn't think anything about how I really was her reincarnated, but after a while, I realized—"

"Right, Sis," said Sophia with her eyes rolled up.

"Anyway, we had to set up some kind of lives for ourselves so we could fit in, so I enrolled at the local college as a freshman. The very first day, I saw a poster about tryouts for this Broadway type of production. I showed up that evening, and I wore a short white dress, just like that other Marilyn would."

"I bet that turned some heads."

"It turned all of them. I've been told my legs are quite a sight."

"They sure are. They're scrumptious! How about mine, though?"

"Yes, of course!" said Marilyn. "Your legs are so hot! But one guy really caught my eye. I think he was a senior, and he couldn't stop staring at my legs. After the practice, he and I hid ourselves away and let everyone else leave. The theater had only some dim security lights on, and I walked out to stand at the center of the stage. I wore heels too . . . did I mention that?"

"Yep, you always mention that, and you always wear heels too."

"Yes, I do, don't I? So do you, Sissy. Anyway, I stood there looking out over the dark and empty seats, thinking about what I was about to do and also about how I'd like those seats full, watching me with him. Is that a bad thing?"

"No, I don't think so. Cameras like us. The audience sure would have been shocked, though. And scared!"

"Don't you mean they would have been turned on?"

"Well, maybe in the beginning," said Sophia, "then they'd sure be shocked and scared."

"Yes, they sure would. Anyway, I felt him coming up behind me. I wanted to stand over an exhaust fan, or a grate, or something like that, because that's what I like to do."

"That's what Marilyn does."

Marilyn nodded and said, "Right, that's what I do."

Sophia shook her head with a grin and let her continue.

"There wasn't any wind to lift up my dress, so I pulled it up myself. I just pulled it all the way up to my waist, and I was wearing the tiniest of white panties. I knew what he saw: my long legs in high white heels with only that thin piece of cloth in the way. That boy didn't have a chance."

"No one could resist that! So, what did he do?"

"I felt him kneel behind me, and then his hands were on my hips. I swear I felt him shaking a little. He pulled down on the thin elastic, working my panties down slowly, and I shifted my hips from side to side to help him. He took his time, too, like he was hypnotized."

"He kind of was, Sis," said Sophia. "That's what we do."

"Yes, we do, don't we? So, he finally dropped my panties down around my ankles, and I kicked it off into the shadows. Still holding my dress up, I turned to face him. He held me by my thighs and got the first taste of my heat, which at that time was only a normal temperature, of course."

"Not for long, though, right?"

"No, but it really got hot when he laid himself down on his back. For a human, he sure was ready, if you know what I mean."

"Do I ever. I always get that reaction too."

"I know you do, Sissy—you're absolutely stunning!"

"Of course—we're twins. So, what happened next?"

"I didn't waste any time. I knelt on each side of him and made sure we had a good connection. He didn't give me enough—I'm not sure any human male can—but it still felt good, and I liked the smile on his face."

"Then, you started giving it to him good, right? And then—"

"Yes, and then, I felt my heat turn on. Like it's supposed to. Only then did I wonder if a human can take that kind of heat, but it felt so good that I couldn't stop. I was really giving it to him, up and down, over and over, and I felt the temperature climbing. My thighs were starting to singe him, and I felt my hands getting hot on his chest too. I smelled burning hair first."

"The heat does make it feel so much better."

"It really does, Sissy. I was hot all over, but then he got this anguished look on his face, and I knew it was too much for him. Right then, I learned that humans are so fragile, but I still couldn't stop."

"So, you didn't stop, did you?"

"I sure didn't. I knew it hurt by the look on his face, even with that big smile of his, but he didn't want to get away. He never stopped smiling, even when the glow from my heat lit up the stage floor all around us. And . . . the pleasure I felt when I let it loose all the way. God, Sissy, it was delicious. I felt bad for him, but I was crazy with pleasure, and I only smiled at my hands burning into him too."

"He still didn't try to get away?"

"No, he loved it. He still smiled, but really, he was mostly dead at that point. I still didn't stop. I kept working on him and squeezed him with all the heat I had. I knew he was frail and that I'd killed him, but it felt so good that I didn't care. At the time, I figured it was his own fault for being so weak."

"They sure are weak, aren't they?"

"Oh, yes, and I didn't feel bad about killing him until after I'd had a monster orgasm. I swear, Sissy, it was like raw electricity racing all through me, but especially you know where."

"I do know where. It's like that for me too. We're sure built to feel good, aren't we?"

"Yes, we are," said Marilyn. "Do you think human men can sense that?"

"Yep, Sis, just by looking at us. When you finally finished and stood up, and you looked down at him, what did you see? Oh, this is the best part!" Sophia said while struggling to not laugh out loud.

"He was all burned up everywhere I'd touched him, even the bright palm prints on his chest, and he was smoldering everywhere. Once that fire gets going, nothing stops it!"

"It's really something."

"I stood right above him, over the smoking ashes, and a few drops fell onto what was left of him a couple of times. Each drop made the sweetest sizzling popping sound. I didn't plan that. It's just that we . . . you know . . . we really get into it."

"Keep going. Keep going."

"Okay. He was still burning, but I wanted to hurry it up so I could get out of there. So, I lay down on top of him so that my arms and legs were over his. I was still tingling all over, and I just let go. I let my heat all the way out, and I roasted him to ashes everywhere. I felt myself sinking closer to the stage every second."

"You were still looking at him, right? How did he look?"

"Oh, Sissy, he still had the cutest smile!"

"Until you burned him down to nothing?"

Marilyn nodded her head with a smile and said, "Yes, and it didn't take long."

"He got more happiness than he could survive, right?"

"He was just a weak human, but he sure did die happy!"

With a more serious expression, Sophia said, "They're all going to die anyway, Sis."

"I think that even if he knew what would happen to him, he still wouldn't have turned back."

"Of course . . . who would? You're really hot, Sis."

"So are you, Sissy!"

"I think you're hotter than the other Marilyn ever was."

"Aw, thanks. Ever since then, that's all I do. I keep the temperature down and treat them real nice. I always feel that heat itching to cut loose, but so far, I've been good. It was just that one time before I knew what would happen."

Sophia tilted her head and said, "You know what the humans call that?"

"Yes, you've told me before: spontaneous combustion. That's not a good name for it, though. I'd call it orgasmic combustion."

"Clueless humans have no idea."

*   *   *

The jet had leveled off, and their attendant brought two glasses and a bottle before returning to the galley.

Marilyn filled their glasses, handed one to Sophia, and said, "As long as we're reminiscing, tell me about your first time, okay, Sissy?"

"You know that I could do it the same way as you, right?"

"Yes, and sometimes you want to, don't you?"

"Sometimes, but I'm more of a touchy-feely kind of girl, especially with a fresh manicure."

Marilyn took a look down at her sister's nails and said, "Oh, how cute. Looks like you're about ready for someone, then."

Sophia glanced quickly at the cockpit, then back to her sister and said, "The pilot?"

"Oh, Sissy, you'd better not!"

"Okay, let's let him live. That first time, huh? That was on the same day you made your debut on a stage. I didn't want to follow you off to college, so I took a job at that diner we just left."

"I remember that it wasn't spontaneous combustion. They figured the guy had some freak accident with the oven, wasn't that right?"

"Well, I wanted to cover my tracks some. I thought another pile of ashes right after your little romp at the college would be too shocking for the town to accept. So, I scooped up what was left of him and stuffed it all in the pizza oven."

Marilyn giggled and said, "Tell me again, and don't leave out the good details!"

"Alright, I was working a late shift with this cute guy named Dustin. He was finishing up in the kitchen, and I cleaned up the last of the tables. After all the customers had gone, I locked the front door and wanted only to find Dustin. Just like you, I didn't know human men were so weak. Why weren't we told about that?"

Marilyn shrugged and said, "I guess they wanted us to figure this world out on our own."

"Yep, and we sure did. We each killed a guy first, though. We roasted them alive."

"But they did love it, Sissy."

"Yep, they sure did," said Sophia. "That got us a good name too."

"Yes, the Kildare Killers."

They clinked champagne glasses.

"If we ever have a moment of weakness and cut loose with the heat, whoever we pick will love it, too, won't they?"

"Yep, you know it," said Sophia.

They toasted again, finished their drinks, and poured more.

"Anyway, I hurried back into the kitchen to find Dustin. I was wearing all black—"

"Like always."

"—and he couldn't take his eyes off of my thighs because my short skirt barely covered anything. He liked the boots, too, I could tell, but all that skin really drew him in."

"You do have flawless skin. Really hot," Marilyn said while peering down at her sister's legs.

"You too, Sis. So, there wasn't any reason for small talk or seduction or anything like that. He knew what he wanted, and he knew I wanted it too. He backed me up against the counter, and I pulled my skirt up. Can you imagine the look on his face when he saw I wasn't wearing anything under the skirt? Now, *that* was a big smile."

"Who wouldn't smile at a sight like that? Anyone would!"

"Thanks, Sis . . . same to you."

They tapped their drink glasses together.

"Dustin dropped his pants, and boy, was he ever ready for me. He got close and poked around while we both giggled, then he got himself all the way in, right where we both wanted him to be. With his right hand, he held my left thigh and raised my leg up. His left hand found my breasts, and he probably thought he was squeezing them too hard, but he couldn't have known how rough we like it."

"We do like it rough."

"Even though we're so soft," said Sophia. "Why is that?"

"I think we like being reminded how soft we are, Sissy."

"Yep, that's probably it. You're quite profound sometimes. Anyway, I held his head in what he probably thought was a gentle, kind of romantic way while he was giving me everything he could."

"Which wasn't enough, was it?"

"No, it never is. Not on this planet."

"It's still pretty fun, though, isn't it?"

"Yep, it really is. Earthmen do make a good effort. So, I started heating him up, and he got this scared look. Then, he felt the barbs holding him in."

"I've never used my barbs. I should try it sometime. He'd never be able to pull back out," Marilyn said with a grin.

"Not all the way. He could still keep plenty busy; he just couldn't get away. Do you think any man would ever want to escape us?"

"No, I guess not, Sissy. I promise I'll try that sometime soon."

Sophia nodded and said, "Yep, you should. At first, he was just confused because he could feel me holding him in, but it still wasn't enough to hurt."

"And then it *did* hurt, didn't it?"

"Oh yeah, and you know how that destroys a man's will, too, but not his excitement. I think somehow, the pain of it gets them going even more. Such strange creatures. Anyway, he was terrified, and he still couldn't get back out of me. That's when I felt my heat going mostly into my hands. I didn't know that would happen. I really didn't."

"Your hands got hot!" Marilyn said and clapped her hands.

"Oh, did they ever."

"Did you have a cute manicure, Sissy?"

"I sure did. He couldn't move his head or even scream, but his eyes looked from one side to the other as he felt my palms burning into him. It smelled so good to me. Just drove me mad with pleasure, even though I felt kind of bad for him."

"Yes, but not bad enough to stop. What is it about the smell of humans like that?"

"I don't know, but I absolutely love it."

"I think we just like being that hot, Sissy. The aroma reminds us of how hot we are."

"See? There you go again, being all philosophical. So, I could feel this massive orgasm building, and poor Dustin, he was just about to have his, too, despite all the pain and burning. Even though he was almost dead. I sent more heat to my hands and prayed the smoke alarms wouldn't go off. They didn't. My burning hands pulled him in close, and he got all my heat. I mean all of it, Sis. It was the sweetest explosion I've ever felt."

"And Dustin? Tell me again what he did!"

"Alright, he was dead and burning and smoking, and he *still* gave me everything he had. How can they still finish when they're dead, Sis?"

"We'll never figure it out. Very curious creatures. God, it's exciting just thinking about doing that again someday."

"I know, Sis. I've never felt anything that good."

"Until the next time you did it?"

Sophia shook her head and sighed deeply.

"No, there hasn't been a 'next time' for me either. Not with the barbs and burning and all that fun stuff. I held him there for a while, just savoring the tingling running all through me. Only then did I realize I'd made a real mess of the place. So, I picked up the smoldering pieces of him, swept up all the ashes, and I jammed it all into the oven, which

I turned up as high as it could go. I don't think anyone had any idea how that had happened to him."

"I like that. You framed the oven."

"I sure did."

Still grinning, Marilyn said, "They never suspected you, did they?"

"Nope. It scared the shit out of everyone so bad that they just wanted to get what was left of him into the ground. Nobody figured a girl as cute as me would ever do something like that to him."

"You really are cute, Sissy."

"So are you, Sis," Sophia said with a big smile. "I believe we can get away with just about anything here."

"I kind of love Earth sometimes, Sissy!"

Chapter 3 – They're Sending Something

"I like how no one ever questions where we get all our money," said Sophia.

"They know we're actresses and models, and by the way we spend, we must be awfully good at what we do."

"Well, we are good, Sis. Having a wealthy benefactor sure helps too."

"How come he never suspects, Sissy? Can't he tell no human women can look this good?"

"It helps that we've never met face to face," said Sophia.

"Yes, but he's seen so many photos of us. He should at least wonder."

"I think he must know," said Sophia, "but he doesn't dare bring it up. He's just happy to help us out, and he's not about to ruin that. So, just take his money. It helped with our mission, back when we still cared about it."

"I do like the money," said Marilyn. "I'm not always sure we should take it, though."

"Hey, it makes him happy to give it to us. He said so. Come on, our limo must be waiting."

"Do you ever think about . . . you know . . . with him too?" Marilyn said while unbuckling her seat belt.

"Sure, pretty often, Sis."

Sophia looked across the aisle at her sister.

"But then, he'd be dead and gone. We need to be smart and just leave him as a friend."

"Well, Sissy, we wouldn't have to kill him. We could just do it like human girls with him."

Sophia nodded and said, "You know, maybe we should give that a try sometime. How about both of us?"

"Oh, yes! Even without our extra heat, he might not survive that."

"No, Sis, he might not."

Marilyn gave her sister a big grin, stepped into the aisle, and said, "Hey, I wonder if he'd just give us even more money?"

*   *   *

Marilyn and Sophia exited the jet and were soon planted in the comfy backseat of a limo speeding up Interstate 405.

"We won't even be on Sunset for about an hour, Sis," said Sophia. "We need sleep, too, just like the rest of them. We might have to be at our best for whatever Dayzee's dealing with."

Marilyn yawned and said, "All that champagne got me a little drowsy too. I think I will take a nap."

"The driver will wake us when we get to the Prism."

"Unless I give him some special treatment along the way. You know I'm thinking about it."

"Don't you dare," Sophia said while shaking her head. "Let's keep this one, alright?"

"He's so cute, though. I can hardly help myself."

"Well, I don't feel like calling for another car. There's no time. So, leave this guy alone, alright?"

"Sure, Sissy, but I'm getting itchy, and when I'm feeling that itch—"

"You'll get what you need sometime soon. Me too. But for now . . . sleep."

*   *   *

"Just drop us in front, Alfred," Sophia said with a big grin.

"You know that's not my name."

26

"You don't want to argue with me, do you?"

"No, ma'am. Course not."

"Good, Alfred. Park close by and wait—I don't know what to expect or how long we'll stay."

"Yes, ma'am."

The sisters climbed out into the warm sunshine of West Hollywood and took a long look around before walking toward the Prism entrance. Marilyn wore a short white dress, tight everywhere and cut low, and her white heels were high and spiky. Her long blond hair had just a hint of waves and cascaded down behind her. Sophia wore one of her many short black skirts with black boots. Her red blouse was thin, matched her lips, and asked little of anyone's imagination. Her silky black hair hung far down her back.

A man leaning his back against the brick wall lowered his newspaper and smiled. He wore a slick black suit jacket, a crisp white shirt, and faded blue jeans. After hurriedly folding his paper and tucking it under his arm, he walked up to them and smiled at Sophia.

"It's you! Loved your latest film, Sophia. You're even hotter in the flesh."

"Huh, I think I'm hotter than you can imagine," Sophia said with a wink to her sister. "What's on your mind?"

"I have an exciting new project coming up. With your talent and knockout looks, you'd be perfect for it. Tell me how I can talk you into it."

She fished a card out of her small purse and handed it to him.

"You'll have to talk to my agent. If you can convince her that the project is worthwhile, then we can talk. Right now, my sister and I—"

"She sure looks like Marilyn!" the man said while staring and smiling.

"She *is* Marilyn. She's gorgeous, isn't she?"

"Hell, yeah. I'm sure we can find a part for you too, Marilyn. I mean, a star like you—"

"Being a star is good, but trust me, the dream is more exciting."

"Oh, please, Sis. There you go again."

"Well, Sissy, I'm just telling the truth." She turned to the producer. "We have the same agent. I bet you have something really special—"

"Alright, we have business in the Prism," Sophia said as she grabbed her sister's arm. "Talk to our agent."

With that, they both turned and strutted across the hot concrete with their heels clicking and the man staring at them with a grin. Sophia swung open the heavy wood door, and Marilyn walked in first as the dark world trapped between the lounge's thick walls swallowed them up.

*   *   *

"Look," said Sophia, "it's like she's never moved."

"She does look good on her favorite barstool, doesn't she?"

Dayzee sat with her back against the bar, a drink in her left hand, and a pen for autographs in her right. She wore a tight white blouse and a black skirt, and her black stockings ended in short black boots with high heels. Long blond hair puffed out and fell past her shoulders.

"She sure does," said Sophia. "She's always got adoring fans around her too."

"Well, she's a big star. Maybe we should give her a minute, Sissy?"

"No, come on. We need to hear her story. We did travel all the way from Ireland for her."

"We should have moved permanently to LA like Dayzee did," said Marilyn. "Just because we were dropped in Kildare doesn't mean we have to call it home."

"That's true, Sis, but I like it there. When our work is done, I think I might stay there."

"If you do, then so will I. I bet our 'friend' will even bankroll us."

"He'd love to, and if he doesn't make that offer, we'll convince him."

"We could so do that, Sissy."

The jukebox played low classic rock, enough to cover the sound of the girls' heels.

Marilyn said, "Uh-oh . . . that's not good. She's not smiling. She always smiles."

"Oh yeah, well, something serious must be going on."

Dayzee set her drink down to cover a yawn just as the music paused, and at the sound of sharp heels tapping on the bar's wood floor, she turned toward the sound, and her yawn turned into a big smile.

When the twins got close enough, Dayzee shooed away her amorous pursuers and said, "It's so good to see you two again. Thanks for coming!"

"It's good to see you too," said Sophia. "Are you alright? What's going on?"

"I knew this would happen eventually. I've been pushing it too much, and now—oh, how rude of me! How was your flight, girls? How have you been?"

"The flight was good," said Sophia, "and we've been doing well. It feels good to be back."

"We do like Ireland," said Marilyn, "but there's not much happening there. Just now, out on the sidewalk, I think we scored another film. Can you believe it?"

Dayzee looked from the beautiful blond to the beautiful brunette with a big smile.

"Of course, I can believe it. You girls are stunning. I'm so glad you're here."

"Alright, what's going on now?" said Sophia.

"I really need your help. Have a seat, and I'll fill you in."

Marilyn took the stool to Dayzee's left and Sophia the one to her right. Dayzee spun around to face the bar and set down her empty glass. She leaned back quickly and looked past Marilyn, then she snapped her head around to look to the right before leaning back in toward the bar.

"What's that all about?" said Marilyn. "You seem kind of jumpy."

"Yeah, you could say that. I'll explain."

"Good to see you two again," said the barkeep while he struggled to not look any lower than their chins. "The usual, girls?"

"Yes, Mack. Set us up. Another for Dayzee too."

"You got it, Marilyn. I can't imagine anyone wearing that dress better than you."

"It's kind of my trademark. When I'm wearing a white dress, I feel so sexy."

"Well, yeah, you really are, and—"

"A little thirsty here, Mack," said Sophia with a grin.

"Oh, right. Yeah. Okay, coming right up."

He turned and hurried to mix their cocktails.

Sophia said, "So, Dayzee, what's this all about?"

Dayzee looked quickly to her left and right, past the girls.

"Girls, I think people are finally catching on. I thought in a crazy town like this people would be too busy thinking about themselves, not worrying about my business."

"Catching on to what?" said Marilyn.

"I never told you girls about what I figured out. Maybe I should have because it's the most amazing thing."

"What are you talking about?" said Sophia.

"It happened by accident. That tonic we take, the one they taught us to mix up, you remember that, right? The one that gives us all those things we can't get from ordinary food on this planet?"

"Yep, sure," said Sophia, "but what about it?"

"I was at a house party a few years ago, and I was overdue for a dose, so I mixed it up. I'd just dropped it into my drink when a guy I was kind of flirting with snatched up the glass and downed it."

"Goodness. Did it kill him?" said Marilyn.

"No, it didn't seem to affect him at all. If anything, it just made him hornier. Because right after that, he invited me up to his room."

"And you went?"

"Of course, Fia. We had a rocking time, and then I wanted to finish him off, so I pushed him down onto his back. He was so, so eager . . . more than I would have imagined possible, and I climbed right up onto him. No heat, just me."

"That's hot enough, Dayzee!" said Marilyn.

"You really are hot," said Sophia.

"Thanks, girls, so are both of you. Anyway, I didn't want to kill him. He was making sweet compliments, telling me how he liked watching me bounce around while I rode him up and down."

"Sounds like a fun guy. Is he cute? Fix me up with him."

"No, Fia, I can't. He didn't live much longer. He stopped talking, and I noticed his eyes staring without blinking again. But he never lost it, if you know what I mean. So, I didn't stop. It seemed the more dead he got, the more excited he got. It was the damnedest thing."

"How is that possible?" said Marilyn.

"It was the tonic. It had to be. But that's not the best part. Somehow, I could feel how close he was to delivering. I took my time and savored it, and finally, I felt him give me all he had. And you know what? He gave me back the tonic, too, along with the usual human man stuff. I felt it."

"Oh, no way. You felt the tonic too?"

"Really, Mare, that's where it ended up—deep inside me. Then, I felt my skin tighten up, and I felt younger somehow. After I left him and looked in the mirror, I saw that I really did look younger."

"But it killed the guy?"

"I thought so, at first. I mean, he was really dead, but while I was looking in the mirror, he came back to life. It was like a miracle!"

"Good," said Marilyn. "You're not a killer, Dayzee."

"No, but you are. Your sister too."

"It was just that one time for each of us, Dayzee. We didn't mean to—"

"Okay, okay. I'm just teasing. The point is that doing that keeps me young. I've learned to cut back on the dose since then, and they don't die. They just come close."

"Damn, Dayzee. Now that you mention it, it looks like you haven't aged at all. That's why?"

"Yeah, girls. I don't think anyone else even knows it works like that."

"So, all we have to do is what . . . stand on our heads and pour the tonic in there?"

"No, Fia, that wouldn't do it, although that could be a fun time. Don't ask me how I know, but I do: that tonic was somehow processed by a human male. Something about his hormones or sexual parts . . . I don't know. But believe me, if you cook it through a man like that, it keeps you young."

"You sure as hell don't look old. Sis and I are aging a little, but you look like when we first got here."

"No, Fia, I don't age anymore. I think that's the problem. I haven't changed at all since I hit this town. I was supposed to age with each passing Earth year, enough to be believable."

"And you haven't, have you?" said Marilyn. "You look absolutely amazing."

"Well, now it's catching up with me. People are getting curious. They're asking questions. I think what just happened a while ago is because of that."

"What just happened?" said Marilyn.

"I was shot at. Somebody took shots at me while I was treating myself to another dose."

"Oh my God. Were you hurt?"

"No, Fia, but the poor guy took a hit. Then, a couple seconds later, he took another. Then, when I was almost done, I—"

"Wait," said Sophia, "you didn't stop? You didn't run out of there right away?"

"Heck, no. I kept going until I finished."

"You're too much, Dayzee."

Sophia said, "What does that have to do with people getting suspicious? You think that's connected somehow?"

"Yeah, I think maybe the Guild sent someone to kill me. You know that I haven't done a damn thing for that project in a long time. I think they sent someone to take me out. That's how they end projects sometimes."

"I forgot all about that project," said Marilyn. "Sissy and I have been too busy too."

"I gave up on it a long time ago, girls. We've been here a long time, and all I'm doing is having fun."

"Same with us, Dayzee," said Marilyn. "Maybe they're after us too?"

"Probably, girls. I didn't even think of that when I called you. I was worried about someone taking shots at me, and I just knew I'd be safer with you two around. It wasn't until later that I started thinking it might be the Guild."

"We'll help if we can," said Sophia. "What can we do?"

"Things have changed. After I called you, the Boss set up a meeting with me. It's good that you're here too. We need to find out if the Guild put a hit out on me. If it's not the Guild, then I don't know who it can be."

"Maybe a jealous wife?"

"Yeah, Mare. That's a possibility—I'm no angel. But now, I have to explain myself to the Boss."

"Oh, God, that's why you wanted to meet here, isn't it?" said Marilyn. "When is he coming?"

"Any minute now."

"The usual way?" said Sophia.

"Yeah."

They all turned their heads to look at the giant statue across the room staring back from beneath the large brim of the hat it wore. Without any of them looking away, they continued.

"Of all the places on Earth, why did they put the portal here?"

"Oh, Mare, I think it has something to do with gravity and magnetic fields and that kind of nonsense. Whatever the reason, there it is, right there by that big guy."

She pointed at the statue and downed her drink. The twins followed with theirs. Three pairs of beautiful eyes stared.

Out of nowhere, a dignified man with a light blue sport coat, gray slacks and shirt, and graying hair stood near the statue as if he'd always been there. He already had a drink in his hand and smiled at his team seated at the bar. He walked over to them as he sipped his cocktail.

"My girls, you look as lovely as ever."

"Thanks, Boss," said Dayzee. "We, um, we're happy to see you."

"Why don't we find a table where we can talk?"

"Sure, Boss," said Sophia.

Soon, they were seated at one of the bar's many high-top tables with fresh drinks before them.

Dayzee started. "Boss, tell me you didn't send someone to kill me."

"No, Dayzee, no one has come for you. Not yet anyway. That's why I'm here—to warn you."

"They're sending someone after me?"

"I'm afraid so."

"If the Guild didn't send that sniper, then why—"

"Sniper? Oh, Dayzee, that's not their style. Someone took a shot at you?"

"A couple of shots. Hit the guy that I was . . . you know. That didn't stop me, though. I finished anyway."

"That's my Dayzee. The shooter wasn't from the Guild. I did suggest you be more discreet. Maybe someone's wife took out a contract on you?"

"Oh yeah, that must be it. Wonderful. So, besides whoever the Guild sends, I also have some maniac with a rifle chasing me down."

"It appears so. You must know that you've brought this on yourself. You do know that, don't you?"

Dayzee waved for another cocktail and set her empty glass down hard.

"I'm not going to stop. No one on this planet seems able to resist me."

"Dayzee, you used to be my best field agent. You and these beautiful twins. You were never here to make hundreds of films and go to all the Hollywood parties. This is supposed to be a research project."

When the bartender brought Dayzee's drink and set it on the table, Marilyn held the top of his hand and said, "My sister and I would like another too."

He didn't pull his hand back. He only gazed into her eyes with his jaw hanging down.

"Think you'd like to serve both of us, Mack? At the same time? Think you'd like to try that sometime?"

"I, um, I—"

"You look nervous! I'm kidding, Mack. Just a drink for now, okay?"

"Sure, Marilyn. Yeah. Coming right up."

He turned and scurried away as well as a man that large and muscular could scurry.

"That could be fun, Sis," said Sophia. "Maybe we should try that sometime and see how long he survives."

"We could sure give him some thrills because—"

"Okay, you two. See?" said the Boss. "This is the problem. All three of you look so much better than human women that these men can't help themselves. You obviously don't remember that you're here for my research project. You were supposed to blend in."

Dayzee shook her hair back and shifted her breasts in her tight shirt with both hands.

"We're not exactly built to blend in," said Dayzee, and the three women all laughed and smiled at each other.

"Why do you think we dropped all of you in Ireland?"

Dayzee finished adjusting her breasts but still held them and stared at the Boss. The twins looked at each other and shrugged before turning and waiting for his answer.

"Prior to your assignment, the Guild performed a planetary scan of the deep desires of the inhabitants on this planet. They scanned both male and female and any other variations that they could find."

"Oh, that telepathy stuff?" said Dayzee.

"Yes, exactly. Well, guess what they found. It's universally understood here that the most beautiful naturally occurring females are from that area—from Ireland. We placed you three there with the hope that you'd have a better chance at blending in. All three of you are just too attractive to be indigenous. And it goes way beyond how you look."

"Sissy sure is hot," said Marilyn. "Dayzee too."

"So are you, Sis. Oh, and then Dayzee left for Hollywood. This is all starting to make sense."

"Huh," said Dayzee. "Yeah, girls, and ever since, I've been doing that thing with—"

Dayzee froze.

"Since what, Dayzee?" said the Boss.

"Nothing. Just, um, since I've been making movies."

"Look, the Guild has run out of patience. None of you have filed reports in forever. But the biggest issue is you, Dayzee. You're in films, you're—"

"We're in films too, Boss," said Marilyn. "Why, just today, Sissy and I got an offer for—"

"Yes, I know, but not hundreds like Dayzee. Dayzee, you're at all the parties, you're all over that exhibitionist thing they call their Internet, and anyone can see that you never age. How would you explain that to them?"

Dayzee shrugged and said, "Yoga?"

The twins giggled and Dayzee grinned. The Boss didn't smile.

"And how would you explain that to the Guild?"

The laughter stopped. Dayzee stared at the Boss a few seconds before answering.

"Maybe it's the perfect weather here? Yeah, that must be it."

"Right. Funny. This isn't a joke. I tried to talk them out of it, but I couldn't. They're sending something to terminate you, Dayzee."

"No, you can't be serious. And what do you mean, 'something?'"

"I wish I could tell you more, but I don't know what it is. Something from one of the labs. All I know is that it's deadly and capable of almost anything. It can take over anyone around you . . . any human, that is."

"We'll stick around and help you, Dayzee," said Sophia. "All of us together can—"

"No, you don't understand. It's coming for all three of you. Yes, you should stick together, but maybe think about laying low, you know? You, Dayzee, maybe stop with the films for a while, and Marilyn and Sophia, can you stay out of the spotlights for a while too?"

"Oh, Boss," said Marilyn with a pleasant smile while gently shaking her head, "you know we can't do that."

"And we're not going to," said Sophia.

"Movies are my life," said Dayzee. "I'm not stopping. I don't think my fans will let me."

"The cameras will always be all over Sissy and me," said Marilyn. "We're all stars, and we have the right to twinkle!"

"You really are a star, Sis," said Sophia. "You too, Dayzee, and we'll never disappoint our fans."

The Boss let out a big sigh and said, "I was afraid you'd all feel that way. So, I'm leaving a protector with you. Look, I know all of you are deadly in your own alluring ways, but you'll need some solid muscle, at least to deal with any humans that complicate things. Like that sniper, Dayzee."

"Fine," said Dayzee. "Who are you giving us?"

"His name is Bruno. He's the most dangerous guy I could find on such short notice. I gave him your files, so he knows something about you. I know you're wondering, so I'll just tell you: your sexual tricks won't kill him, but it sure will weaken him. Even if he wants a go at any of you, you need him strong. Do *not* weaken him. Got it?"

"Sure, Boss," said Dayzee. "We'll keep the big guy in tip-top shape. It's a good plan because we'll be busy dealing with what the Guild sends after us, and Bruno can handle everything else. You know, I feel better already."

"Maybe your drinks are finally kicking in," said Sophia with a smirk.

"Won't argue with that. Alright, Boss, when is the tough guy coming?"

The Boss looked at his watch and began counting with five fingers, then four, then three . . .

All eyes looked at the big statue guy wearing a hat, and out of thin air appeared a man with long brown hair and a burly brown beard. His black boots looked heavy, and his jeans looked thick, too warm for Southern California in October. His black t-shirt stretched over impressive muscles, and he wore a ball cap with "Not My Planet" printed on the front. He stood about three feet tall.

The three women looked at their Boss then back at Bruno. No one spoke as he approached the table, taking a biker's beer out of his hand on the way. He dragged a chair with him and set it between Marilyn and Sophia. He put his beer down, sat, and looked from face to face. Even the jukebox remained silent.

But the biker didn't.

"Hey, you little shit. Gimme back my beer."

Bruno tipped his hat and said, "Pardon me, ladies. Boss."

Bruno climbed down from his chair, grabbed the beer, and walked out to meet the genuinely large man. He stopped a few feet from him and craned his neck to look all the way up at him. Then, he proceeded to chug every last drop.

"Why, you stupid little—"

Bruno dropped the bottle, and with blinding speed, he stooped down and grabbed the man's ankles. In a heartbeat, he had stood and lifted the man straight up, and he held him there as the bottle spun on the floor until it stopped.

"What the f—"

"Hey! I'm not very fond of the word 'little.'"

Bruno flexed his knees just a bit, and on the way back up, he rammed the man's head into the ceiling. Some of the lights in the bar flickered from the man's head tangled in the wires above the wood ceiling, and they must have wrapped around him because when Bruno let go of his ankles, he stayed there amid a cloud of dust and falling plaster chips. The jukebox roared to life.

"Barkeep, another beer," he said as he waved to Mack. "Put it on his tab. As long as he's hanging around a while."

"Sure thing, pal. Nobody liked him anyway."

Bruno looked first at the surprised women, then he turned to look at the Boss.

"What?"

"I suspect it's going to be one hell of a Halloween," said the Boss.

"Oh, that's right," said Dayzee. "That's today. Well, we'll just have to rock and roll through it!"

Chapter 4 – A Clean Sweep

Back at the table, Bruno took his seat, and moments later, Mack brought him a fresh bottle of beer.

"Well, that was impressive. Hi, I'm Marilyn."

Bruno stood and reached toward her, so she gave him her hand. He kissed it while looking into her eyes and said, "I'm very happy to meet you, Marilyn."

"You're stronger than you look."

"I believe you are likely even more beautiful than you look."

"Oh my . . ."

He kissed her hand again and let it go. She gave him a warm smile.

Bruno turned and said, "And you are Sophia? A pleasure to meet you too."

"Likewise. I feel safer already."

"You *are* safer. And you,"—he turned toward Dayzee—"are the famous Dayzee Dazzle. No camera could ever capture your radiant beauty."

"Well, you do know the right things to say. I'm intrigued, Bruno. How did you get so strong?"

"My last assignment was in a place where gravity is crushing. It almost killed me, but I adapted. On a planet like this,"—he raised his hands to each side—"my strength is unmatched."

"Oh, and the hat," said Dayzee. "'Not My Planet?' What's that all about?"

"It's not just about messing with these Earth people, is it?" said Marilyn.

"It can't be," said Sophia, "because you couldn't have had time to get that printed up for this trip."

"You're both right," he said while looking from one twin to the other. "I had that made after my first off-world assignment, so no, it's not just about Earth. It's more just about missing home, that's all. I must say, though, I've become a big fan of this planet from knowing all you lovely ladies."

"My, oh my," said Marilyn. "You're really something!"

"Welcome to Earth," said the Boss. "Ladies, Bruno probably can't kill whatever the Guild is about to send your way, but he can help with everything else. Let him help."

"The way he's looking at me, I think he might want to help himself," said Marilyn with a teasing smile.

"Okay, Marilyn, don't even get started with him. That's not why he's here. Go take Mack if you have to, but Bruno is off-limits. Got that?"

"Yes, Boss," she said without looking away from Bruno. "But I like that if I were to lift my dress—"

"Which you always do," said Sophia with a smiling sneer.

"Yes, well, he's already right there. You'd like that, wouldn't you, Bruno?"

Bruno turned to look at their Boss, who frowned and shook his head.

"I would. Of course, I would. But I'm here to protect you, nothing more."

"Good. Remember that," said the Boss. "What they need most from you is your strength. Don't dwindle it away with whatever naked treats they offer you."

Bruno bumped his bottle, chased it as it rattled across the table, and quickly caught it.

"Right, Boss. I need to stay strong. No naked treats for me."

"Good. Okay, I need to leave. Don't trust anything around you, ladies. Whatever the Guild sends will be deadly and disguised as someone you might never suspect. Let Bruno watch your backs, and—"

"He sure would like the view," said Marilyn. "He might want to do more than—"

"That's enough, Marilyn. You and Sophia are here to help Dayzee, and—"

"And he's here for all of us," said Dayzee. "We got it. Have a safe trip."

The Boss turned and gazed at the statue.

"That thing is creepy as hell."

He chugged what was left of his cocktail and walked back to the statue against the far wall. In the blink of an eye, he was gone.

"I still don't get why that's here," said Sophia.

"The portal, you mean?" said Dayzee. "It was here long before the Prism. It just worked out that way. Maybe somebody sensed that there was something bizarre about that spot, so they plunked that statue right there. Alright, I bet you have a limo waiting out front?"

"Of course, I do," said Marilyn. "Let's go. But hey, where are we going? Are we really going to lay low?"

"Such a sweet kid," Dayzee said as she shook her head and smiled at Sophia. Then, they both turned to Marilyn.

"No, Mare," said Dayzee. "That's not our style. Let's go have some fun. Just stay alert, and watch for that thing, whatever it is."

"Where are we headed?"

"There's a pool party happening right about now just down the street. Let's get that limo and go."

They all got up and began the walk toward the door.

Sophia said, "Dayzee, we didn't bring suits with us. We planned on shopping for new clothes after we got here."

"Since when do either of you want tan lines anyway?"

Marilyn and Sophia looked at each other and grinned.

"Remember Halloween? No clothes—that's your costumes."

Dayzee held the door, and they all stepped out into the southern California sunshine.

"She makes a good point, Sis. Turns out we have all the suits we need."

"Oh, you're right about that, Sissy. But you know what? That limo might be a little crowded with all of us in there. Hey, Bruno, can you drive that thing?"

"Sure, I've received an Earth vehicle download. Why?"

"Just hang on a sec."

"Really, Mare?"

"I can't wait, Dayzee. Come on . . . it won't take long."

Marilyn strutted over to the passenger side front door and tapped on the glass. The driver powered the window down and said, "Yes, Marilyn?"

"Slide over to this side for a minute. I need something from you. You can't really say no, can you?"

"No, ma'am, I sure can't," he said with a shaky voice and lifted his legs out from under the steering wheel. Within seconds, he was seated right where Marilyn wanted him.

She opened the door and said, "You've been a good driver for us. Would you like a little treat?"

"Yeah, yeah, ma'am, you know I would."

She placed her right heel up inside on the limo's carpeting near his legs and said, "Touch my leg."

He reached out and caressed her thigh gently, then he began rubbing up and down on the front, then the back.

"Feels good, doesn't it?"

"God yeah, it sure does. You're so soft and smooth."

"Go on and see what else you might find. You know you want to."

"Oh, come on, Mare," said Dayzee. "You know what's going to happen."

"I'm not going to hurt him, I promise. I just need a little bit of fun, and then he can go have himself a drink inside."

"Can't you wait for someone at the party instead?"

"He doesn't want me to wait. Do you, Mr. Driver?"

He shook his head and reached up between Marilyn's thighs, and when he found what he was looking for, Marilyn let out a soft squeal.

"Oh, you sure found something nice. You like that, don't you?"

"God, yeah. You're so warm."

"I bet you'd like me to sit on your lap right now, wouldn't you?"

"Sis, you shouldn't—"

"Shush, Sissy. He's a big boy. He knows what he wants. Don't you?"

"Oh, yeah."

"You'll need something to lock me in just the right place on your lap. You wouldn't want me to slip away once I'm on you, would you?"

He shook his head while he unzipped with his left hand, and his right kept exploring.

"Oh, that's really good. Slide forward just a bit now. Yes, just like that."

"I can't watch this," said Dayzee, and when she turned to face the bar, so did Sophia and Bruno. "It'll just make me hornier too."

Marilyn lifted up her dress and straddled the man on the front seat of the limo. After she wiggled her way down onto his lap, she let her dress fall and cover them.

"I'm sure not falling off of that, am I? You really have me now, Mr. Limo Driver."

She began to rise and fall and squirm from side to side, all the while playing with his hair and looking into his eyes. Sophia, Dayzee, and Bruno laughed but never turned to look. No one walking along the sidewalk glanced inside the car either.

Then, the driver's smile left him. His hands snapped up to grab Marilyn's throat, and he began to squeeze. When she coughed once, Sophia turned to look, and she laughed and pointed.

"Oh, now they're really playing, aren't they?"

Marilyn started to gag, and her sister said, "Wait, this isn't all fun and games!"

She reached in and tried to pull his arms away, but he was far too strong.

"I'll get him," said Bruno.

"No, I don't think this is a human thing anymore. I'll get it," said Sophia.

"Oh, it's the thing the Boss said was coming after us!" said Dayzee.

Sophia climbed in behind the driver and placed her fingertips on each side of his head. Instantly, they all smelled the burning flesh as Sophia blasted her heat up all the way. She burned her way through skin and bone and brain until her fingers touched. Though its head had been burned beyond recognition, its hands still strangled Marilyn.

Dayzee reached in through the open door and gripped the thing's throat. She turned up the heat, too, and within seconds, she'd burned completely through its neck. Sophia now held a roasting head above the smoking stump of the driver's neck. Still, the hands squeezed Marilyn's throat, causing her eyes to pop out as she made faint gurgling sounds.

"His heart!" said Bruno. "Burn that fucker's heart!"

Dayzee laid her palm over the corpse's heart and ramped her heat up high. It was a strange, sick smell as the heart meat fried and roasted, and Dayzee soon felt her hand on the seat of the car.

The dead thing's hands released Marilyn, and she fell out of the car, where Bruno caught her. She gagged and coughed while he sat with her in his arms.

Sophia climbed back out and said, "What the hell? So, that thing is really here already? And it wants all three of us?"

"Sure looks like it," said Dayzee. "At least now we know how it wants to kill us: it'll take over someone, anyone, and even after they're dead, it'll keep attacking."

Marilyn coughed again and said, "I couldn't have stopped that thing. I panicked and didn't even think of trying to burn it. I'm glad you were both here."

"Oh, you know what, girls?" said Dayzee. "We should try to stick together all the time."

"You mean," said Marilyn, "all the time? Like, in the same bed at night too?"

"Now you're just being silly," said Dayzee.

"Bruno doesn't think so," said Marilyn. "Look at that smile. I bet he's imagining it. Aren't you, Bruno?"

"Uh, yes, Miss Marilyn. How could I not?"

"Well, since it's your job to protect us, you'd have to—"

"Mare, just stop," said Dayzee. "No, we should be okay in separate rooms at night. Let's just stay close, though. But if one of us lines up some entertainment, the other two will have to be there too."

"So, if it goes bad," said Sophia, "between the three of us, we should be okay. That's a good plan."

"And even if it doesn't go bad," said Marilyn, "that'll be one lucky guy!"

"Just one, Sis?"

"Oh, you make a good point," said Marilyn.

"Bruno," said Dayzee, "drag that thing out of there, and let's get going."

"And do what with it? Just leave it smoldering on the sidewalk?"

"Sure, this is Beverly Hills, and—"

"It's West Hollywood," said Bruno. "I've received the geographical download too."

"Well, close enough. Look, crazy things happen here every day. All I know is that pool water is going to feel heavenly now."

*   *   *

"No, don't drop us, Bruno. Let's stick together. You were smart enough to know that I had to burn that thing's heart to make it stop," said Dayzee.

"Seemed logical to me. I thought about snapping the arms off, but that might have hurt Miss Marilyn."

"You'd never want to hurt me, would you?"

"Not a chance. Okay, I'll park over here. You ladies just have all the fun you want. I got you covered."

"We know you do, Bruno, and we do appreciate it," said Sophia. "But you'd like us much better uncovered."

"Don't you start teasing him too," Dayzee said while shaking her head and grinning.

Bruno grinned too.

"I don't see a pool," said Marilyn. "Is this the right place?"

Dayzee pointed up, and they all looked at the top of the building.

"A penthouse pool? How cool. Whose place is it?"

"He's a producer I've worked with. You'll both like him. Especially you, Mare. He looks more like a rock star than a producer."

"Ooh, I think I will!"

"This is why I like hanging around here and not running off to a place like Ireland. It takes time to make all these contacts, and now you girls get to enjoy the fruits of my labor. Come on."

They took a quiet ride up the elevator and walked out under a white tarp roof that flapped gently from the breeze. To the left was a bar with two waiters in Hawaiian shirts and white shorts. To the right, a man strummed an acoustic guitar and sang just loud enough to set a good mood.

Straight ahead, a large oval pool waited, blue water sparkling in the sunshine. Lawn chairs and tables beneath umbrellas circled around, and dozens of men and women in swimsuits sat and stood talking, enjoying their drinks. Expensive jewelry was on display in every direction. Beyond the railing which held it all in, the Hollywood hills spread out to the shimmering horizon.

"It's hard to believe something just tried to kill me," said Marilyn.

"Well, don't let down your guard," said Dayzee. "Do have some fun, though."

"I will, but what's our plan?" said Sophia. "Just go about our business until that thing finally finds a way to kill all of us?"

"We need to come up with two plans. Let's get some drinks, find a table, and I'll tell you what's ahead of us. You'll like it."

*　*　*

The umbrella above them blocked the late afternoon sun, but the breeze was still hot enough that they all eyed the pool.

"Okay," said Dayzee, "here's the first thing: we need to get you girls going on the fountain of youth."

"Fountain of what?" said Marilyn.

"Oh, you're such a sweet kid. Think about it, Mare. The man drinks the tonic, his body does to it whatever it does, you lay him on his back, and when he finally—"

"Nice fountain," said Sophia. "I want one. No way in hell I want to get any older either."

"You won't, dear. My beautiful twins will stay gorgeous forever. You probably would anyway, but this fun little routine will make sure of it."

"And it's just the usual tonic? The one the Guild taught us?"

"Yeah, that's all. But you have to do it the right way. I don't think either of you will mind that, will you?

"Not me," said Marilyn.

"Me neither," said Sophia. "I'll get a shot of that every day just to be sure."

"No, you'd better not," said Dayzee. "That's too much. Maybe your age would start going backwards!"

"Could it? You can't be serious!"

"I really don't know, Fia. You'll know when you need it, so don't go crazy with it."

Sophia shrugged and scanned the bodies in and around the pool.

"Now, the other thing. We can't just run from whatever the Guild sent. We need to find a way to kill it."

"Any idea how?" said Marilyn. "We don't even know what it is."

"We'll figure it out, girls, and when we do, we'll still have one more job."

"Yes," said Marilyn, "then we can wear down this guy,"—she pointed at Bruno—"and see just how weak we can make him. Think you'd like to get real weak, Bruno?"

He only stared into her eyes and nodded with a silly grin.

"Sure, we'll find time for that," said Dayzee. "All three of us. There might not be anything left of him! But what I'm talking about is the Boss. We need to deal with him too."

"What do you mean?" said Marilyn. "He's been helping us, telling us about the Guild and the thing that they—"

"Think about it, Mare. The Boss sent that thing. He probably sent that sniper too. He knew that I'd call you two for help. Whatever that thing is, maybe it can't survive long on Earth, so he needs us together. I think its job is to kill one after the other after the other. A clean sweep. No trace of us left."

"Why would they want us dead, Dayzee?" said Sophia. "Sure, we haven't been working all that much, but why would they want to kill us?"

"It might not be about us at all," said Dayzee. "I think this is just how they end projects."

"You think the Boss sent it?"

"Yeah, Mare. I'm sure of it."

"We sure have a lot to do, then."

"We sure do, Fia, but first, I'm hitting that pool, and girls? Try not to kill anyone, okay? At least not right away?"

"Hmm . . . we'll try," said Marilyn. "But we *are* the Kildare Killers."

"I know you two only killed the first time you were here before you learned how weak these men are."

"But we've earned that name," said Sophia. "When we kill, it's truly spectacular."

"You are so right, Sissy. It feels so good too!"

Chapter 5 – That Fountain Thing

"You sit tight, Bruno," Dayzee said as she rose from her seat. "You Kildare beauties, take a stroll with me. Let's get you out of those clothes and wrap you up in towels instead. You can slip those off at the side of the pool, and when you're under the water, no one will notice."

"Until they bump into one of us," said Sophia. "I'll make sure someone does. All they'll find is skin and more skin."

"Me too, Sissy. I'm still itching for some fun. That dead guy turned out to be just a tease, and—"

"Girls, try not to burn anyone up, okay?"

"Like we can stop ourselves," Marilyn said with a shrug.

"That's funny," said Dayzee. "I know you girls can control yourselves."

"Oh, you know what, Dayzee?" said Sophia. "That water might keep things cool. Could that work? Maybe we can have some fun and not incinerate anyone. At least not today."

"That's brilliant, Sissy! Yeah, that just might work. You got your eye on anyone?"

"I sure do. That guy over there that looks like some kind of bodybuilder. I wouldn't mind getting my hands on that."

"Keep those hot hands underwater, and he might have a chance!"

"How about you, Sis? What looks good to you?"

"That rock star guy over there. You see him? With the hair?"

"That's your type, alright," said Dayzee. "He's the guy I was telling you about—I'll introduce you later. Okay, we need to get you two undressed. Come on over behind that trellis. Bruno, have a drink and keep an eye on us. We need to have some fun."

"Yes, ma'am."

"No, Dayzee. Right here. Hold this towel up for me," said Marilyn.

"You love torturing Bruno? Is that it?"

"Well, he can close his eyes if he wants to."

She looked down at him with a smile and saw a huge grin, and his eyes stretched as wide open as he could get them.

"Look, he doesn't want to close his eyes! Here, hold this up."

Dayzee and Sophia pulled the towel open to block the view from the pool, but not from Bruno, and Marilyn did a slow striptease, giggling with every bit of her that got exposed. She glanced over her shoulder once and didn't catch Bruno's eye—she only saw him looking up from her heels, along her bare legs, all the way over every generous curve, and finally to her long blond hair.

"See anything you like, tough guy?"

His mouth moved silently, and he finally found Marilyn's big eyes.

"Oh, yeah. My God."

"I guess it's look but don't touch for you. Right?"

"I . . . I—"

"I'm glad you have my backside. I mean my back," she said with a giggle.

"Oh, please," said Dayzee. "Do you really have to torment the man?"

"Yes, she does," said Sophia. "Wrap yourself up, Sis, then it's my turn."

"Oh, you girls . . ."

Marilyn got herself covered and wore only a clean white towel and high white heels. She held one end of another towel and Dayzee the other, and Sophia turned to face Bruno as she unbuttoned her blouse.

"Fia. Really, that's too much. You should at least turn around. He can only take—"

"Do you want me to stop, Bruno?"

He didn't hesitate a second. "No!"

"See, Dayzee? He knows what he wants. He deserves a good look."

She unbuttoned slowly and pulled her blouse apart enough that only two tantalizing parts of her were just out of sight. She gazed into his eyes and opened the shirt all the way, pointing right at the staring man so close.

"There. How do you like those, Bruno?"

"I . . . if I could—"

"They're just teasing you, Bruno. Okay, back to focusing on your job. You need to—"

"There's still my skirt, Dayzee," said Sophia. "That will have to go too."

"And anything under it," said Marilyn.

"You're funny. Such a sweet kid," said Sophia. "Okay, I just need to stretch this a little bit to get it over my hips. There. There it goes. Now, I'll just shimmy it down. A little bit more. Just a bit more. And see, everyone? Nothing under it!"

Bruno's shaking hand rattled his beer bottle on the table until he lifted it up, and he stared at everything except Sophia's eyes. She dropped the skirt down around her heels, and she stepped out and kicked it aside.

"Show's over," she said as she let Dayzee and Marilyn wrap her up. "For now anyway."

She blew him a kiss and turned toward the pool. When she started a slow strut, Dayzee and Marilyn joined her.

"You two kind of drove him crazy."

"Yeah, but we didn't kill him. That's the main thing."

"Try not to kill anyone here, alright? That wouldn't help my reputation with these people."

"Well, if the water's cool enough . . ."

"Let's hope, Sis," said Sophia.

"Girls, don't even try that. You might get it all boiling."

At the edge of the pool, the twins removed their heels and sat, dunking their legs in the water. Dayzee stood next to them and began removing her clothes.

"No towel, Dayzee? You're just going to stand there naked?"

"Wouldn't be the first time. No, girls, my underwear can pass for a bikini. A really teeny one."

They all laughed and soon, a nearly naked Dayzee sat with them.

"Let's just try to pick the right time, then you two slip in, and I'll keep your towels out of the water."

They looked around for a few seconds at the other guests glancing their way, then Sophia said, "Waiting is for chumps. I'm getting wet."

She dropped her towel behind her and splashed in. Marilyn shrugged at a staring Dayzee and did the same.

"I'm going to mingle a little. Try not to cause too much trouble, alright?"

"Sure, Dayzee. We'll cause just the *right* amount of trouble," said Sophia.

Dayzee shook her head with a grin, stood, and walked along the pool back toward the bar.

"You know, Sissy, all we need to do is catch the eye of the ones we want, and they'll come to us."

"You mean 'for us,' don't you?"

"Yes, Sissy, or maybe 'with us!' Look, they're both looking this way."

"This is just too easy. I like Earth."

"Me too."

Within seconds, the two men stood in the pool in front of Marilyn and Sophia, who were both stooped down so that only their heads broke the water's surface. From being so close, the men could see their bare breasts just under the water, and they turned to each other for a quick grin.

"You girls want some company?"

"Of course, we want some company. We're stripped naked already, aren't we?" said Marilyn.

"You boys up to it?" said Sophia before she reached out for her muscle man under the water and said, "Oh, this one sure is."

Marilyn did the same and said, "Mm . . . mine too. You happy to see me, Rock Star?"

"You know it. God, your hand is warm."

"I can get a lot warmer. Sound like something you'd like?"

She turned to her sister, and they shared a grin.

"I'm ready to find out."

"Hmm . . . the water might be cool enough."

"What?"

The twins giggled, and Sophia said, "We're just a little too hot sometimes, that's all."

Rock Star said, "You damn sure are. Hey, both of you, give us a peek?"

They flashed each other a quick grin then turned to look at the two men. They both rose up just enough that the lazy lapping of the water coated them and flowed back off over and over.

"We make quite a pair, don't we?" said Sophia. "We like doing everything together too."

"God," said Rock Star, watching the water drip off of Marilyn. Without looking back into her eyes, he said, "Let's go inside."

"Won't the owner mind?" said Sophia, as she held her man with both hands under the water.

Rock Star didn't answer as he continued to stare at Marilyn's breasts dripping pool water, so Sophia reached over with one hand to help her sister.

"Hey," she said, and he turned to look. "Are you really the owner of this fabulous place?"

"Yeah, I *am* the owner."

"Oh, nice. Sounds like you got a real handle on things. Well, so do we."

"Damn, you sure do. Wanna go inside, already?"

Marilyn turned to her sister and said, "We did tell Dayzee we'd be good."

"We did."

"Wait, why would you be good? What are—"

"Oh, Mr. Rock Star," Marilyn said, "even when we're good, we're still quite bad."

*　　*　　*

The girls turned to see Dayzee standing at the edge of the pool right behind them.

"Girls, I need a word. Guys, do you mind? Just a sec."

"Sure," said Rock Star. "Anything for you, Dayzee."

"You're the sweetest. Thanks!"

The two men backed up a few steps, then turned and walked to the other side of the pool. Dayzee stooped down on her heels.

"You're going to fall out of that bra, Dayzee," said Sophia.

"I hope so. Listen, girls, now's a good time. Why wait?"

"A good time for what?"

"Your fountains of youth, Mare. I have everything you need. I'll mix it up and meet you inside."

"How do you know which room we're going to?" said Sophia. "This place is huge."

"At least one of you will end up in his room—the biggest, most luxurious one."

"Oh, and you know where that is?" Sophia said with a chuckle.

"It's been a little while since I've been there, but yeah, of course, I do. For a while, I thought he was the one."

"The one for what?" said Marilyn.

"Nothing. Just someone to get me the next big part, that's all."

Dayzee stood and said, "You two go on ahead. It'll only take me a second or two."

She stood and helped both girls quickly wrap in their towels after they'd climbed up out of the water.

"Alright, they're coming back. I'll see you two inside."

*　　*　　*

Back at their table, Dayzee searched through her tiny purse and found that she didn't have the potion ingredients.

"Damn, Bruno, it's not here," she said and turned to see the girls leading their guys under the canopy. "It must have fallen out in the limo."

"What's that, Dayzee?"

"It's something the three of us need to stay healthy here. It must be in the car."

"If you want, I'll run down and get it."

"Damn, that thing could attack again any second."

She looked again at the entrance to the condo.

"We can't stick together this time, so why don't you stay close to those two? Maybe stay out of sight, but stay close enough in case they scream for help."

"As you wish," he said and began a brisk walk.

While watching Bruno off on his mission to protect the twins, she grabbed one of the white towels and wrapped it around herself.

*   *   *

Dayzee stepped out of the elevator at ground level, walked through the lobby to the front door, and peeked both ways before venturing outside. She saw the limo close by and began walking toward it, with her heels clicking sharply on the concrete walkway.

Just as she reached for the front door handle, the glass shattered, and a gunshot rang out and echoed up and down Sunset.

"Damn it! Not again!"

She yanked the door open just as another bullet struck the hood.

"You're still a lousy shot!" she said while looking all around.

She pulled the door shut and scurried over into the back seat.

*   *   *

The men led the two girls into the plush bedroom, and Sophia closed the door. They'd slipped back on their heels, and they dripped a trail of water from their soaking wet towels.

Sophia turned toward her sister, brushed her hair back over her shoulders for her, leaned in close and said, "Sis, where's Dayzee? She wanted us to do that fountain thing."

"Hey," said Rock Star. "If you want to kiss your sister, we sure won't stop you."

"Damn right," said Muscles.

"Sure, we kiss all the time," Marilyn said and stepped closer to Sophia.

They held each other around their waists, and Marilyn whispered in her sister's ear, "Maybe Dayzee got distracted, Sissy? I can't wait. I'm so itchy I can't stand it!"

"Me too, Sis. Okay, let's have some fun, but not too much, alright?"

"No burning?"

"No, Sis. No barbs either. Now, give me a kiss, and let's give these earthmen something to remember!"

They brushed their lips quickly and giggled before turning to the two men for real kisses.

*　*　*

Dayzee scanned the back seat and floor, then peeked over to search the front passenger seat. She saw the small bag with their essential mixture wedged mostly out of sight next to the console. She grabbed it up and leaned back, taking turns looking in every direction.

After ten minutes without any more bullets striking the car, she pulled gently on the rear passenger side door latch, kicked it open, and pulled her leg back inside. Nothing happened. No more shots.

She took a deep breath and leaned out, then quickly back in. Still, no gunfire rang out, so she hurried onto the sidewalk and slammed the door behind her.

With the potion ingredients in one hand, she ran as well as she could, dressed in a towel and heels, back to the front door. The door had just swung shut when chips of concrete outside sprayed up from another hit.

"That was close," she said out loud, then added, "I guess he's lousy at reloading too."

*　　*　　*

Marilyn pulled the door closed and stood in the hallway with Sophia. Each wore their heels again and only their white towels. They fought to contain their laughter.

"I knew we could do it, Sissy. I felt my heat so close to taking over, and I almost let it loose, but I didn't."

Sophia grinned at her sister and said, "Same here, Sis. You saw me touching his face, didn't you? I'm sure he felt how warm my fingertips were, but still, he had no idea what I could have done."

"My guy had no idea either. I wanted so bad to burn him. And my barbs—I really wanted to try that on him."

"I still had a pretty good time. How about you?"

"It was okay, and it helped when I glanced at your cute fingernails and thought about your hands getting hot. But it was nowhere close to what it could have been. Like if I would have—"

"Incinerated that weak human?"

"Yes, that. Maybe next time?"

"We've been good for a long time, Sis. We should give ourselves a special treat soon. What do you think?"

"I don't think I can help myself!"

*　　*　　*

Only a couple of steps down the hall and toward the pool party, Marilyn and Sophia found Bruno waiting for them. A second later, Dayzee ran up to them out of breath.

"Girls, sorry I'm late. I had to run down to the limo for the stuff, and that lunatic was somewhere on one of the buildings taking shots at me!"

"I heard that, Dayzee, but I thought you could handle it, so I stayed close to the girls."

"Good call, Bruno. Why bother protecting me from a sniper? Two gorgeous naked girls in heels sure need your help more."

"Sorry, Dayzee. They really are hot, though."

"I guess I don't blame you." She looked the girls over with a smile. "It's fine, Bruno. I just get bitchy when I'm shot at."

Before even greeting the twins, she took a few sniffs of each.

"Well, you smell only like girls. That's a relief."

"Not like burning flesh? Is that what you mean?" said Sophia.

"Yeah, I thought for sure you—"

"We were good," said Marilyn. "But oh, we wanted to."

"Did we ever," said Sophia.

"It's probably good to not kill them all, girls. I'm glad you had some fun, but where are your guys? Are you sure they're still alive?"

"They're fine. They're still inside the bedroom. I think we wore them out because they were out cold," said Sophia.

"And we did it just like normal human women would," said Marilyn.

"I was gone only about ten minutes! You couldn't wait?"

"Nope," said Sophia while Marilyn shook her head.

"Fine. Here."

Dayzee handed each of them a small bottle and a plastic bag with powder inside.

"Mix this up, and let's get back inside."

"It's a little late. Sissy and I really took care of them."

"I'm not sure these guys are up to the job now," said Sophia. "We really wore them out."

"They'll be ready for you again. The potion really gets their attention up. They could be just about dead—no wait, they *could* be dead—and you'll still have your fountains. Let's get you started on this."

Dayzee grabbed a bottle of whiskey and some glasses, and the three women headed toward the bedroom with Bruno close behind.

* * *

Dayzee knocked on the door only once before it opened, and the two men were about to step out into the hallway.

"Oh, well, hello there," said Rock Star while rubbing his squinting eyes. "Good to see you again. You have a white towel on too. Looks hot as hell with those heels."

"Glad I caught your attention. Are you going to invite us in?"

He glanced down at the whiskey bottle in Dayzee's hand.

"Sure, come on. We were just about to head back out to the pool, but I did work up a thirst."

"Good, you've earned it. Let's all have a drink in private, and I'll tell you what we have in mind."

Dayzee poured and mixed their drinks while Marilyn and Sophia kept them occupied.

"We want you again. Right now," said Marilyn as she let her towel drop to the floor. She noticed only a slight reaction from the men standing before her in swimsuits.

"You wouldn't ever tell us no, would you?" said Sophia as her naked sister slowly opened her towel and tossed it aside.

The two men looked at each other then back at the twins.

"I, um, maybe you should let us—"

"A toast," said Dayzee as she handed everyone their drinks.

They all downed the concoctions quickly, and within seconds, both men looked down at their renewed enthusiasm. Their swimsuits were stretched out and expanding even as they watched.

"Good boys," said Marilyn, and she led her man back to the bed.

*   *   *

Marilyn said, "We want you two flat on your backs on the bed. You boys look tired, but we want another ride. Want to make us happy?"

"Oh, hell yeah," said Rock Star.

Muscles nodded with a big grin. They both slipped off their swimsuits and lay on the bed, each one with a pillow under his head.

"Oh my," said Sophia. "That's a sight I'll never get tired of."
"They do look happy to see us."
They stood side by side with arms around each other's waist.
"We're twins," said Sophia with a smile. "Twice the fun."
"Gorgeous twins," said Rock Star.
"God yeah," said Muscles.

*   *   *

Seconds later, Marilyn straddled her rock star and Sophia her muscle man. Both women bounced around, both smiling, and Dayzee stood near the bed and watched. Both men looked over as she dropped her towel and began removing her bra and panties.

"Maybe you two could take turns giving me some attention, too, while these beautiful twins are busy on top of you. How does that sound?"

She lifted one knee up onto the bed, but she froze at seeing the rock star snap his head to one side then the other. His smile had turned to a grimace, and then the muscle man acted the same way. Both men's eyes were closed, but they started a low snarling.

"Bruno! Bruno, get in here!"

The door exploded in, ripping the hinges from the jamb and sending splinters of wood across the floor.

"Quick! Hold them down!"

"What the—"

"There's no time for questions. Get up there, and hold their arms down!"

Both men started reaching for the twins, but Bruno was too quick. In each of his hands, he held two of their wrists, pinning them against the cushioned headboard. The bones in their arms made snapping sounds like twigs as Bruno's grip crushed them.

"Don't stop, girls. They might be possessed, but they'll still give you what you need."

"But you said Bruno couldn't stop that thing, right?" said Marilyn while she continued to bounce.

"Oh, you know . . . you're right. Bruno, quick, before they become completely possessed."

"What, Dayzee? What do you want me to—"

"You have to kill them!"

"Dayzee, no," said Marilyn. "Don't make Bruno kill them. Please!"

"They're possessed! He has to!"

"I can hold them, Dayzee. They're not going anywhere. Maybe we don't have to kill them?"

"I think they're already dead, Bruno. But sure, give it a try. Girls, don't worry—Bruno's got it."

"I'm not worried," said Sophia, "and I'm not about to stop. Oh, this is good. They're like bucking broncos."

"They really are, Dayzee."

Marilyn and Sophia never even slowed down.

"Ooh, I think it's even better now that they're possessed by that thing," said Marilyn.

"I think so, too, Sis. I like what Muscles is doing for me now . . . much better than before!"

They both kept bouncing on the writhing men.

"Hmm . . . I think I want to burn him," said Marilyn. "He might already be dead, right?"

"Me too, Sis."

Sophia reached for her man's face.

"No, girls. You'll burn down the building. Some other time, alright? Maybe they'll somehow be okay?"

"Okay. I guess I don't want to destroy this place. I sure do want my fountain, though. I think he's getting closer."

"Mine too, Sis. I can tell. He's getting so close now . . ."

Bruno had found a way to hold all four arms in one hand, climbed back off of the bed, and stood by Dayzee, who was still completely naked except for her heels. She looked down at the man as he stared at the scene of two beautiful twins riding the convulsing men and enjoying it immensely. He started to shake.

"Oh, Bruno, that sure is a sight, isn't it? Come here."

She turned the man into her and found what Marilyn had said before to be true. He was already at just the right height. She turned his cap around, held his head gently against her, and let out a short gasp. The sight of the girls getting their first fountains brought out a smile, and the first wave of pleasure filled her.

"Mm . . . one more bounce, and mine's going off," said Marilyn. "It's too bad that thing got him, but still . . ."

"But still, it feels so good. Mine is just about there too. Let's do it together, Sis."

"I like that idea."

She reached her arm around Sophia's waist, and Sophia did the same. They got their timing right and bounced one more time, then again, then they both squealed as their fountains came alive.

The twins turned face to face and saw the dazzling light blazing from each other's eyes.

"Oh, Sissy . . . your eyes!"

"Yours too, Sis!"

Dayzee watched them and pulled Bruno in tighter, and he gave her just what she needed to peak just as both girls took their first fountains amid their own explosions of pleasure.

Both girls turned toward Dayzee, and she raised a hand to block the light from their eyes. When the tingles had started to trail off, Sophia looked lower to see what Bruno was busy doing to Dayzee.

"Hey, I thought we shouldn't, you know, not with—"

"Oh, I guess I didn't make that clear. He can do things to us as long as he doesn't have too much fun himself."

"Bruno, you're okay with that?" said Marilyn.

"Mm–hmm . . ." he said without turning away from Dayzee.

"He's okay with that," said Dayzee. "He is *so* okay with that."

"Our eyes, Dayzee. What the hell was that?" said Marilyn.

"It's from the fountain, girls. That's just the way it works. Don't ask me why."

"Now, I get it," said Sophia. "Dazzle. Dayzee Dazzle. Am I right?"

"Uh-huh. That's right, Fia. You could be the Dazzle Twins now, if you want."

They each still had an arm around the other's waist, and they turned to look at each other. They giggled for a few seconds before Sophia turned back to look at Dayzee.

"Nope. We're still the Kildare Killers. You do all the dazzling, Dayzee."

Chapter 6 – Down Sunset Boulevard

Back off the bed and standing up on their heels, the twins let Dayzee help wrap them back up in their towels.

"We should probably get out of here," said Sophia. "It's a shame that thing the Guild sent to kill us ended up taking those two instead. I liked them."

"I liked them too, Sissy. Hey, I think I just saw Rock Star breathe. Maybe they're only sleeping?"

"You know, you might be right," said Dayzee. "Bruno, let go and see what happens."

Bruno released their arms, and they didn't move. The men lay there quietly, except for an occasional snore from Muscles.

"I know you all heard that!" said Marilyn.

"What's going on?" said Sophia. "Did we cure them? Did we somehow kill that thing?"

"Oh, I don't think you killed the thing, but maybe it gave up on these two."

"Didn't you break their arms or wrists or something?" said Sophia.

"You know," said Dayzee, "I think that stuff might heal them. I'll find out at the next party."

"Right," said Sophia, "if we're not all dead by then."

"We still need to get out of here, ladies," said Bruno. "Let's make it quick. That killer might invade these two again."

"They did a fantastic job with their fountains," said Sophia. "I feel younger already!"

"Told you so," said Dayzee.

Marilyn said, "Bruno's right—we should go. Let's just get our clothes from the—"

"No, there's no time," said Dayzee. "I have clothes for both of you, and wouldn't you like to go on a shopping spree later? My treat!"

"Sounds good to me," said Sophia. "Let's go."

"I can always use another white dress," said Marilyn. "A really short one!"

*   *   *

"I'm glad we made it out of there, girls. You both got what you needed? Can you still feel it?"

"Oh yeah, Dayzee . . . he gave me all of it," said Marilyn.

"Mine too. Dead men might not tell tales, but they sure still like getting some tail."

"That's a pretty good one, Sissy!"

"What's another word for a dead guy, Sis?"

"What?"

"A stiff. Get it? Even though they were dead, they were still plenty—"

"Oh, girls," said Dayzee, "they were never really dead. I'm glad the producer isn't dead, at least—he was about to offer me a part in his new production."

Sophia said, "I feel that fountain stuff, Dayzee. I feel better than I have in a long time. Do I look any different?"

Dayzee stopped them on the sidewalk before they got to the limo. She looked from one girl to the other.

"You two were already gorgeous, but you're even more so now. You really do look younger. Do you feel younger?"

"I feel a hell of a lot younger!" said Marilyn. "Let's do something fun! Bruno, I want you to drive fast, okay?"

"That sounds awesome, Sis! Yeah, Bruno, let's see what that thing can do!"

"Kids," Dayzee said as she shook her head and smiled at Bruno. "What do you think, Bruno? Girls just want to have some fun, right?"

"Okay by me. So, about that . . . that upstairs thing . . . when I . . . when we—"

"Ah, Bruno, you'd like another round of that, wouldn't you?"

"Yes, ma'am. Oh, God yeah, ma'am."

"With me too," said Marilyn. "It was my idea," she said with a giggle.

"And me. You want to enjoy us all sometime, tough guy?" said Sophia.

"Yeah, but you promise you won't burn me up?"

"No promises, mister," said Sophia. "I'm betting you're willing to take that chance. You still in?"

It took him no time to nod and say, "Hell, yeah. Anytime. All of you."

"It's a date," said Marilyn. "But right now, let's get this heap rolling. And I mean *fast!*"

*　*　*

Dayzee sat in front, Marilyn and Sophia took the back, and Bruno slammed his door shut and grabbed the wheel.

"So, Marilyn, you want me to—"

The car lurched forward with a loud crash as a custom car rammed them from behind. They all turned around to look and saw a wild-eyed man with ragged hair, wearing a flannel shirt with cut-off sleeves, staring through the windshield at them.

"Another crazy trying to kill us," said Sophia. "This is already getting old."

"How do you know he's not just drunk, Sissy?"

"Look at his head, Sis. It's laying over on his shoulder. Another dead guy, I bet."

"Another stiff, Sissy?"

"Oh, you know, I bet if we were to—"

"Girls!"

Dayzee turned toward their driver and said, "Bruno, think you can hustle back there and finish that thing off?"

He reached for the door handle and said, "Sure, Dayzee. I can just reach in and snap his neck. No, wait . . . that's already broken. So, maybe I should—"

"You should drive!" said Marilyn. "This is perfect! He'll chase us, and we can see what kind of driving you can do!"

"I like that idea, Sis! Yeah, Bruno . . . drive!"

"That car looks fast, Sissy, so Bruno will have to drive like a wild man!"

"If he outruns it, I'll give him a big kiss, Sis! More than that if he—"

"Girls! Bruno, care to humor them?"

"Whatever you want, Dayzee."

Bruno chuckled while shaking his head, turned back around, and started the car just as they got rammed again. He shifted it into drive and buried the accelerator, squealing the tires and leaving long black streaks on Sunset.

"Drive, Bruno!" said Marilyn.

"Yeah, drive!" said Sophia.

The limo screamed down the road, sideswiping parked cars and setting off alarms as the pursuing car raced close behind and rammed them again, bouncing them all around inside.

"Can't you go any faster? What planet are you from anyway?" said Sophia with a loud laugh.

"Good one, Sissy!"

"I've never driven one of these things before!"

"You damn well better learn quick!" said Dayzee.

"Yes," said Marilyn, "you want us all to survive, don't you? So you can . . . you know."

Bruno nodded his head with a grin and glanced up at the rearview mirror. Marilyn was looking back and blew him a kiss. Dayzee turned and looked back over the seat.

"Girls, Bruno's powerful as heck, but he can't kill this thing. All he can do is trash up the body that the thing is using. You remember what worked before, right? With the heat?"

"Yes, sure, Dayzee, but how can we get close enough? That thing is crazy!"

"You got that right, Mare." She turned to Bruno. "Just keep driving, and give me some time to think, alright?"

"You got it, Babe."

"It's Dayzee."

"Right. Dayzee."

"You're still working for us, remember?"

"Yes. Yes, of course, Dayzee."

"Good boy."

The limo's engine roared, and though the dead guy didn't ram them again, he stayed close as both vehicles raced east down Sunset Boulevard. Sophia turned to look.

"That must be the owner of the car in the front seat too. Looks like he's dead. So, that thing must have killed him and then took the car? These things can think like that even after they go crazy?"

"Maybe," said Dayzee. "Or maybe it killed them both and took over just the driver."

"Hey," said Marilyn, "can that thing take more than one at a time?"

"Oh, hell yeah," said Dayzee. "It just did that upstairs."

"Right now, it's still just the driver, right, Dayzee?"

"Looks like it, Mare," said Dayzee.

"What are we going to do?"

"I'm thinking, Mare. Somehow, we need to trap that thing so you girls can go to work on it."

"We might have to do this the hard way. Bruno, can that thing hurt you?"

"I doubt it. I can take a lot of abuse."

"Hmm . . . maybe we'll see about that someday."

"Sign me up," said Sophia. "I want to abuse him."

"Oh, me too!"

"I want to abuse the hell out of him," said Sophia.

"Me first! I know some sweet ways I want to—"

"Girls, take a break! How about it, Bruno? You'll be alright?"

"Anything you want, Dayzee. I'll be fine. What do you have in mind?"

"I say just slam on your brakes and bring that hot car to a stop behind us. Then, before it can get out, you get over there and smash the door so there's no way it can get out."

"I can do that, but then what?"

"If the window's up, smash the glass and hold that thing still. Are you strong enough?"

Bruno shook his head and smiled.

"Sweetie, I could—"

"Dayzee."

"Dayzee, I could pick that car up and slam it around if you wanted me to. I could bust that thing up, too, but burning is probably the best bet."

"Oh, this plan is really coming together! Flip that car over hard so that its roof is crushed in. That should hold that thing in there. Then, keep an eye on Fia when she goes to work."

Dayzee looked back over the seat.

"Okay, Fia, get that hand warmed up. You have some heart to burn."

"I'm more used to breaking hearts," she said with a smirk.

"You're right about that, Sissy. But soon, we'll be calling you a heartburner!"

"Well, Sis, think about what you burned first of that guy on that stage back in Kildare. Think about what we could call you?"

"Because of what I burned? Is that what you mean? Oh, you know, maybe I'd like being called a—"

"Hey! You two! You're like little kids back there! Stay focused, Fia. Bruno's going to set it up for you. Lean back against your seats—we're going to get hit!"

Bruno floored the brake pedal, and the limo screeched to a stop. A fraction of a second later, the speeding car crunched its front end into the limo's rear bumper. Without a word, Bruno jumped out, and in a flash, he was at the driver's side door of the car behind them.

All three women turned to watch as Bruno crouched down and tipped the car up with both hands. From there, he snapped it up into the air, where it seemed to hang for a second before it spun around lazily and landed on its roof.

"Go, Sissy! Burn that bastard!" said Marilyn.

"There's no need to swear, Mare," said Dayzee. "but she's right, Fia. Go burn that thing's heart."

Sophia swung the door open and ran to the car. Dayzee and Marilyn followed close behind.

"That thing's going wild in there, Dayzee," said Bruno.

Inside the car, it was a blur of arms swinging and banging into the dash and punching holes in the windshield, leaving blood dripping down the glass and shredded skin clinging to the sharp edges.

"Sheesh . . . what a mess," said Sophia.

"Grab its arms, Bruno," said Dayzee. "Hold it still!"

"Okay, Dayzee."

Bruno reached in and chased the arms around for a second until he got a good grip on the thing's wrists. Then, it started shrieking and bellowing and banging its head on anything close enough.

"Quick, Sissy . . . burn that thing!"

"Okay, Sis. I got this."

Sophia's hand was already glowing as she reached it into the car. She found the right spot, and it blazed up brighter, looking like someone had lit a flare in the front seat. Most of the intense light became muted by the dark smoke drifting out through broken glass all around, and the sound of sizzling came with a blast of a sickly-sweet barbecue aroma.

The arms slowed, then stopped altogether. Sophia withdrew her hand, and Bruno let go of the thing's wrists.

"We did it," said Dayzee. "Nice job, Fia and Bruno. Are you both alright?"

"I'm fine," said Bruno.

"You're mighty damn strong," said Dayzee.

"Thanks. Yeah, on Earth, I sure am."

"Fia? What's wrong?"

"It's just the smell, Dayzee."

"It's not that bad. It's just—"

"No, it's not bad at all. It's just making me want something. Something I haven't had in—"

"Sissy, we'll get that soon, okay? I promise. We've been good for a long time."

"Well, alright. Since you promise."

She took a deep breath and let it out slowly.

"Alright, we should probably get out of here, girls."

"You're right. This is more than usually happens on Sunset. But still, no one is even paying attention," Sophia said with her hand raised up close where she could inhale the hot scent.

"You gotta love this place, Sissy!"

"This town is in for a rough ride," said Dayzee. "Now that you two are back."

They all laughed as they walked back to the limo.

*   *   *

After Bruno had closed everyone else's door and got in himself, he started the engine and waited with both hands on the wheel.

"You're wondering what's next, right, Bruno?" said Dayzee. "The thing is . . . I don't know."

She looked over the seat at Marilyn and Sophia.

"Girls, we have a few hours to kill before the backyard party starts at the Prism. Why don't we all go back to my place and hang out awhile? We need to figure all this out."

"Yep," said Sophia, "this isn't going to be easy. I thought I killed that thing twice already."

"But you didn't, Sissy . . . not really. I think you just killed whatever body the thing took."

"That's right," said Dayzee. "All you did with your wickedly hot hands was kill the poor loser that was in the wrong place at the right time."

"Any ideas?"

"No, Mare, I don't have a clue. But I know someone that would."

"The Boss?"

"Yeah, Fia. But why would he tell us? Remember, I think he's the one that really sent that thing after us."

Marilyn said, "I don't get it. If he sent the thing to kill us, why'd he send Bruno to help?"

"Alright," said Dayzee, "maybe he didn't send that thing. But he probably really does know what it is and how to kill it. I can tell he knows more than he's letting on."

"If he does know about it, you should ask him. Make him tell you," said Bruno. "I have a feeling you can be pretty persuasive."

Dayzee turned to look at Bruno and got a huge smile.

"Why, Bruno, you're pretty amazing, you know that? I think you're right!"

"I think he's right too," said Marilyn. "He's earned a treat. From all of us."

"There'll be time for that later. You can wait before you, you know, get to know us all better, can't you, Bruno?"

He gripped the steering wheel so tightly it started to bend and twist.

"Hey," said Dayzee. "Easy on the car. We still need it."

He stared straight ahead, but he couldn't help but smile and nod. Dayzee turned to the girls.

"He likes that idea."

She reached over and got a hold on his trousers.

"Boy, does he ever like the idea. He'll just have to wait."

"Like a dead guy," said Sophia with a smirk.

"Like a stiff, Sissy!"

Dayzee turned to look out the windshield, but she didn't let him go.

"Home, James."

"It's Bruno, Babe."

"It's Dayzee, James."
"Yes, of course. Home, Dayzee."

Chapter 7 – Mansion in The Flats

"See, this is part of what's pissing off the Boss."

Sophia pointed at the mansion as Bruno turned into the drive and piloted the limo through the thick stone towers framing the massive wrought iron gate.

"Well, life has been good. Why shouldn't I have a nice place?"

"Maybe because we're supposed to keep a low profile?"

"Fia, I'm not about to live in the shadows. I was going to get back to the mission someday. Maybe. Meanwhile, this has all just been too much fun. I kept getting good film offers, so I never—"

"Yes, and you were never aging," said Marilyn.

"And now, neither will you two. You think *you* can stay away from the cameras? Bet you can't."

"Of course, I can't. I want a house just like yours, Dayzee."

"Call our friend, Sis. I bet he'd find a way to set you up."

"Oh, you think, Sissy?"

"What friend?" said Dayzee.

"We have a serious fan, Dayzee. We're not going to bug him for a house, though, are we, Sis?"

"No, I don't suppose so."

Bruno pulled the limo into the garage and shut it down. He let out a deep breath and turned to Dayzee.

"Yes, you can come inside too. Where the heck else are you going to go?"

"Thanks, Dayzee."

"But you should dump this limo first—it's all beat to hell. Even the steering wheel."

"Oh, sorry about that."

"It's fine. Just go and find a fresh one. Think you can do that for us?"

"Of course. Anything for you." He looked over his shoulder. "And you two."

"I like how he said 'anything,' Sissy."

Marilyn giggled as they both opened their doors. Dayzee got out and slammed her door shut too. Bruno backed out far enough to be able to take the circular drive to the exit gate, and with a roar of the engine, he was gone.

"We tease him too much. We can't really let him, you know, take care of all of us, can we, Dayzee?"

"Yeah, we sure can, Mare. It won't weaken him, and if anything, it'll just make him more protective of us."

"Oh, that sounds about right. We take care of him, and he'll take care of us!" said Marilyn.

"Alright, let's get inside and come up with a plan," said Dayzee.

"And a drink. I'm ready for a strong, tall drink."

"Strong and tall sounds good, Sissy."

"Just don't ever talk like that around Bruno, alright?"

"Sure, Dayzee. He's plenty strong, but tall? Not so much."

"He sure is just the right height, though," said Dayzee with a smile, and they all filed into her mansion in the Flats.

*　　*　　*

Sophia stood near the wall of glass and sliding doors and looked out at the pool, still blue under a sun that would soon dip behind the thick line of evergreen trees and shrubs ringing the backyard. The fading sunlight glinted off of the windows of both guesthouses toward the rear of the property.

"Here's your order, pretty girl," said Marilyn as she handed Dayzee her drink and walked to join her sister.

"Thanks, gorgeous."

Dayzee sat at the bar at one side of the great room and looked at Marilyn and Sophia looking out at the grounds.

"There are plenty of bedrooms upstairs. You can pick out whichever ones you want. But first, we need to do some thinking."

"I've done a little bit of thinking on it, Dayzee," said Sophia, "and I think we should lure the Boss back to Earth somehow. And when he gets here, we'll just capture him. We'll take him prisoner."

"You think it would be that easy? Girls, he might have some tricks of his own that we don't know about."

"Yeah, he might, but he'd never kill us, and you know what else? I know he's flirted with us all at one time or another. We could dangle some bait in front of him and probably get him to do whatever we wanted."

"What exactly do we want? What would we do with him?" said Marilyn.

"Torture him," said Sophia.

"Oh, Sissy . . . really?"

"Yep, Sis, but in a nice way. Ooh, the things we could do to him. He wouldn't stand a chance."

"And then," said Dayzee, "he'd tell us what we need to know: how to kill that thing."

"Yeah, Dayzee," said Sophia, "and then, we'll have to kill him too."

"We'll have to, Sissy?"

"Well, Sis, I guess we won't *have* to, but I want to. Don't you?"

"If he really did send that thing to kill us? Yes, I sure do. How about you, Dayzee?"

"We'll all kill him. After he talks."

"And after we have some fun with him, right?"

"Yes, Sissy. If he's going to die anyway, we can send him off with a smile!"

"You girls. I just love you two . . ."

*　　*　　*

Dayzee led the way up the grand staircase that was wide and curved gracefully, and they all stopped to peek over the railing at the intricate tiles that spanned the expansive foyer.

"I see just the right spot for a Christmas tree. A really tall one."

"Oh, Mare," said Dayzee, "we don't have time to think about Christmas right now. It's not for a couple of months anyway. It's still only Halloween."

"I know, but I like planning these things out. I know just the outfit I want to wear to get some nice photos by the tree."

"Let's find you girls the bedrooms you want, and then, I don't know about you two, but I'm going to take a dip. How does that sound?"

"Count me in," said Sophia before looking to her left and into one of the bedrooms. "I'll take this one. I like all the mirrors and—"

"Of course, you do, Sissy! You're gorgeous!"

"—and that vanity near the window is perfect. You know, Dayzee, cameras come out of nowhere for us. A girl's got to be ready."

"Good, that's your room for as long as you want it. How about you, Mare?"

"Hmm . . . let me take a look."

As they kept walking down the hall, Marilyn glanced into a room on her right and said, "This one. This is the one for me. I know it's weird, but I like having a view of the front of the house. I like seeing if anyone's coming to visit."

She walked over to the wide windows, looked down at the driveway, and froze on the spot.

"Uh-oh."

"What, Sis?"

"We *do* have visitors. Three cars—two of them just like the one Bruno flipped around. That dead guy in the car must have been in a gang, and I think they followed us back here."

"Wasn't Bruno supposed to be watching for crap like that?" said Sophia.

"Maybe you two shouldn't be teasing him all the time. How could he not be thinking about you instead of doing his job?"

"Oh, yeah. All the naked treats we keep offering him."

"Exactly, Fia."

"You might have a point, Dayzee," said Marilyn. "He can't help but think about Sissy without her clothes. I know I do a lot! She's absolutely stunning!"

"So are you, Sis—you're gorgeous! Everything about you is—"

"Girls! We have a problem! Try to focus!"

Marilyn continued to gaze out the window and said, "Whew, what a relief. Bruno just pulled in behind them all with the fresh limo. He'll handle it."

"Hey, how did he find a limo that quick?"

"Easy," said Dayzee. "He just took the first one he found. Who's going to stop him?"

Dayzee and Sophia joined Marilyn at her window, and all three watched through the glass.

"Look, he just got out of the limo," said Dayzee. "and there's what . . . ten or twelve of them? Uh-oh, they're starting to laugh at him. Oh, girls, they really have no idea what his deal is, do they?"

"Oh," said Marilyn, "I know what he'll be thinking about while he mows them all down."

"What's that, Sis?"

"All three of us standing around him naked, with no place to go, no reason to stop, and he can just take turns enjoying us."

"Well, who wouldn't enjoy that, Marilyn?" said Dayzee.

"Anyone would want that," said Sophia. "Anyone at all."

With relaxed smiles, they all turned to watch.

*　　*　　*

Three doors opened on each of the three cars, but the drivers remained in each.

"Look at that, girls. They have a plan—like a cute little military operation. They're ready for a getaway."

"Pretty smart for a bunch of dopes," said Sophia.

Nine men approached Bruno, who had exited the stolen limo and closed the door. He'd moved out into the grass and stood waiting for them. The girls upstairs could hear their taunts and laughter through the open windows. One man, the largest, stood within striking distance of Bruno, while the others moved into positions to surround him.

"What do we have here? You're just a tiny little man, aren't you?"

"You should go. Look,"—he pointed to the open exit gate—"the door's open wide for you."

"Oh, you're a comedian. I like that. You're surrounded, so how about if we let you leave? Maybe go back to kindergarten?"

"Or run home to momma!" said one of the others.

"Yeah, it's time for your nap!"

The laughter carried up to the window.

"School sounds good. Your lesson begins now."

Bruno unleashed a blinding uppercut with his right, which would have hit the man in his chin if Bruno were a bit taller. Instead, he'd nailed the guy's crotch and lifted him up off of his feet before he let him crumple back to the ground. He lay on his side and held his smashed parts, and if he said any more, the women couldn't hear it.

Another man stepped in close behind him, and Bruno spun around and dropped to one knee, delivering a left jab to the middle of the man's thigh. It snapped and formed a new joint, sort of a second knee, that bent the wrong way.

The thug stared with his mouth open and wobbled a few times before falling to the grass. Bruno stood back up.

"Oh, you see what he's doing, girls? He's not picking up cars or anything because that would send them running. He's letting them think they have a chance."

"He's not just ridiculously strong—he's pretty smart too!"

"He sure is, Sis. This is fun. I hope more gangs come after us!"

"Girls, no. As much fun as this is, we have more important things on our schedule. We need to—"

"Look, Dayzee! One of them grabbed his neck!"

Bruno reached up to grasp both of the man's wrists, and it appeared he was struggling with him, but the women knew it was only a ploy. After a few more seconds, Bruno again dropped to one knee and pulled the man over his shoulders, spinning him high through the air and slamming him hard enough that he lay deep in the lawn in his own profile stamped into the yard.

The remaining men looked at each other, and they'd fallen silent.

"They're starting to see something isn't right," said Dayzee. "Look. They're scared, but none of them wants to be the first to run."

"Could they really outrun him anyway?" said Marilyn.

"I doubt it. I think they're all dead, girls. Soon, anyway. I bet they're starting to see that now too."

"Oh, look," said Marilyn. "Now, the drivers are getting out."

"Yep, Sis, but they're staying by their cars. You can almost see them shaking from up here. What a show!"

They watched as the remaining seven attackers stayed in their ragged circle around Bruno, and he looked up at the window. He gave them a thumbs-up and took slow, confident steps toward the rear of the first car in front of the limo. The ragged circle of attackers followed.

"Any guess what he's going to do this time, girls?"

"I can't imagine. How about you, Sissy?"

"Nope. We did see him flip that car, though."

"Right, Sissy. Maybe he'll crush them!"

"I doubt it, Sis. I bet he wants to show us something new. I think he likes showing off for us."

Bruno had reached the rear bumper, which was old style—thick and heavy and plated in chrome. His slow-motion pursuers formed a semicircle around him on one side, but none seemed eager to get too close. He sat back against the bumper and gestured for the men to come closer. They didn't.

"Dayzee, what the hell is—"

Too quickly for anyone to really watch it happen, and with the shriek of metal ripping and bolts shearing, Bruno stood holding the bumper over his left shoulder like a baseball bat, and the car bounced and squeaked a few times before settling. He gave a look up at the window.

"Oh, I think he just winked at us!"

"He did, Dayzee! He really did!"

Without warning, Bruno swung the bumper like a major league star through the entire line of men, crumpling them all and sending the head of the last in line high into the air. The girls all watched as it sailed toward them, then up and over the roof.

"Dayzee," said Marilyn, "I think it was watching me on the way over!"

They looked back down and saw seven dead bodies, one of them a head shorter than just a second before, and the three drivers hurried into the cars and locked their doors.

"Oh, bravo, Bruno," said Dayzee.

"Hey, I like that. That's what we should call him after he, you know, when we finally let him—"

"Yes, Sissy, 'Bravo Bruno' is a wonderful name for him!"

"All that strength, Sis. Think about that. When we finally give him his shot, think about all that destructive power inside him, and all the while, he'd stand there happily—"

"Girls! Try to stay focused! He's not done yet!"

Bruno walked calmly to the driver's side of the nearest car and looked in on a terrified man who'd just started the engine. Before he could try to back up or pull forward, even though there was no room in either direction, Bruno crashed his right forearm into the roof above the man's head. The car folded nearly to the driveway like a cardboard box, and something red and gooey leaked out below the deformed door.

"Oh my God . . ." said Dayzee.

"Sheesh," said Sophia.

The engine was still running, so Bruno hopped up onto the hood and punched straight down, silencing it. From there, he hopped down to the next car, stood near its bumper, and looked in at the driver. He was just barely tall enough.

"Good thing it's a lowrider, huh, girls?"

"That's funny, Dayzee."

They all shared a laugh and a quick look before turning back to the scene on Dayzee's driveway. When he grabbed under the bumper and lifted the car up, Dayzee said, "Oh no, I hope he doesn't mess up the driveway stones. I had those imported last year—they're hard to replace."

"Hey, can you get some from back home? Is that possible?"

"I doubt we could transport them all through the portal at the Prism. But how cool that would be! No one on Earth has ever seen stones that change colors on their own. I'd love to find a way to—"

"Dayzee . . . look!" said Marilyn.

Bruno tossed the back end of the car up, and while it hung in the air pointing straight up, he got a grip on the front bumper.

"Oh my God, he sure is strong."

"Bravo Bruno, Mare," said Dayzee.

He raised the car higher until his arms were straight up and holding the car above his head.

"Oh, he just winked again!" said Dayzee.

Then, he didn't seem to care about gravity because he swung the car down onto the first one in line. Both cars flattened, their engines died, and the deceased drivers leaked out and left puddles on the driveway.

"He's cleaning that up. I swear, he's cleaning that up," said Dayzee.

"I have an idea," said Sophia. "Yep, he needs to clean up the bodies and also get rid of those crunched-up cars."

"So, what's your idea, Sissy?"

"He needs to trade that limo for a tow truck. Three trips to a canyon somewhere, four bodies in each car, and—"

"Everything except that head that flew away somewhere?"

"Yep, Sis, everything except that runaway head."

"Well, Sissy, it's more like a flyaway head."

"Yep. When someone finds that, they'll just think a mountain lion is on the loose. No one would give Bruno a second glance while he drags all this crap out of here. He could tow it all away. Problem solved."

"Maybe we can hope that we won't need him until he gets the yard all cleaned up?" said Dayzee.

"Yep. We'll just hang out in your pool until he gets back, and then—"

"Then, we're off to rock and roll at the backyard Halloween shindig at the Prism!"

"That's right, Mare, but we sure do need Bruno with us for that."

"Yes, Dayzee. We need Bravo Bruno."

Chapter 8 – About that Pool

When Bruno walked into the house from the garage and found his way into Dayzee's large great room, she already had a drink waiting for him.

"Thanks, Dayzee. I did work up a bit of a thirst out there."

"We watched all of it from upstairs. Pretty impressive work, Bruno."

"Just doing my job, ma'am."

He gave her a quick bow and sat at her bar. She poured herself a shot of whiskey and downed it.

"Fia, why don't you tell him your idea?"

Sophia stood to his right, and Marilyn sat on a stool to his left. Dayzee served them each their favorite cocktails.

"So, Bruno, you left a lot of dead bodies on Dayzee's driveway."

"Yeah, I really did, didn't I?"

"You junked up their cars too," said Marilyn.

"You're the right guy to clean it up," said Sophia. "I can think of three more things you might like to give a thorough cleaning, and we all really want you to because—"

"Okay, Fia," said Dayzee, "try to stay on topic."

"Right. Alright, here's my idea: swap your limo for a tow truck, load some bodies in each of their cars, drag them out of the city, and push those smashed-up cars into a ravine somewhere. How does that sound?"

"Easy enough. Will you be okay while I'm gone?"

"Yes, we sure will," said Marilyn, and he turned to look her way. "We're going swimming. I don't know about these two, but I'm going au naturale."

"Me too," said Sophia. "How about you, Dayzee?"

Dayzee nodded and finished her drink. "Oh, yeah. It's heated to just the right temperature. We'll be fine back there. Just close the gates on the way out."

"Sounds good. How about one more for the road?"

Dayzee poured another and set it in front of him.

"While you're working, tough guy, think about that pool. Think about all of us wearing nothing, all wet, frolicking around in the warm water, and—"

"Mare," said Dayzee, "you really need to give it a break. Why are you torturing the poor guy?"

"Um . . . it's kind of like foreplay. You don't mind, do you, Bravo?"

"'Bravo?'"

"Oh, sorry. I mean 'Bruno.'"

"Yeah, it's kind of like foreplay, I guess. But it's a lot like torture too."

"You don't want me to stop, do you?"

"Not a chance, as long as you're all safe until I return."

"Deal."

*　　*　　*

"Let's go upstairs and find you girls some cover-ups so you can get out of those clothes."

"That's a good idea, Dayzee," said Marilyn. "What do you have?"

"None of my clothes will do, and I don't want pool water getting on them anyway. But there are some shirts up there that you'd both look really cute in."

"Whose shirts?" said Sophia.

"Oh, you know, just leading men that I'd taken an interest in, even if only briefly."

"Leading men, huh? And you led them here? *You* did the leading."

"I sure did, Mare, but only the hottest ones. I like leading on leading men."

"I bet you like that they come and go, huh?" said Sophia.

"It's all for the best. If I settled down and got boring, I wouldn't get cast as often as I do. Come on, let's go see what's up there."

*　　*　　*

All three still wore their heels, Marilyn her short white dress, Sophia her short black skirt, and Dayzee her even shorter black skirt. Their graceful strides up the elegant curving stairway led them to Dayzee's palatial bedroom, where a giant four-poster bed sat against the far wall, and plush seating and gleaming furniture filled out the space.

"Your walk-in closet is bigger than most bedrooms!" said Marilyn. "I could get used to living like this."

"Stick around, and you will, instead of running off to Ireland all the time."

"She does make a good point, Sis. We should plan on staying awhile."

"Sure, that sounds good—I want my own mansion."

"Here's something good for you," said Dayzee as she handed Marilyn a long-sleeved white shirt on a hanger. Marilyn held it up and looked in the mirror.

"I think this might work. Whose is it?"

"Oh, I can't name names. You've heard of him, but that's all I can tell you. Go ahead and try it on."

"Get going, Sis—we'll watch."

"Well, okay . . . I do like having an audience."

She handed it back to Dayzee and gently rolled the straps of her dress down over each shoulder.

"Take your time, Mare!"

"Hmm . . . okay, Dayzee."

She began slipping it down, revealing her large breasts, then her flat belly, then her tiny white panties. When her dress dropped to the floor, she stepped out of it and hooked her thumbs in the thin elastic band just above her hips.

"We did say naked, didn't we?"

"Oh yeah, Sis. You need to get naked. Keep going."

Marilyn grinned, shrugged, and said, "If I must."

She pulled the tight band down over her hips and wiggled from side to side.

"Oh, that's hot, Sis."

"Glad you like it. You'll have to do the same thing."

"Um, no. Not wearing anything under the skirt, remember?"

"Oh, that's right. Even better."

She kept going until her panties slid down along her smooth thighs and dropped around her ankles. She lifted one heel up and set it back down farther to the side and kicked the tiny garment toward the dress on the floor.

"Oh, just hold it a second. You're absolutely beautiful, Sis."

"You really are, Mare. That other Marilyn has got nothing on you. She never did."

"Ooh, tell me more," she said and giggled.

"You want to stand there naked while we tell you how beautiful you are?"

"Well, of course, Sissy!"

"You do look simply stunning without any clothes, Sis. You're quite a sight."

"Okay, you two. Here, Mare."

Dayzee handed her the shirt, which she put on and buttoned up halfway, leaving a good view of her cleavage.

"That's hot too. Those are really nice, Sis."

"Yours too, Sissy. We're twins. Okay, it's your turn. Take your time."

"Oh, I will. I'll show you how I undress for a man when I feel like he deserves a special treat. How does that sound?"

"I like special treats too, Sissy!"

"Then, this is just for you, Sis."

"What about me?" said Dayzee. "I want a special treat too!"

"Here's a treat for both of you, then."

Sophia looked from one to the other as she slowly unbuttoned her tight blouse. She didn't open it all the way, but her perfect skin was visible all the way down between the generous curves of her breasts, down over her belly, and all the way to the top of her skirt.

First, she pulled down on each side, showing them how excited she'd become for her slow striptease.

"Oh, wow, Sissy! I bet the guys love that!"

"They sure do. Then, I do this."

She didn't uncover her breasts, but she held them through the cloth, squeezed them together, and bounced them a few times. She leaned her head forward and lifted them up, then she paused to look at Marilyn and Dayzee.

"Oh, you could, couldn't you?" said Dayzee.

"I sure can."

"You've done that, Sissy?" said Marilyn.

"Yep, many times. It drives them crazy."

"Of course, it does!"

"It kind of makes me crazy too."

"Sissy, do you ever do that just by yourself? Just because you want to?"

"Mm-hmm. I sure do."

"That's really hot!"

"Then, I finally give them their first look."

Sophia pulled her blouse open to reveal two perfect, large round breasts, each looking quite happy with so many eyes on them. She slipped the shirt back over her shoulders and pulled her left hand free, leaving the blouse to drop and hang up on her right. She twirled it a few times and sent it across the closet.

"Oh, Sissy, they're perfect!"

"Just like yours. But this helps even more."

She reached back and crossed her arms behind her, arching her back and sending her breasts out even farther as she faked a pout.

"Oh my God, Sissy, I'm doing that next time."

"I'm not done yet, Sis. Watch this."

With her arms behind her back, Sophia spun herself from side to side, causing them to dance back and forth, bringing huge smiles from her twin and Dayzee.

"Really hot, Fia. And the whole time, they have no idea how hot you really can be!"

"They don't, Dayzee, but I've been good. All except for that first time."

"You miss it, don't you?"

"Yep, I sure do, Dayzee, but I'd rather not kill anyone."

"You like being a Kildare Killer, though."

"I sure like that name. Alright, now it's just the skirt. Because, you know, that's all that's left."

"I like that about you, Sissy."

She reached inside the top elastic and spread it out to get it started moving down over her hips. All the smooth skin of her belly came into view, and before long, it was nothing but skin all the way down to the crumpled-up skirt around her heels.

"Now, that's a sight," said Dayzee.

"She's right, Sissy."

"You're too hot even without the extra heat. I guess you leave them happy, either way."

"Haven't heard any complaints yet. How about you, Sis?"

"No, not a single one. Not even from the dead guy."

Dayzee handed her a black long-sleeved men's dress shirt, and she quickly slipped it on. But she didn't bother to button it.

"How do you look so hot in a men's shirt, Sissy?"

"I've always thought a woman could be really sexy in a man's shirt, like this."

"You weren't wrong, Sissy. How are you so perfect?"

"We're not from this planet—that helps. Your turn, Dayzee. You need a cover-up, too, don't you?"

"Girls, it's my house, and I feel like walking through it naked."

"Except for the heels?"

"Always, Marilyn. That's always a good idea."

Dayzee stripped all her clothes off, tossed them aside, and stood naked in her closet, with the twins each wearing only a men's shirt and their heels.

"Any Earth guy that happened to see this would lose his mind."

"Wouldn't he, though, Sis?"

"Oh, I'm about to lose my mind too," said Marilyn.

"Alright, girls, this has been fun, but it's time to hit the pool. Changed my mind," she said and took another shirt off of its hanger.

*   *   *

"Where are the cameras?" Marilyn said as she followed Dayzee and Sophia back down the stairs. "Shouldn't there be cameras for us?"

"Maybe next time, girls. I know a photographer that could take some amazing photos of all of us."

"Good," said Sophia. "Make the call. Sis and I came to help you, but we want some thrills too. Let's get it all on film."

Through the house, they walked until they'd reached the sliding glass doors that led to the patio. Dayzee slid it to the side and said, "Girls, time to get wet."

"Ooh, I think I kind of already am," said Marilyn.

"I think you always are, Sis."

They walked down the flagstone path and got to the edge of the pool before any of them saw it.

"Sheesh," said Sophia. "It's the head. Wow, it floats."

"God, I'm not getting in there now, Dayzee," said Marilyn. "Especially not with it leering at me."

"Oh, Mare, I really don't think it's—"

Dayzee stopped herself and turned her head to listen to something.

"I've been keeping track. We must have spent more time undressing and complimenting each other upstairs than we knew."

"I call that quality time," said Marilyn.

"So do I. Anyway, I think Bruno is on the last of the cars."

"And bodies."

"Yeah, bodies too. The point is, he needs to keep busy. We shouldn't call him back to fish that thing out of there."

"I'll get it," said Sophia. "Do you have a net or something?"

"Yeah, it's hanging on the side of the pool house. You're really okay with doing that?"

"Not really, but I do want to swim."

"Oh, Sissy, you can't really get in there now, can you?"

"It's loaded with chlorine, girls," said Dayzee. "It should be fine. And heads are biodegradable, which helps."

Sophia brought back a small net on a long pole and soon had pulled the head back toward the edge. She dragged it across the concrete, leaving a trail of water but no blood.

"Well, I guess it's nice and clean now. Just toss it behind the bushes, Fia. The local cats will have a feast."

"The cats eat human heads?" said Marilyn.

"I suppose. If they're hungry enough."

"What about the skull? They won't eat that, will they?"

"No, Mare, probably not. Let's just remember to have Bruno bag it up before the yard crew comes out again. Now, about that pool . . . who's—"

"Dayzee, could we make a Halloween decoration out of it?"

"Mare, that's probably not a good idea. Now, who's going in with me?"

"I am," said Sophia. "I'll take that chance."

"Me too."

Dayzee kicked off her heels, tossed her shirt onto a lounge chair, and began a slow walk down the wide stairs leading into the shallow end. Marilyn and Sophia removed their shirts, too, left them with

Dayzee's, took off their own heels, and they joined her in the warm water.

"Oh, this feels so good," said Marilyn, "and it does seem pretty clean."

"It does feel good, Sis. You want your hair braided?"

"Oh, Sissy, even that phony Marilyn wouldn't want a braid in a pool."

"Okay, you're probably right. How about braiding mine, then?"

"There are some built-in seats on the side if you want to get more comfortable."

"That's a good idea, Dayzee. Come on, Sis."

Sophia led Marilyn to the closest one and sat her down, then she turned and sat in front of her.

"Thanks for the braid, Sis," said Sophia as she sat on the edge. "I'm almost falling off this seat, though."

"Oh, Sissy, there's room. Come on . . . back up some more. Don't be shy."

Sophia wiggled herself back, pressing into her sister.

"You can do better than that, Sissy."

Sophia chuckled and wedged herself in tightly.

"Oh, that's nice. All better. You sure feel nice and warm, Sissy."

Sophia squirmed her hips each way and said, "I bet that's even warmer now."

"Sissy, you better stop."

"Why's that?"

"I might start liking it *too* much!"

"If only I had a camera right now," said Dayzee. "That's a dream shot right there. I'm going to call my photographer friend when we get back inside. Jiff is his name."

"Does he take videos too?" said Sophia and she wiggled around more.

"Sissy, you better stop!"

Sophia held still and said, "We could probably find some really nice poses if we wanted to, don't you think, Sis?"

"I never thought of that. Yes," said Marilyn, "we should try that sometime—sounds like a lot of fun."

"Let's practice later, even without the camera guy. What do you think?"

"Okay, we really should practice."

"Ooh," said Dayzee, "I don't want to miss that."

Marilyn finished the braid, and Sophia waded out into the deeper water. Dayzee stood with water halfway up her breasts, and Sophia said, "That's a good photo too. Just like that."

Dayzee looked down and said, "Yeah, the water's just the right temperature. We really need Jiff to follow us around, don't you think, girls?"

"Except when Bruno's killing people, you mean?" said Marilyn.

"Well, yeah, we don't want to record that. But the rest of the time? Just think of all the good shots up in the closet, the three of us walking through the house, then all of us in the pool. Can you imagine?"

"I sure can. We've already got a big list for Jiff."

"You're right, Fia. We also need to lure the Boss back here and get some answers out of him."

"And torture him," said Sophia.

"Then, we could finally use our heat again. My barbs too—I want to try out my barbs."

"Yeah, Sis. He sure deserves it. It would hurt really bad, and maybe he'd die, but he'd—"

"Girls, let's try to stay focused. Okay, that's the first thing—capture the Boss, and make him tell us how to kill that thing."

"We sure don't want a photographer for all of that!"

"No, Mare, we sure don't."

"Unless we were sure we could keep all the photos because I'd like to see how we look doing all that to him. Hey . . . videos too! We could have your friend take videos of us and the Boss, and—"

"Fia! Just stop a second, alright? We're not getting any photos of that. Jiff can't even be there. So, once we find out from the Boss how to kill it, then we'll have to do that. We'll need to actually kill it."

"That might not be easy," said Marilyn. "Can we be sure the Boss will tell us the truth?"

"He will with my barbs in him," said Sophia. "Oh, he'll sing like a little birdie."

"Can I do that part? Can I try out my barbs on him? I'd love to because—"

"Girls! Slow down! Alright, we'll get the truth from him, and then we'll do whatever it takes to kill that thing."

"And then?" said Sophia.

"Then, it won't matter if we weaken the hell out of Bruno. He's already been such a big help. After that's all done, we can—"

"Hey, wait a minute," said Marilyn. "We can do that other thing with him like he did at the pool party. All three of us. He really wants to!"

"Yep," said Sophia, "we could give him a little taste of—"

"Oh, hold up—both of you. Strike that word from your vocabulary and any word that means the same thing, alright?"

"Little?"

"Yeah, Fia. He's not the tallest guy around, and maybe . . . well he might not . . . I mean—"

"Oh, that's true," said Marilyn. "We don't really know. What did you feel back in the car, Dayzee? When you grabbed him?"

"He was just starting to react, so I knew he liked the idea, but I let go before I could be sure."

"So, we don't really know?"

"No, Mare, so just be sensitive to that."

"Okay, easy enough, Dayzee. But how about if we let him take care of all of us when he gets back? We could all get out of the pool, all naked and dripping wet. We could call him over to the pool, and then Bruno could—"

"I could what?"

*   *   *

Three sets of eyes smiled at their defender as he stood at the pool's edge, looking down on them.

"Your timing is impeccable, Bruno," said Dayzee.

"I took care of the cars and the bodies, and I even got us another limo. I'll hose down your driveway soon, but I wanted to let you know that all of that is gone."

"You've performed such a valuable service for us already."

"Yes, and not just lip service," Marilyn said with a twinkle in her eye. "You've been such a—"

"We're ready for tongue service," said Sophia. "Right here. Right now. How does that sound, tough guy?"

"Um … yeah, I'd love to! Who's first? You know, I guess it doesn't matter because—"

"Let us get out of the pool, and we'll just take it from there."

"But you like it in there, don't you ladies?"

"We don't want you to drown, Bruno," said Dayzee. "I think it would feel heavenly underwater like that, but you—"

"You don't understand. None of you do. I told you I got my strength from that other mission the Guild sent me on. You remember that?"

"Sure, but what does—"

"It was mostly a water planet, Dayzee. A big, gigantic, crushing gravity monster of a planet. Do you remember how they sent me on missions deep underwater? They fixed me up. I can breathe underwater."

They all looked at each other with grins and eyes wide open, then they all looked back up at him.

"Well, aren't you full of surprises! We're ready for you," said Dayzee. "Not a stitch of clothing in here. Just a bunch of naked girls for you to enjoy."

"I can't wait!"

"Are you ready for some naked treats?"

"Yes, ma'am, Dayzee!"

"But you can't enjoy it too much, remember? We still need you strong, alright?"

"I promise. This will just be another service I provide."

"I don't think this is what the Boss had planned for you, is it?"

"No, Lady Sophia, but I like to go beyond the call of duty."

"Oh . . . 'Lady Sophia.' I like that."

He tossed his hat over his shoulder, walked down the stairs fully clothed, and only his long hair floating on the surface could be seen. They watched him approaching them.

"Did you hear that? He called me 'Lady Sophia.' I like his style."

"He's pretty amazing, isn't he?"

"Yeah, Mare. But, girls . . . no heat, okay?"

"Oh, okay."

"And no barbs, Fia. That would just be horrible."

"I promise. I'll just be a normal human type of girl for him."

When he got close enough, they surrounded him, and he tread on the surface, spinning himself around to look at each of them.

"Who's first?"

"That would be me," said Dayzee. "It's my pool, and I want to feel your hands on me somewhere the whole time, you understand? I don't want you getting creative with yourself down deep in the water."

"I will. You'll always feel my hands on you too."

"Good. Or keep your hands on one of us, at least. Between the three of us, we need to feel both of your hands."

"Oh, what a hardship to have to touch all of you!"

He smiled and nodded and sunk below the ripples. He'd turned to face Dayzee, and she felt his hands reach around and hold the backs of her thighs as he stepped in close and gave her a slow, gentle start.

"Oh, that's good, girls. I like it underwater like that."

"Is he doing a good job? Does he know what he's doing?"

"Oh, does he ever, Mare. You'll see."

Dayzee looked up at the sky with a smile and held her breath. A minute later, she started to lean to one side, and both sisters grabbed an arm to steady her. She shook a couple of times and said, "Oh my, oh my, oh my . . ."

She looked back down and said, "That's a good start. Who's next?"

"I am," said Sophia, and Dayzee reached into the water and turned him toward her. The sisters hadn't let go of Dayzee, and she held onto both of them. As the man hidden under the water, providing another valuable service to them, continued his efforts, each of them held onto each other to form a ring.

"Oh, that *is* good underwater. I can tell he's really liking it. That makes a big difference."

"Do you feel his hands on you?"

"Yeah, Dayzee, he's holding my ass. He's squeezing it in his strong hands, and he's like a vise holding me up against him. Wow, I couldn't get away if I tried."

"You're not even trying, are you, Sissy?"

"Hell no, Sis."

"You're not going to heat up, are you, Fia?"

"No, Dayzee, I promise I—oh my!—I won't."

Marilyn let go of Dayzee long enough to splash some water on her sister's chest, and even Sophia looked down to watch the streams of water run down over every little detail, some drops beading up in just the right places before falling back into the pool.

"Just to keep you cool, Sissy."

She splashed her sister again. Then, she flicked some water onto Dayzee too. Dayzee returned the splash, and they all had pool water dripping off of their breasts while their servant tended to Sophia beneath the surface.

"Mm . . . I just might heat him up. You two better keep me cool. Don't stop."

They laughed and splashed, each watching streams of water dripping off the other two, and before long, Sophia stopped splashing and started to shake.

"Oh, this is it. I'm just about there. Don't let go—I might fall over!"

"Do you still feel his hands?"

"Oh yeah, Dayzee. He's rubbing up and down my cheeks and still holding me tight against him. Oh, wow . . ."

"I'm almost there just watching you, Sissy!"

"Hey, Mare, just think about what you're getting real soon. You are so going to like it."

"He really can stay underwater, can't he?"

"He's pretty damn amazing, like a—"

"Hold up," said Marilyn, "it's Sissy's time. Look at her! That look on her face right now . . . it's so hot!"

"Oh . . ." said Sophia, and they had to hold her up.

Twenty seconds passed with no one splashing and two watching Sophia grinning with closed eyes.

"Whew, that was splendid."

"Is he done, Sissy?"

"Oh, I guess, Sis. I like that he's gradually slowing down, not just stopping altogether. Mm . . .that's nice . . ."

After another minute, she reached out and turned Bruno to face her sister.

"Your turn, Sis. And here,"—she splashed water all over her chest—"this isn't because you need it . . . I just like the sight of it."

"Both of you keep splashing me. Oh, I feel his hands on my thighs. He's not holding me tight like he did with you. Oh, there he goes. That's really good."

Her sister gave her another splash and said, "He's not holding you like a clamp?"

"No, he's not. He's touching me so softly. And he's—hey, keep splashing."

Both of them splashed more on Marilyn's chest and smiled at the sight.

"That's really hot, Fia. You have a really hot sister."

"Don't I know it. He's what, Sis?"

"It's like he's under there worshipping me. His hands are flat against my thighs, and he's right there, and he's, oh my, he's . . ."

"Well, that was quick," said Dayzee.

"That's my Sis—she's never too far from one. Or more."

They splashed her a few more times as she shook gently while they helped to hold her up.

As the last of the water dripped off of her in places showing her satisfaction with his work, she said, "Ah, that was so good. I'm sorry it's over."

"He's not coming up for air, is he?" said Dayzee. "I say we give him another round!"

Chapter 9 – Those Dead Bodies

"Your clothes will be out of the dryer soon, Bruno. And I must say, you look damn good in just a towel."

"Thanks, Dayzee. Would you believe I never work out? This is all genetic work from the lab."

"Well, whatever it is, it's damn impressive. You're the best pool boy ever!"

"I like being your pool boy. I'm happy to protect and tend to you in the pool—all of you."

Marilyn and Sophia had each gone off to their rooms to get ready for the evening out. They hadn't been to a party at the Prism since leaving for Ireland several years earlier. Their bags were in their rooms, and they were each getting dressed and ready for a fun night out.

"Good, we'll need you to get busy in the pool again real soon. How does that sound?"

"You know I'd love it. And if the twins are busy, or if they're gone, you should know that I'd be happy just to be your pool boy too."

"We wouldn't even need the pool, would we?"

"No, ma'am. We sure wouldn't."

"So, tell me, Bruno, how is it that you can breathe underwater? How did that happen?"

"It sure wasn't an accident. They worked on me in the lab before I was sent to that planet. Basically, they gave me something kind of like gills, like fish here on Earth. It's not noticeable until I'm in warm water for a while, but then it becomes really obvious."

"Don't be mysterious, alright? What exactly did they do to you? I didn't see anything different about you. I still don't."

"Well, you wouldn't right now because I'm on dry land. If you wouldn't have been splashing around—which I'm really sorry I didn't see!—you probably would have noticed."

"We can certainly splash around just for you to watch. Would you like that?"

"Like you can't even imagine!"

"It's a date. I think we all liked it as much as you! But what would I have noticed?"

"They took a part of me, that part that you wanted me to leave alone when you made me keep my hands on you. That. That's how I breathe underwater. After it's been wet for a while, it swells up, and—"

"Wait, wait, wait. It swells up?"

"Yeah, it gets really big. Solid, too, and I can get my oxygen that way if I need to. It's really pretty amazing because—"

"Wait, wait, wait again! When it gets wet? That's what you said?"

"Yeah, like in an ocean somewhere, or even in a pool, as long as the water's warm enough, or maybe in a—"

"In a girl?"

"You know, I'm not sure about that. They never told me, and when I was on that mission, I never got the chance to—"

"Oh, Bruno, we're going to find out. We are so going to find out. You might be just the kind of man we're all missing while we're here on Earth."

"All three of you? You think the twins will want to try that too? Really? This is the best damn assignment I've ever had!"

"Me first, though. I'll test you out. Maybe more than once. Maybe a *lot* of times. I need to be sure before I recommend you to the girls."

"That's very unselfish of you, Dayzee. You obviously think of others first."

"Are you being a smart ass?"

"Maybe a little."

Dayzee smiled and said, "You've earned it. Anyway, you're exactly right. I'm just thinking about what's best for them, with just a bit of selfishness for myself."

"I'm here to serve you in whatever ways I can. I can kill for you, or—"

"You can fill my needs. I think maybe you can really *fill* my needs."

* * *

At the sound of heels clicking on the tile floors, they both turned and watched Marilyn and Sophia strut into the room and toward them at the bar. Marilyn had chosen a different short white dress, showing off almost every bit of her bare legs. Her heels were high and white, too, and her long blond hair fell gracefully down over her shoulders and back.

Sophia had found a short black dress, and her legs were bare, too, ending in tall black heels. Her black hair fell straight behind her, far down her back, and her big blue eyes sparkled above her red lips.

"Wow, girls. That's quite an entrance."

"Never a photographer around when you need one, huh, Dayzee?"

"It's on our list. I'll call Jiff soon. You two, keep our guy company while I take a minute or two. I'll be right back."

Dayzee's heels clacked on the floor as she walked away wearing only her pool cover-up, and she disappeared around the corner.

They both turned to Bruno, who sat at the bar holding onto his half-full glass of whiskey.

"So, tough guy," said Sophia, "I think you might be the ultimate pool toy."

"Pool boy. Pool toy. Either way, I'm here to take care of all of you."

"Except that we need you strong, remember? At least for now," said Marilyn with a smile. "After we take care of a few problems, I'll need to be taken care of too."

"Me too. Hell, even just another round in the pool would do me just fine. You're coming to the Prism with us, right?"

"Of course. You girls are too hot to go out on your own. No one knows you're not from Earth? Really?"

"You'd think they'd know something was up, right?" said Sophia. "But no, I don't think anyone has even suspected that."

"You said they can't survive your heat? How has that worked out?"

"Oh, Bruno," said Marilyn, "my first time, I had no idea. No one told us. I really roasted that guy. I absolutely loved it and didn't care until all the pleasure was gone. Only then did I feel bad for him. I haven't turned up that heat since."

"Me neither," said Sophia. "It was just one time for me, too, and it was just like for Sis—it was so, so good."

"I can take the heat. You both know that, right?"

They looked at each other long enough to share a smile.

"Yes, you certainly can. You're on our list of things to do. Hey, that's kind of funny," said Marilyn.

"My Sis is a comedian without even trying. But she's right. It's just that we need you strong, like tonight at the party. We might have that thing coming after us again, and if there are just regular old humans giving us problems, well, that might be too much."

"That's why I'm here, ladies."

All heads turned when Dayzee made her grand entrance. She wore black boots up to her knees, fish-net stockings with garter straps, and her black skirt was short and showed off her legs. A black and white tank top barely kept her from spilling out, and she'd woven strips of black ribbon in her long, wavy blond hair. Her eyes were big and bright, and she paused a short distance from them, turned away and smiled at them over her shoulder with her hands on her hips, then turned and walked up to the bar.

"Wow, Dayzee. You sure know how to attract attention," said Marilyn. "That's almost too hot for a place like the Prism."

"You know me, Mare—always look your best. You two look great, so I can't be looking like an average earthgirl on the street."

"You think some of your producer friends might be hanging out?" said Sophia. "Since we're here for a while, we might as well pick up some gigs."

"You never know, girls. It's Halloween—anything can happen. Is everyone ready?"

They all nodded.

"Is the car ready, James?"

"It's Bruno."

"Pool boy, maybe?"

"I like 'pool boy.' Sure, that works."

"Is the car ready, pool boy?"

"Yes, ma'am, but I'm still wearing just a towel."

"Silly pool boy, your clothes are dry. Get dressed, and let's get going!"

*　*　*

Dayzee took the front seat with Bruno, and the twins lounged in the back. On the way toward the exit gate of Dayzee's estate, she screamed, "Stop! Stop the car! Look!"

They all looked through the windshield and along the driveway, and near the road, they saw a headless body staggering toward them.

"Hey," said Marilyn, "maybe he fell apart so he could fall back together as something better!"

"How long have you been saving that line, Sis?"

"You can't imagine how long, Sissy."

"Bruno, you said you got rid of them. What the hell is that?"

"Um, Dayzee . . . I might have lost a body here or there. I was a little distracted. I knew you were all heading for the pool. I thought about how you'd all look naked, really wet, too, with all that water dripping off of every part of you, and—"

"And what? You just tossed the corpses anywhere around the Flats? How many of the dead guys made it to the canyons?"

"Uh, I'm sure every one of the cars made it. I dragged each car far out of the city, and I—"

"That's great, but what about the corpses? What about all those dead bodies, Bruno?"

"I think most of them made it. Probably. Well, some of them. I think some of them made it. Look, I didn't want to mention it because I didn't think it would matter, but—"

"But what, Bruno? What the hell?" said Dayzee.

"Okay, it was really strange. Right after I pulled out of the drive with the first car, I looked in the rearview, and it looked like one of the dead guys was climbing out of a window. Or falling. I thought maybe he was just falling. And if he just fell out somewhere, that would be fine, too, because no one would—"

"Wait a minute. You left a trail of bodies out there?"

"Well, I don't know about a trail so much. But—"

"So, it's not just this headless one coming up the driveway?"

"Sorry, Dayzee, I really don't know. I dumped that first car and came back for the second. I checked, and all four bodies were in it. I think them climbing out had something to do with the car moving."

"What about it?"

"It seemed to animate them somehow. Dayzee, they started leaning and hanging out of the windows, too, and they just fell wherever along the road. Same thing with the last car."

"Bruno, I'm shocked!" said Dayzee. "How could you let this happen?"

Bruno looked away from Dayzee's eyes to study her up and down, then he twisted and examined both twins with his eyes stretched open, then he turned back to Dayzee.

"Naked treats. I was thinking about naked treats. Look at yourself, Dayzee. Look at those twins back there."

He gestured over his shoulder, causing Marilyn to giggle. Dayzee started to smile and shook her head.

"Yeah, I get it. Those beautiful twins sure are distracting."

"So are you, Dayzee."

"Thanks, Mare. Bruno, where do you think all those guys are? Are they near or far?"

"I don't know, but I guess this headless guy was the closest one to your house."

"Hey, maybe he's just looking for his head?" said Marilyn.

"Most men are looking for head, Sis."

"Aren't they, though? That's not all they want, though, because even after I've—"

"Quiet, back there! I need to think!"

They sat in the idling car and watched a bloody man with no head bumbling closer to them with every choppy step. Dayzee turned to Bruno.

"Okay, drive past that thing. Don't hit it, alright? Just drive past it, and let's see what it does."

"I bet he'll keep looking for head, Sissy."

"Really, Sis, guys are crazy for it. There was this one time when I was on set, and I—"

"Quiet!"

Bruno took his foot off of the brake and let the car idle until it was alongside the walking corpse, then the car passed it, and they all turned to look out the window. The body stopped and turned, then it began its short, stumbling steps toward the car.

"Look at that, girls—it's coming after us! That man doesn't care about his head!"

"First time ever," said Sophia with a smirk.

"What are we going to do, Dayzee?" said Marilyn. "Is that stiff going to keep coming after us?"

"Oh, that's funny, Sis. He's stiff and looking for head. You can't make this stuff up!"

"Even when they're dead, Sissy! Sometimes, this planet is just too—"

"Girls! Try to take this seriously, alright?" Dayzee said while looking over her shoulder at them.

She turned back to Bruno and said, "Alright, it's not moving too quick. You really did beat the crap out of it. All of them. None of them will be moving too quick. I say we have a good night out, and maybe those things will never catch up with us."

"But Dayzee," said Marilyn, "all those dead guys are just going to be walking around the Flats on the way to the Prism? How's that going to turn out?"

"Call the dog catcher," said Sophia with a sharp laugh.

"That's funny, Sissy," Marilyn said through her giggles.

"I could run this one down for you, Dayzee. Really smash him up."

"No, don't bother. Let the thing wander around. It'll take a long time for it to get to the Prism. By then, we'll be heading back home. If we have to, we'll finish them off back here if they somehow follow us home. Let's go have a good time and try to forget about them."

"Now, who's being funny?" said Sophia. "We're supposed to forget about twelve rotting corpses animated by something from another world while they all waltz their way to us through the ultra-cool Beverly Hills Flats?"

"They're not really waltzing, Sissy. Maybe more like break dancing? Get it? Because they're broken up, and—"

"Girls, I never should have taught you about the fountain of youth. You're like two Earth teenagers back there. Try to take this seriously. Please!"

"You're right, Dayzee," said Sophia. "This isn't funny, but we are dressed up, and we deserve a night out. We shouldn't let a bunch of dead guys stop that."

"Good. Thank you. Onward, James."

"It's—"

"Bruno. I know. To the Prism, Bruno."

He watched in the rearview, and the three girls turned to watch the corpse continue following after them. Bruno spun the tires and pelted the thing with rocks, twigs, and pinecones. It held up its hands to block the spray.

"He's protecting his head, still! Now, that's kind of funny, Dayzee. You have to admit it."

"When you're right, you're right, Fia. I feel like getting out and throwing garbage at it."

"Ooh, can we?" said Marilyn. "I'm a pretty good aim at throwing rocks, and I bet—"

"I was kidding, Mare."

"Oh."

A speeding limo full of laughter raced toward the Prism, with a headless corpse in slow pursuit.

Chapter 10 – That Creepy Thing

"Don't let us out of your sight, Bruno. I'm feeling a little paranoid, and I'm not ashamed to admit it."

"You have every reason to be cautious, Dayzee. That thing the Guild sent is pretty scary."

"Yeah, and we don't know how much it's capable of. There, up ahead. Let's take that space."

He rolled the limo half of a block past the Prism and parked along the curb. He put it in park and killed the engine, and no one moved.

"I have a question," said Marilyn. "Are we sure that thing can take over more than one at a time?"

"Oh, you're such a sweet kid," said Dayzee. "We already discussed this. Think back to the penthouse pool party. Remember those two guys? Geez, that was only a couple of hours ago, Mare."

"Oh yeah, that's right. So, we can have a small army hiking our way. All dead and trying to make us dead too."

"Yep, Sis. It's good to be back in the Hills, isn't it?"

"Yes, Sissy, but these aren't the kinds of thrills I expected."

"Nope. There sure are plenty of kills, though. Thanks to Bruno!"

* * *

After a short hike past the shops and restaurants lining Sunset, they got to the Prism, and Bruno held the door open. They walked in, all of their heels clicking on the hardwood floor, before the jukebox dropped the next song, and the door swung shut, blocking out what remained of the daylight.

"Hey, my favorite girls," said Mack. "Back already?"

"We wouldn't miss a party here. You know that, Mack," said Dayzee. "How about a round to get us started?"

"Coming right up. And another beer for you?"

Mack glanced up at the hole in the ceiling that still hadn't been patched. Bruno turned and gave it a look.

"Yes, another beer sounds perfect. How's that guy doing?"

"He's okay. He's had bottles and pool sticks broken on his thick skull, so he's used to it."

"He must be pretty angry, though, right?"

"No. Actually, he doesn't remember any of it. I didn't tell him what happened, and he just thinks he pissed someone off again like he usually does. Not much different from any other night for him."

"Oh, well, good . . . I'd hate to have to put another hole in your ceiling."

"How exactly did you do that? That's not the kind of thing we—"

"Oh, that. It's just some sneaky trick I learned at the Shaolin temple a while back."

Mack stared for a few seconds before he spoke.

"Okay. Well, that's that."

He paused, and Bruno stared back calmly.

"Okay, then."

He turned back to the bottles, picked a few, and started mixing up their drinks.

"I should probably pay him to have that hole in the ceiling patched up," said Dayzee.

"Yeah, probably," said Bruno. "Maybe wait until this adventure is over, though, huh? There might be more."

"Oh, right. I could see you destroying this place."

"Here are your drinks, ladies, and a beer for you. Who's destroying the place?"

"No one, Mack. We love this place, you know that."

"Yeah, I do know that. The party's out back. A couple of food trucks pulled in back there, so whatever you have a taste for, you'll probably find it. Have a good time."

"Thanks, Mack. I think we will," Dayzee said while looking out the windows at the sidewalk along Sunset.

They picked up their drinks, and Dayzee led them toward the back door of the Prism.

*　　*　　*

"I'm hungry, Sis. How about you?"

"I wasn't before that wonderful pool party we had,"—she stopped to smile at Bruno, who got a giant grin—"but now I could eat a horse!"

"How about just some normal human food, girls?"

"Sausage sounds good," said Sophia.

All three stopped and stared at her just as Dayzee was about to push the door open.

"No, really. There might be a truck out back. I'm not trying to be funny."

"I know something funny, Sissy. Think of what we could do with a Popsicle. How fast could we melt one? We could have a contest."

"Girls, not now, okay? Or at least wait until we get Jiff to tag along. You two could see who can vaporize their Popsicle the quickest."

"I'm just going to get some pizza," said Marilyn. "But I'll have to be really careful with this white dress."

"Let's just hope the night goes well, and you don't have to worry about getting blood on it," said Dayzee.

"Oh, that's right. That thing's coming after us."

"Maybe all twelve of those things," said Sophia. "Keeping your dress clean might be the least of our problems."

They made it outside and looked around at several food trucks and small groups of people, some standing and some sitting at picnic tables.

"What looks good to you, Bruno?" said Marilyn.

"Besides you?"

"Oh, you really do say the sweetest things. Yes, I mean, what looks good to you to eat?"

"Besides you?" he said with a big smile.

"Oh, I think I felt something. You sweet talker, you. The things you do!"

"You have no idea," said Dayzee.

"What do you mean?"

"Nothing, Mare, let's just eat. Pick out whatever you want. It's all on me."

With hands full of food and drink, they took seats at a table that gave them a good view of the door back into the Prism and the alley alongside it that led to Sunset Boulevard. The food vanished quickly, and there were at least three of them watching all around them.

"I don't think that headless thing could possibly make it this far," said Marilyn. "Something must have happened to it, right?"

"Think about it, Mare: who would even notice? This is Beverly Hills—everyone's too caught up in their own lives."

"Even if someone saw it, they probably wouldn't care, or they'd think it's a prank," said her sister.

"So, that's our conclusion? That if we stay here long enough, it'll show up? What then?" said Bruno.

"You hold it, and we burn it," said Sophia.

"And no one will think that's weird at all . . ." said Marilyn.

"Hey," said Dayzee. "That thing can't move too fast because Bruno busted him up good. So, if it somehow wanders through the Prism and comes at us back here, we'll just lead it into the alley. There are only a couple of deadbeats back there with the garbage, and they won't believe their eyes anyway."

"And if it comes through the alley, then we'll—"

"We'll still lead it right back into the alley, Mare. Alright, we got this covered! I need another slice of pizza. Bruno, what is that you're eating?"

"Oh, this is just vegetables and stuff. I'm a vegan."

"Since when? How did that happen?"

"It's from that world I was on for my last mission. I spent so much time in the water that a flock of fish kind of adopted me. I mean, I didn't swim with them, although I tried, but they always came around me. They started trusting me. It got me thinking. I don't know, but one day, I just decided to change my eating. No more meat for me."

Marilyn got a big smile and said, "Hmm . . . you sure liked the taste of us. I think maybe you'll always need that in your diet!"

"I should be so lucky, Miss Marilyn. I think I will always—"

Loud laughter rang out just inside the Prism's back door, and when it swung open, the headless corpse turned its torso back and forth as if scanning the entire back lot.

"I feel like it's looking at me," said Marilyn.

"Its eyes are somewhere else, but somehow, I think it is," said Dayzee.

The thing stopped with its body turned toward the group at the table.

"Showtime," said Dayzee. "It saw us. I guess we knew this would happen, didn't we?"

"What should we do?" said Marilyn.

"Somehow, it seems to be looking at us. Some headless corpse is looking at us. It's the creepiest thing."

"It sure is, Fia," said Dayzee. "Great—it's starting to walk toward us."

The door slammed behind it, but they could all hear the jukebox continuing to play, and several guests opened the door and stepped around the invader.

"See, girls? Beverly Hills."

"Just tell me what you need from me, Dayzee."

"I will, Bruno. I think, for now, we just need to let it get closer. Look how pathetic it is—it can barely move."

"Yes, Dayzee, but if it got its hands on one of us, it might—"

"Don't worry, Mare . . . we won't let it get you. Okay, everyone ready to hike into the alley? It looks pretty dark back there now."

"Do I have time for that Popsicle?" said Sophia. "I still want to try that, especially when the weather's—"

"Fia, there's a headless corpse coming to get us, and you want a Popsicle?"

"Bad time, huh, Dayzee? Okay, then what's the plan?"

"Oh, shit! Get up, everyone, that thing is picking up speed! Head for the alley!"

"'Head!'" Marilyn said with a cackle.

Partyers moved aside to let the thing pass, and they kept laughing, talking, eating, and drinking. When it passed a waitress with a tray of drinks, it snatched one up. Marilyn turned to see.

"Sissy, watch!"

Sophia stopped and watched, too, as the thing poured the drink over its stump of a neck then dropped the glass with a shatter that was drowned out by the music.

"Where's that camera when we need it, Sis?"

"I don't know, Sissy, but that was one of the funniest—"

"Girls! We have to move!"

Two giggling women followed Dayzee and Bruno around the corner and into the darkness filling the alley. When they walked past a ragged man sitting with a bottle against the brick wall, he grabbed at Sophia's leg.

"Hey, don't touch!"

"Can't blame him, can you, Sissy? You know your legs are magnificent. I'm about to grab them."

"So are yours, Sis. If I was a wino in an alley, and your gorgeous legs were close enough, you know I'd—"

"Enough about the legs already! Alright, let's hold up here. Bruno, do you think you can pin that thing down long enough for Sophia to fry it?"

"I sure can, Dayzee. All of you, stay behind me, and I'll hold it up against this trash container. Who's going to burn it? You, Lady Sophia?"

"Oh, yeah. I'll burn that thing good. Maybe I'll burn that wino, too, because he—"

"No, Fia, you will *not* burn the wino."

"Fine."

"Alright, he's almost on us. Bruno, are you ready?"

"Yes, ma'am. Just a couple more steps."

The dead thing took a few more quicker steps, and Bruno rushed around behind it, where he grabbed both of its arms. It started twisting around and fighting to get loose, but it couldn't break Bruno's grip.

"If it had a head, it would be screaming right now," said Sophia.

"Hey, I wonder if its head is screaming in Dayzee's landscaping? Are they still connected like that?"

"That's actually a very good question, Sis. I wonder if the neighbors can hear? Or what if a cat is gnawing on it, would it be able to scream and—"

"Fia! Today, okay? Let's get this over with."

"Sure, Dayzee."

Sophia closed the distance and hesitated at the sight of its hands reaching for her, even though its arms were trapped and pulled back.

"Alright, here goes."

The glow of her right hand illuminated the alley, causing the grabbing wino to cover his eyes, and Sophia reached out her palm toward the thing's chest.

"Aim for the heart, just like before, Sissy."

"I will. This thing is disgusting, but you know what? I bet it'll still smell like tasty barbecue."

"Just burn it already!"

Sophia brushed back her long black hair with her left hand and jammed her right palm against the thing's heart. It sizzled and smoked, and within seconds, its arms stopped reaching for her. But still, it stood there.

"Go deeper."

"I always say that too, Sis."

"No, I mean all the way through, Sissy."

"Okay, Sis."

Sophia leaned in, causing smoke to billow out, carrying the sweet aroma of burning heart all through the alley.

"Okay, you're through," said Bruno. "Don't burn me too."

"Oh, I won't. Why is it still standing?"

Bruno released it, and it crumpled to the asphalt.

"It ain't," said Bruno.

"You did it, Sissy! You protected us, and you too, Bruno!"

They heard a bottle rattle across the pavement and turned to look. The derelict stared, and his mouth moved, but he didn't say anything.

"He'll never believe it in the morning," said Dayzee. "Okay, Bruno, can you toss what's left of our friend into the trash? We need to get back inside."

While Bruno lifted the body up by one ankle and tossed it into the container like a dead raccoon, Marilyn said, "Back inside? Shouldn't we get out of here before the rest of them show up?"

"I think we might have enough time for our first task," said Dayzee. "Do you remember what that is, Mare?"

"Yes, I do. We need to capture the Boss. Do you know how to call him? I don't."

"There's no definite way to do that, but I think I can figure something out. Come on, let's all go inside."

"After I get my Popsicle."

"Sure, Fia. You've earned it. But then, we have to take care of business."

*   *   *

They took seats at the bar, ordered their drinks from Mack, and mostly watched the silent statue against the far wall.

"Your Popsicle didn't stand a chance, Sissy. And it smelled like blueberries!"

"Hmm . . . I wonder if I taste like blueberries now?"

The three girls turned to look at Bruno. He grinned and shook his head.

"I like blueberries," he said. "And they're vegan."

"I think we might be onto something here. Sissy, I'll try strawberry, and Dayzee, you could—"

"I never should have told you two anything about the fountain. Try to remember why we're back in here while a horde of corpses is heading our way."

"Right, Dayzee, we need to take the Boss back to your place and have some fun with him. I'm using my barbs."

"Yes, you will. Maybe all three of us should give it to him, but we need to get him through the portal first."

"Yep, but how?" said Sophia.

"Every other time he showed up unplanned, it was when I needed him. Like when I was in some kind of distress."

"So, how do we do that? It seems like nothing upsets you."

"You're right about that, Fia. I've been in the Hills a while, and I've seen a lot. I don't know what to do."

They all sat, sipped their drinks, and watched the statue staring back at them.

"That thing's creepy sometimes," said Marilyn.

"It sure is, Sis."

"I have an idea," said Bruno. "And it'll work as long you don't go weak on us, Dayzee."

"What are you thinking?"

"It's complicated, Dayzee, but it should work. The main thing is that you have to keep your promise. If you can do that, then—"

"Alright, Bruno, enough suspense. Just spill it already."

"Okay, Dayzee. You'll have to accept that once we get started, you won't be able to change your mind. Here's my plan: I'm going to keep my hand near the back of Lady Sophia's neck. It'll just look to everyone like I'm being friendly. But you'll give me orders to strangle her if Miss Marilyn does anything except be a helpless girl and get herself into some serious trouble. She's going to walk over and flirt with those guys playing pool. They look pretty rough, and when she eventually laughs at them and tries to walk away, I believe they'll attack her right here in the Prism. We all know she could fight back, but she'll know that if she tries to burn any of them to save herself, you've given me orders to strangle her sister."

The three girls stared at him without saying a word.

"That should upset you, don't you think?"

"But then she'll really be in danger. How's that going to help?"

"Easy. You'll get upset, the Boss will show up, I'll let go of Lady Sophia, and Miss Marilyn can burn her way through them. Or better yet, she can still be a damsel in distress, and I'll go handle them for her. We better be ready to all get the heck out of here quick, though."

"That's crazy."

"It'll work, Dayzee, but you have to understand that we'll let it play out. You won't be able to change your mind, so I'll have to keep following your orders."

"Girls, what do you think?

"It's easy enough for me, Dayzee," said Sophia. "I don't even have to get up. I'll just have another drink and enjoy the show."

"Oh, you know," said Marilyn, "it sounds kind of exciting. I can act that part—I bet I can play a convincing victim. Let's do it!"

While Sophia ordered her next drink, and Marilyn looked with a grin across the bar at the boisterous group of men, Bruno looked at Dayzee and shrugged.

"Okay, fine."

"You have to promise."

"Fine. I promise I won't change my mind until the Boss shows up."

"Now, give the order."

Dayzee took a deep breath, expanding her chest and causing Bruno to smile at the sight, then she let it out slowly.

"Bruno. Strangle Sophia if Marilyn doesn't play the helpless victim for those thugs at the pool table."

"Here we go," said Bruno. "Showtime!"

He reached up and laid his hand at the back of Sophia's neck. She only brushed her silky black hair up and over his hand and took another sip of her drink.

"Oh, Sissy, I think I want to meet those guys over there. You think they'll like my legs? This dress sure does show them off."

"They'll want more than just to look at your legs, Sis. I'm not sure that's the safest thing to do."

"Look at them, Bruno," said Dayzee softly. "They snapped right into their roles. True professionals."

"No, I think they're gentlemen," said Marilyn. "I'm absolutely sure they'll treat me like a lady."

She finished her drink and set it on the bar.

"So, what happens if they get rough?"

"Oh, I don't know. I wouldn't be able to stop them. Never mind that, Sissy. I'm sure they're really nice."

Sophia only shrugged and grinned at her twin sister and took another sip.

"Sissy, does my hair look good?"

Sophia pulled her twin's hair back over her shoulders and arranged it neatly.

"There. You look fantastic—too good for them, Sis."

"Don't be silly—I'm sure they're very polite guys. If I want to walk back here, I'm sure they'll be considerate and let me leave."

"We'll watch from here, Sis, but you're on your own."

"I'm a big girl. I'll be fine. What's the worst that could happen?"

Chapter 11 – What a Tease

"Oh, my sister really does look good from behind, doesn't she?"

"Yeah, she really does," said Dayzee. "She sure knows how to move it too."

*   *   *

Marilyn's slow strut brought her up behind one of the large men shooting pool. His back was broad and stretched his black t-shirt, and tattoos covered his arms and neck. When he pulled his cue stick back for a shot, Marilyn grabbed it.

He turned quickly with fire in his eyes until he saw her. A smile spread across his face as he looked down on the beautiful blond in a short white dress.

"Well, hello there, sweet kitty."

"Hi! I'm sorry if I messed up your shot, but I wanted to come over and say hi."

"I'm glad you did. I can shoot pool anytime, but a hot chick like you doesn't come along all that often."

"Hmm . . . coming often sounds so good. Maybe that's something we could discuss sometime."

"Oh yeah, we sure as hell will."

He reached out and pinched some of her hair and rubbed it between his fingers. Without looking, he laid his cue on the table behind him and sat back against it.

He let go of her hair and said, "You're not very shy, are you?"

"Oh, no. I sure ain't."

"Get in here a little closer."

Marilyn stepped in so close that her bare thighs were brushing against the greasy denim of his jeans. She stood with her heels together and reached up with both hands to hold her hair above her shoulders.

"Do you like my dress?"

*   *   *

"God, what a tease she is!" said Dayzee.

"That's my Sis."

"She's practically shoving her boobs in his face!"

"Yep. She's just getting warmed up. Look at him stare."

*   *   *

The man looked only at Marilyn's breasts, which were mere inches away from his wide-open eyes. Marilyn's assets were straining to fall out, and his bulging eyes had stopped blinking.

"I love how you fill up that dress. Damn, I want a better look at what's under it. Helluva body you got."

Another man had come up behind her and leaned in close, taking deep breaths of her.

"Your friends seem to like my dress too. I wonder if they want a peek at what's hiding under it, just like you? What do you think?"

The man finally looked back up into her eyes, just as his buddy reached around and had one hand on each of her breasts. While those hands kept themselves busy, the first man reached down for her hips. Then, he slid his hands down her thighs until he held the bottom hem of her dress. Marilyn only smiled as she kept holding her mane up with both hands.

*   *   *

"How do you feel about that, Dayzee?" said Bruno. "She's in the thick of it now."

"Eh. She looks like she's having fun teasing those boys. How about you, Fia? What do you think?"

"I agree. She's having a good time over there. This plan will never work. Mack, another drink for me."

* * *

"Let's see a little bit more of you. You don't mind, do you, Honey?"

He began pulling Marilyn's dress up, exposing more of her bare thighs. The man behind her continued to fondle her breasts, and he'd begun slipping his right hand in from the top. He played with her under the dress, squeezing her and rubbing his rough hand across her.

She dropped her hair and said, "Oh, you know, this is a lot of fun, but I just remembered that I need to make a phone call. My darling poodle needs a pedicure appointment."

"What?"

"Don't worry. I'll be right back as soon as I can."

She tried to push down on his hands as he kept pulling her dress higher. With one hand, she tried to pull the other man's hand out from inside her dress, but she didn't have any success with either of them. The fondling and undressing continued, completely ignored by everyone in the Prism except for Dayzee, Sophia, and Bruno. Even Mack looked only at Sophia and never glanced over.

* * *

"Look, Dayzee. She's trying to get away, but they won't let her."

"Yeah, but they're not really being rough with her. They're all just playing around."

Sophia said, "Dayzee, they're feeling her all up and stripping her. She can't fight them, either, because if she does, Bruno's going to strangle me."

"Oh, Fia, it's still just like a fun game to you girls. Who wouldn't feel her up? She's gorgeous."

"Yep, you're right about that. You and I should try that sometime."

"Have you had too much to drink, Fia?"

"Nope. She's just gorgeous. I always feel that way."

"Huh. Alright, let's just watch. Your sister sure does look hot over there, doesn't she?"

"Well, yeah, she really does."

*   *   *

The man in front of Marilyn had yanked her dress up to her waist.

"Oh, now that's a pretty sight."

He called over his shoulders to his friends, "Hey, guys, check this out. Her panties are so thin that you can just about see right through."

Laughter and cheering followed, and Marilyn stopped fighting with her dress. Instead, she placed both hands on his chest and tried to push herself away. The man behind her kept enjoying her breasts.

"Oh, Honey, you're not going anywhere. Not until we're done with you."

"Stop. I changed my mind. I'm not really that kind of girl, and my poodle needs me!"

"You sure are that kind of girl, and no one gives a shit about your damn dog. Hell, we're all going to take a turn."

He glanced around the bar and said, "No one's even watching except your friends, and they don't seem to care what happens to you. Let's do this right here."

The man behind her let go of her breasts and grabbed both of her wrists. He pulled her arms behind her and held them there. The man in front of Marilyn let go of her dress and reached up to feel her breasts instead.

"Oh, man. These are really nice. We all want a better look."

He reached for the dress and began pulling it down over her shoulders. Marilyn turned to look at her companions at the bar and mouthed the word "help."

*　　*　　*

"She's really getting into some trouble now, Dayzee. You can see that, right?" said Sophia.

"She'll give in and burn a couple of them," said Dayzee. "I know she will."

"Then, I'll strangle her beautiful sister, just like you ordered me."

"Ow! Hey, take it easy, Bruno! Dayzee, put an end to this!"

"I changed my mind, Bruno. Let Fia go. Do *not* strangle her!"

"It's too late for all that. I have my orders."

"Dammit, Bruno!"

Dayzee began taking quicker breaths and turned to watch Marilyn surrounded by men holding her and stripping her down.

*　　*　　*

Just after he'd pulled the dress down enough to uncover Marilyn's breasts, he said, "Oh, now that's just wonderful."

The man behind her pulled her arms tighter together, giving them all a better sight. Whistles and laughter filled the room, and Marilyn again turned to look at Dayzee. The man holding her shook her roughly, causing her to look back at the man in front of her.

"Okay, back her up a second."

The man behind her took a step back, and Marilyn shuffled on her heels to back up with him. The man in front stepped out of the way, and immediately, she got pushed down onto the cloth of the pool table with her heels still on the floor and her legs straight and spread apart.

"You guys, take her arms."

Hands from each side grabbed her wrists and pulled her arms straight out to her sides. Her hair fell over and covered her face, and no one at the bar could see any longer if she begged for help.

"Your damn poodle's just going to have to wait."

*   *   *

"They're getting close, Dayzee," said Bruno. "They're really going to do it right here in this bar. You're right about Beverly Hills—no one cares!"

"Stop this, Bruno! I changed my mind about all of it—we'll find another way to—"

"Ow! Bruno, that hurts!"

"Let Fia go, and tell Mare she can defend herself. Do it now, Bruno!"

"Can't. Miss Marilyn's about to get it from all of them, and you can't help her."

"Oh . . . Bruno, please!"

"Ow! Dammit, Bruno!"

*   *   *

Marilyn tried kicking her heels up behind her, but all she could hit was the legs of the man behind her.

"You two, hold her ankles too."

Two men stooped down and held her heels to the floor. She now had her arms spread to the sides as she lay across the table, and her legs were held in place on the floor by strong hands around her ankles.

"Alright, get out of the way," he said as he pushed the second man away. "I'm first, just like last time. Just like every time!"

He stood close behind Marilyn and folded her dress up on her back, showing them all the tiny piece of cloth held on by a thin strap and barely covering her.

*   *   *

"Bruno, she's really in trouble! Make it stop!"

She grabbed Bruno's hand, the one about to strangle Sophia, and tried to pull him away.

"Wasting your time, Dayzee. I'm too strong for that. There's no saving Miss Marilyn now. That sweet girl is about to get violated by all of them. She thought it was a game at first. You saw her face—she doesn't want any of it now."

"So, help her!"

"Ow, Bruno—that really hurts!"

"She asked for it, and now she's getting it. A whole lot of it."

*　　*　　*

"Oh, that is one fine ass."

He grabbed the elastic strap and pulled her panties down to just beneath her cheeks. Cheers, whistles, and laughter erupted.

"Aw, look at that. You're offering that to me? Okay—if you insist!"

Marilyn arched her back and turned her head from side to side, and she fought to move her arms and legs, but she was held down tightly by too many men.

"That's even better. I like when they fight."

He pulled her panties halfway down her thighs and left it there. With slaps to his back and voices encouraging him to keep going, he began to unzip.

*　　*　　*

"Bruno, this has to stop!"

"Sorry, Babe. Miss Marilyn's really trying to get away—she doesn't want it—but it's way too late for that."

"Bruno! Goddammit, Bruno! BRUNO!"

"What's wrong with Bruno?" said the Boss as he tapped Dayzee on her shoulder.

Dayzee spun around and gazed at the gray-haired man in a blue sport coat standing right behind her. He took a quick sip of his cocktail and looked calmly at her. She snapped her head back to Bruno.

"Go help her. Now!"

Bruno let go of Sophia's neck, and she reached up and rubbed it before saying, "Hey, maybe at least let the first guy go? That's kind of hot."

"That's not even funny, Fia," said Dayzee. "Bruno, quit screwing around—go save her!"

*   *   *

Before the man got anything out of his open zipper, his big boots left the floor, and he waited there high in the air with his arms waving around.

"What the—"

When he tipped to one side, and his face broke through the nearest wall, his question went unasked. Bruno looked at the four men holding Marilyn in place, saw their scared faces, then took a moment to admire the view. He let out a deep sigh and smiled at the sight.

"Okay, you can all go if you want. Get your asses down Sunset and find some other game to play."

One said, "We ain't going nowhere, tiny. You got lucky with Big Jake, but you don't have a chance against all of us."

Bruno again took a second to admire what waited there out in the open for anyone to take. He shook his head and sighed again, watching Marilyn writhe on the table, unable to free herself.

"Boys, you're making a mistake. I'm very fond of this young lady. Let her go."

The four kept holding Marilyn to the table, and two other men approached Bruno. With blinding speed, he jumped straight up and punched each man's face, and when they dropped unconscious to the floor, all four men let Marilyn go. Without taking their eyes off of Bruno, they all scurried out of the bar and onto Sunset.

He looked down again at her and saw that, even though she wasn't being held there, she seemed to be in no hurry to get up. He heard her voice.

"I bet that looks mighty good, huh, tough guy?"

"Miss Marilyn, that's . . . that's—"

"They almost had me. That would have been something to watch, huh?"

"Oh, um, that would have been . . . I mean—"

Marilyn laughed and said, "Okay, how about pulling my panties up for me?"

"Really? You'd let me, um, you want me to—"

"Maybe I better just take care of it myself, then."

She stood up on her heels, reached down for her panties, and soon had herself covered. Her dress fell back over her, and she appeared as if nothing had happened.

They walked back to the bar, and Marilyn said, "Oh, hi, Boss. Nice of you to drop by."

"What was that all about?"

"Oh, nothing. I just got into a little bit of trouble, but our hero, Bruno, saved me."

Then, she whispered in her twin sister's ear, "What was the hurry? I could have taken a few of them first."

"That's what I told them. You looked really hot like that too."

"I felt really hot. Hey, when we do some photo shoots, maybe something like that, Sissy?"

"Oh, okay, Sis . . . that's a great idea."

"What are you two whispering about?

"Oh, nothing," said Sophia. "Boss, we need to show you something back at Dayzee's."

"What? I don't know about that. I never get too far from the portal. You know that."

"Yeah, we noticed," said Dayzee. "Why is that?"

"I haven't been conditioned like the rest of you, Dayzee. I get weaker the farther from the portal I go. How far is your house?"

"It's real close—right there in the Flats. Come on, I'm sure everything will work out just fine."

The Boss looked at Marilyn and said, "How are you, Marilyn? Are you okay?"

"I bet she's damn itchy," said Sophia.

The Boss turned and said, "What's that?"

"My Sis is itchy. She's always itchy."

"Oh, I bet. She should make a plan for that."

"She has a plan," said Dayzee.

"I do," said Marilyn.

"We all do," said Sophia.

The Boss looked at the twins before turning back to Dayzee.

"Twins, huh?" said Dayzee. "Go figure. Alright, we need to leave."

*   *   *

Out on the sidewalk in front of the Prism, they all heard sirens wailing in the distance to the west.

"Bruno, which direction did you take those, you know . . . cars and stuff?"

"West, Dayzee. You don't think . . ."

An ambulance with lights blazing approached from their left, sped past them down Sunset, and took the turn left several blocks down. But it didn't travel too far down the street, because they could see the flashing lights bouncing off the buildings lining the street in that area.

"Yeah, I do think. Let's get to the limo."

They took their first steps to cross the street when a fire engine zipped past them, also heading west.

"It's like Armageddon." said Sophia. "Let's stick around and see what happens."

"Good idea, Sissy. We'll wait until we see them getting close, then—"

"Girls, you really need to stop! We can't stick around here and—oh, too late . . . look!"

129

A loose band of corpses ambled toward them from the west, with police and firefighters and medics circled around them, pointing and laughing, some asking them to stop.

"Heck, they're not going to stop," said Sophia. "Hey, can they even hear?"

"Fair question, Sissy. All we know about them is that they're looking for head!"

"Just like a man. Even when they're dead, they still want—"

"Fia. Mare. Just stop. Can you believe that? They're just writing tickets and stuffing them in their pockets. Even the one without a head?"

"Only in Beverly Hills," said Sophia.

"West Hollywood," said Bruno.

"Whatever," said Dayzee.

"It's still Sunset Boulevard, Dayzee."

"Well, that's just wonderful—no one's going to stop them. Look, let's get to the limo. Boss, are you feeling okay? You look a little pale."

"I think I'll be okay. I'm just feeling kind of tired."

"Home, James."

"Dayzee, you know it's—"

"Alright, it's just a joke. Take us home, Bruno. It's been quite an evening so far."

"At your service, Dayzee."

Chapter 12 – That's Weird as Hell

"What are all these stains on your driveway, Dayzee? Did one of you hit a deer or something?"

"Something, yeah. It's supposed to rain later. That'll help."

Bruno pulled the limo into the garage and killed the engine. Everyone got out except for the Boss, who stayed seated in the middle of the backseat.

"Boss, are you okay?" said Marilyn. "Do you need some help?"

"Yeah, I think so, Marilyn. I'm really tired now."

"Okay, just take my hand. We'll get you into the house."

Marilyn and Sophia helped the Boss into the house, but before Dayzee followed, she stopped.

"Bruno, do you remember that head that you sent flying over the house?"

"Yeah, I sure do." he said with a satisfied grin. "I'm kind of proud of that."

"It really was a nice touch. You have a flair for theatrics. Well, we found it in the pool after that, and it ended up behind the shrubs back there. Do you think you could bag that up and set it out with the trash? Tomorrow is garbage pickup day."

"Sure, Dayzee. As long as no one makes jokes about me wandering around the yard looking for head."

"Oh, Bruno, you know I can't promise you that," she said and shook her head with a smile.

He stared at her without a smile of his own, she patted his cheek, and she turned and entered her house.

* * *

"Where's Bruno?" said Marilyn. "Is he still shaking from what he saw of me?"

"Oh, Mare, we all saw you."

"I'll never forget the sight, Sis. I think it was even better because you were pretending to be helpless."

"In a real way, Sissy, I *was* helpless. I knew you'd get hurt if I fought back too much. I really was helpless!"

"And you liked it?"

"It was a fun game, Dayzee, all except for thinking Sissy might get hurt. I don't ever want that."

"What if the Boss never showed up, and they kept going? What would you have done?"

Marilyn paused and smoothed down her dress with a grin. She kept fussing with the bottom hem, and finally, Sophia spoke again.

"You would have liked it, wouldn't you? You just don't want to admit it."

"Well, if that ever really did happen to me, I—"

"You wouldn't stop it. I know you, Sis, and you looked really hot like that."

"I felt really hot!"

"Alright, you two, let's get back to the Boss. I left him on the couch, and he sure looks tired. He's probably fast asleep already."

"No, Dayzee," said Sophia, "we can't just let him take a nap. Don't you remember all the fun things we planned to do to him?"

"You're right, Fia, so why don't you go mix up a special drink for him?"

"Oh, really? You want to dose him up with that?"

Dayzee shrugged and said, "Why not? What's the harm?"

"Fine by me," said Sophia. "Where do you keep all your stuff?"

"It's in the bottom drawer behind the bar. Let's get him lit up and have some fun. Oh, and we'll get some answers too."

"Will that make him a fountain of youth?"

"No, Mare, that only works on human men, but still, it'll get him going. You want something to sink those barbs into, don't you?"

"I really do. I can't even imagine how that feels."

"It feels really good, Sis. You'll see. Well, it won't feel good for him."

"He's going to tell us everything when my barbs dig in," said Marilyn.

"He will, and even if he tells you everything, Dayzee and I will still take our turns."

Marilyn shook her head slowly and said, "Maybe we shouldn't kill him, Dayzee?"

"Mare, if he did send that thing here to kill us, then he's not our friend. He brought this on himself."

"Okay, that makes sense," said Marilyn. "We might as well make it fun for us."

"That's right, Sis. Now, come on—let's get him a stiff drink."

"That's funny, Sissy!"

*   *   *

Behind the bar, Marilyn glanced up to see Dayzee sitting beside the Boss on the couch.

"Sissy, come back here."

She joined her twin, and they both looked over the bar at the gorgeous blond movie star sitting beside their Boss.

"He really isn't all that bad looking, is he?"

"He's alright, Sis. He is pretty buff."

"Where did she say the stuff was?"

"Bottom drawer, Sis."

Marilyn stooped down, opened the drawer, then stood back up with several vials and plastic bags.

"Whoa, Sis . . . what are you doing?"

"He's pretty old, isn't he? I mean, look at that gray hair. He really does need a stiffer drink than a younger man, don't you think?"

"Yeah, you're probably right. He does look pretty old. Okay, mix all of it up."

"Oh, Sissy . . . all of it? Really?"

"Sis, he's going to be dead soon anyway. Let's take that chance and see what happens."

"Alright . . . here goes."

Marilyn mixed all of the vials and packets of powder before pouring it all in with some whiskey in a tall glass. When Sophia reached for it, her sister held her arm and said, "Did you ever wonder what would happen to us with a monster dose like this? What would that do to us?"

"Now that you mention it, I am kind of curious. Let's plan to try that sometime but not now.

"Maybe it makes us super horny," Marilyn said with a big grin.

"You looked plenty horny enough bent over that pool table, Sis."

"I'm still thinking a few more minutes would have been—"

"Just a few?"

"Well, how long would it take? Let's see . . . there were almost ten of them, so—"

"Sis, you wanted them all to have a shot at you?"

"Well, I don't know. I was just thinking out loud."

"Forget that, for now. We need some answers from the Boss."

"I'm going to play with my barbs. Finally!"

"You'll love it, Sis."

*　*　*

"Aw, Boss, here's your drink," said Dayzee. "As tired as you are, a little bit of whiskey might help."

He took the glass and fought to keep his eyes open.

"I am indeed tired, Dayzee. Too far from the portal, I think. Maybe you should hold the glass, because I'm,"—Dayzee took the glass from his hand—". . . I'm . . . I need to lie down for a second."

He fell back onto the cushions with his eyes closed.

"Is he dead already?"

"No, Mare, but he sure is tired. Girls, tie his wrists and ankles together, then tie him to the couch."

"Sure, Dayzee," said Sophia. "I bet this happens all the time here."

"No time for joking. Just get him tied down."

"Who's joking?"

The twins soon had their Boss tied down on his back, and Dayzee leaned in with the glass.

"Fia, hold his mouth open, and I'll pour it in."

Dayzee poured the entire glass, then Sophia held the Boss's mouth closed.

"That ought to do it," said Marilyn. "A big dose for an old man. That should—"

"What are you talking about? What did we just give him?"

"Well, he's so old that I thought—"

"He's not old, Mare! He dyes his hair because he likes the color!"

"Oh. Um. Well. I mean—"

"How much did we just pour down his throat?"

"It was . . . it was probably more than . . . I mean—"

"How much?

Marilyn shrugged and said, "Every last little bit of it."

"Mare, that could kill him!"

"Well, weren't we going to kill him anyway? We were going to—"

"Yes, *after* we got the answers we needed. Oh, girls . . ."

They all looked first at the sleeping man's face then to the bulge springing up in his trousers.

"Too late now, Dayzee," said Sophia. "It's showtime."

"We really need that photographer, Sissy."

"Can you imagine that? With all three of us—"

"Stop, you two. We need to wake him up and get some answers before he dies from that stuff. Fia, pull his pants down while I get undressed. I know just the way to wake him up."

"Dayzee, I thought I'd get to use my barbs first."

"You will. I promise, Mare, I won't barb him. You'll be the first to sink yours into him."

"Good. I can't wait!"

As Sophia worked his pants down over his impressive growth, they stared in amazement. Dayzee had removed all of her clothes, except for her heels, and tossed it all over the back of the couch.

"Oh my," said Marilyn. "I guess that's why he's the Boss!"

"He's sure looking like my kind of boss now, Sis. Dayzee, get going on him. Wake him up."

"I am, Fia. I really don't know how long he'll live with what you two gave him."

"In the meantime, you can't argue with the results."

"No, not at all. Help me get up there."

Dayzee held Sophia's hands and swung her leg over the Boss and ended up with one knee on each side of him.

"That's good. Now, I just need to lower myself down on him just like . . . that. Oh, that's a good start."

"More, Dayzee," said Sophia. "Try to take it all."

"She can do it, Sissy. I know she can."

"Oh, I don't know, girls. It's a lot, and I think it's still growing."

"It is! I can see it!"

"One of you, slap him. Wake him up."

Sophia didn't hesitate, and she struck him several times, making loud smacking sounds. The Boss woke and stared up at Dayzee's breasts as she bounced up and down on as much of him as she could take.

"What . . . Dayzee . . . what are you—"

"It's not just me, Boss. The Kildare Killers are in on this too."

He glanced first at their faces; then he looked down on their long, bare legs as they stood next to the couch.

"You must have thought about this all the time, Boss. Admit it."

He looked back up at Dayzee, who now held her breasts in her hands.

"Well, I mean . . . sure, I—"

"Girls, show him what else is waiting for him."

Marilyn and Sophia hurried to get their clothes off, and they threw it all over the couch too. Very quickly, they both stood naked in their heels near the Boss. He looked first at their breasts, then down along their bellies, then stared somewhere just below their navels. Though weak, he still grinned.

"Look at him grin, Sis."

"Who wouldn't, Sissy?"

Sophia leaned over to peek beneath Dayzee's thigh and said, "Oh my, I think he's still growing."

"I know. I can feel it!"

"I want a turn," said Sophia. "Come on, Dayzee, it's my turn."

Dayzee rose up high and hesitated, and the Boss stared into her eyes.

"I'll be back for more," she said and climbed down off of him, and Sophia took her place.

"My turn, Boss. Have you noticed yet that you're tied up?"

For the first time, he tried pulling his arms down and found that he couldn't.

"Keep struggling. I like it."

"I always suspected you were like that, Sissy."

He tested his constraints again and again, and Sophia lowered herself onto him.

"Oh, that's good, Boss. Let me just go for a ride for a while. You don't mind, do you?"

Even though he pulled at his ropes, he shook his head.

"I didn't think so. Here we go. Just up and down. Up and down. That's a good Boss."

"Fia, try digging your nails into his chest," said Dayzee. "You'll like it."

He shook his head as Sophia started to unbutton his shirt.

"There's no time for that," said Dayzee.

Sophia ripped it open and dug her nails into the bare skin of his chest.

"Oh, that sure is nice!"

"Told you."

"How's that, Boss? You like that?"

He didn't speak, but he did groan as he watched Sophia's breasts swaying with her steady motions.

"Okay, Sissy, my turn. Come on, let me have him."

"Sure, Sis. Now, the fun really begins."

She reached down and grabbed his chin and shook his head a couple of times.

"I wonder if you know what's coming."

"I think I know what he hopes will be coming!" said Dayzee. "Go on, Mare, time to let him have it."

Sophia stepped down onto the carpet, and Marilyn took her spot, with her knees on each side of the helpless man tied to the couch.

"Oh, here we go . . ."

She dropped down on him but didn't get any farther than the other two.

"He's still growing, Sis. Come on . . . you can do it."

"I don't know. I think I bottomed out."

"Alright," said Dayzee, "you remember that we have extra room if we need it, right?"

"I've heard that, but I've never believed it."

"It's true. Now's your chance to try," said Dayzee. "You need to relax. Take slow, deep breaths and just move really gently. That's it. Good girl. Just like that."

Marilyn barely moved as her sister and Dayzee stood next to her and encouraged her.

"You can do it, Sis. Just relax."

"What are you three—"

"Shh," said Sophia. "She's concentrating."

Marilyn closed her eyes and took full breaths, expanding her chest and giving them all a good view.

"Wow, Sis. Amazing."

"She sure looks good," said Dayzee. "They're magnificent."

"Oh, they sure are. Come on, Sis. Keep trying."

Sophia fell to her knees and got real close to peek beneath her sister's thigh.

"Almost, Sis. A little bit more."

Marilyn wiggled from side to side and let out a deep breath.

"She did it," said Sophia. "She really did it!"

Then, Sophia sat on the Boss's chest, turned toward her twin, and gave her a tight hug. Still in each other's arms, Sophia leaned back only slightly and looked into her sister's eyes.

"Sis, how does that feel? I knew you could do it."

"Oh, Sissy . . . I think he's still growing."

"Oh my God . . ."

Sophia started to get up, but Marilyn didn't let her go.

"Hold up, Sissy. Think about what a great photo *this* would be!"

"Oh, you are so right. Dayzee, we need Jiff."

They embraced again and played with each other's hair.

"You girls are adorable, and I wish that photographer was with us already. But, Fia, I'm not sure the Boss can breathe."

She didn't let go of her sister, but she said, "Hmm . . . and I bet he doesn't mind too much."

"You're right about that, Sissy. We do need him alive, though," she whispered into her sister's ear.

"Oh, okay. I'll get up, but you're so sweet, Sis, that I could hug you forever."

"Me too!"

"Okay, you two, we have some business to take care of now that we've all softened him up."

"Oh, that's too funny," Marilyn said as she began a steady up and down on him. "We haven't softened up anything!"

"Oh, Mare . . . you know what I mean."

Dayzee knelt beside the couch and leaned in until her lips were close to the Boss's ear.

"The first question is the easy one. It's just yes or no, Boss. Did you send that thing to kill all of us?"

He said, "No," and kept staring at Marilyn softly bouncing on him, with her breasts rising and settling back down.

"Oh, I'm not sure I believe you."

She turned and put her cheek against his, and they both looked up at Marilyn, who was now holding her hair up away from her shoulders with both hands.

"She sure is stunning, isn't she?"

He nodded, rubbing his cheek along hers.

"I bet she feels heavenly, doesn't she?"

He nodded again, but he didn't speak.

"She won't for long, tough guy, if you don't tell the truth. You know what I'm talking about. Did you send that thing?"

Dayzee waited and watched the blond twin relax and lower herself down over the man who continued to grow from the potion overdose.

"He's still growing, Sis?"

"Mm-hmm. He sure is, Sissy. But I'm handling it."

"You're amazing, Sis. Maybe we should mix up a batch if you ever want to, you know, shoot some pool."

"Oh, you know what? That's a great idea! We could spike all their drinks, then when they—"

"'When,' Sis?"

"Yes, *when* they strip me and stretch me out on the table again, I'll—"

"Girls, you really need to stay focused. We can talk about all that later. But right now, Mr. Boss Man, tell me—did you send that thing to kill us?"

He didn't make a sound, but he shook his head from side to side.

"Why don't I believe you, Boss?"

He shrugged and kept staring with a grin.

"Okay, tough guy. Marilyn, you've been waiting a long time for this. Use them. I'd say start out slow. Savor the moment."

Marilyn closed her eyes and pursed her lips to let out a deep breath, and when the Boss began panting and fighting against his ropes, a smile spread across her face.

"Feels good, doesn't it?"

"Oh, yes, Dayzee, it sure does. Each barb is sending me all these tingles."

"The level of his pain equals the level of your pleasure. That's what they do. The more pain he feels, the—"

"More pleasure I feel? Oh, God, no wonder this is so dangerous. I only want to hurt him as much as I can!"

"Go slow, though, alright? At least for now."

"Okay, Dayzee. I'll try, but it feels so, so good . . ."

"How deep are you?"

"I think only the sharp points are in him, but I know they get thicker, and if I give him more, then—"

"Easy, Sis. Take your time. He's not going anywhere. Already, he can barely speak from the pain."

Dayzee turned toward the Boss and kissed his cheek several times. Then, she turned his face toward hers and kissed his lips. His eyes closed, but he didn't resist. She pulled her lips away only enough to speak to him.

"How come you never took me seriously, Boss? We could have been—"

"Dayzee," said Sophia, "what are you talking about?"

"Nothing, Fia. I forgot where I was for a second. Alright, Boss, you need more motivation. Marilyn, give him some more."

She resumed their kiss, and Marilyn drove her barbs deeper into him. His muffled scream ended up in Dayzee's mouth, and when she backed away, she quickly covered his mouth with her hand.

"How does she feel now, tough guy? You must be losing your mind by now. Do you want it to get worse?"

He shook his head.

"I'm not sure I can stop this sweet girl," she said and looked up at Marilyn, who had closed her eyes and bit her lip.

"She's never felt this good. I'm not sure I can stop her from barbing you all the way. Do you want me to try?"

He closed his eyes and frowned but didn't make a sound. A few seconds later, he nodded.

"Good, so you can still communicate. Now, answer me, or I'll switch this hot blond on high. She'd love it. Boss, did you send that thing?"

With tears leaking out to each side, he shook his head again.

"Boss, it's only going to get worse."

"Not for me," said Marilyn with a laugh. "Oh, it feels so good, Dayzee. I'm going to give him just a bit more."

"Do it. You're going to love it, Sis."

Marilyn moaned as her barbs dug in deeper, and Dayzee held the scream inside the Boss's mouth.

"How much more do you have left, Sis?"

"Oh, I think I have a lot. Maybe a little bit more—it feels so, so good."

She moaned more, and he screamed more, and her moan was louder than his scream.

"Okay, okay, Sis—don't kill him, alright?"

"I've heard that's the best orgasm ever, Sissy. Is that true, Dayzee? If I actually kill him this way, it'll be more ecstasy than any other way?"

"It's true, Mare. You can't imagine how good that would feel."

"I want to do it, Dayzee. I think I'm going to do it."

"You hear that, Boss? I don't think I can talk her out of it. The gorgeous blonde wants that giant climax, and for that, you're not going to survive. Last chance. Did you send that thing?"

His smile was gone, and sweat beaded up everywhere on his face, but he still shook his head.

"Oh, Dayzee, I have to give him more."

"Alright, Boss. Maybe I'm asking you wrong. Did you tell the Guild to end our project?"

He froze, staring up at Marilyn.

"She's got plenty more for you. You'll never survive that. She can really drag this out too."

"Oh, can I? Sissy, is that true?"

"Yep, you could keep him there a long, long time."

"Well, Boss man?" said Dayzee.

"Yes. Yes, I did cancel your project, but I didn't think they'd want to terminate you."

"Did you try to stop them?"

"Stop the Guild? How? Of course, I didn't. I couldn't. I sent Bruno instead."

Dayzee leaned back with a big smile and patted his cheeks with both hands.

"Okay, Marilyn, stop. Don't do it."

"I can't stop, Dayzee. A really big wave is just starting to hit!"

Dayzee stood and grabbed Marilyn by her shoulders and looked into her eyes.

"Stop! You've had enough fun for now. Why don't you give your beautiful sister a turn?"

"I haven't used my barbs in a long time either, Sis. Come on. Pull them out of him, and give me a chance."

"Okay, but I must really love you, Sissy, because this is heavenly!"

"I love you too, Sis."

Marilyn got herself free and scooted back to sit down on the Boss's legs.

"You have room. Come on, Sissy, I want to braid your hair."

"Seriously, Sis?"

"I keep thinking about all the ways we're going to get photographed. This is one of them."

"Your sister has some good ideas, Fia."

Sophia got herself in position, and after some deep breathing and relaxing, she'd lowered herself all the way down.

"Oh, Sissy, you did it too."

Marilyn took her sister's hair in her hands and said, close in her ear, "I knew you could do it, Sissy. Now, imagine there's a camera pointed right at you, right when you get those sweet little barbs of yours out."

"Ooh, that would be a hell of a photo, Sis."

"Think about how many barbs you have, Sissy. All those pointy little barbs . . ."

"Oh, Sis, I can't even count how many. Okay, here goes."

Dayzee held the Boss's scream inside, Sophia drove the points of her barbs into him, and Marilyn got started braiding her twin's long black hair.

"You two are absolutely gorgeous."

"She's right, Sissy," said Marilyn before she let go of her hair, leaned in close, wrapped her arms around her waist, and set her chin on her shoulder. "Give it to him, Sissy. This is so much fun."

Sophia sighed but didn't answer, and she looked up at the ceiling with her mouth open. Marilyn rested both hands on her sister's thighs.

Dayzee leaned in close to the Boss again and said, "One more question, tough guy. Tell us how to kill that thing. Every time we've killed whatever it was in, all it did was send the thing packing to the next warm body."

"Or cold body," Sophia said with her eyes closed as she rose and fell the slightest amount, just enough to pull her embedded barbs up and down in him. Marilyn rode up and down with her.

"She's funny, but she's right. So, Boss, tell us—how do we kill it?"

She slid her hand to one side, giving him a chance to speak, but he didn't answer.

Sophia looked down at him and said, "Good, I don't want him to answer too soon."

Dayzee knew to cover his mouth again, and Sophia let out a low moan as she drove her barbs deeper into him.

"This is really hot, Sissy. Keep giving it to him. I still haven't braided your hair yet because I'm too busy hugging you."

Dayzee gave him another chance, and he turned his head toward her. She put an ear next to his lips, and he whispered his answer to her so low that the twins didn't hear him.

"Oh, that's weird as hell, Boss!"

"I want to go deeper, Dayzee. A little bit more. I'm just now getting to the thickest parts."

"Okay, but don't give him too much. I want a turn too. Oh, wait. Hold up a second."

Dayzee took a small pillow, squeezed the edge down, and jammed it into the Boss's open mouth.

"Okay, give him some more but not too much."

"Oh, God . . . here I go," said Sophia as she closed her eyes and drove all of her barbs deeper into him.

"My, oh my, that feels so good."

"I'll braid your hair later, Sissy. I don't want to miss any of this," Marilyn said close to her sister's ear. She swept all of the straight black hair over to the other side and kept her cheek against her sister's. "Now, you can bounce up and down some just for fun."

"No, Fia, don't do it. He'll never survive that."

Sophia paused and looked down on him, but she didn't move much.

"Okay, I need to get off of him before I can't turn back. This feels too good. I know I'll kill him."

"You would, Sissy. I don't know how you can stop."

"Anyway, it's my turn," said Dayzee. "Mare, try to pry your sister away from him. He's mine."

The twins climbed off of the couch, and Dayzee knelt over the man. But before she let herself down, she said, "Girls, I don't know if you knew it, but the barbs don't cause permanent damage. Look."

Both of them knelt next to the couch and examined him closely.

"You're right. No difference, but the pain was real, wasn't it?"

"Yeah, it sure was. The only way it leaves any lasting damage is if you go so far that you kill him, and neither of you did that."

"Wanted to, though," said Sophia.

"Me too. Are you going to kill him, Dayzee?"

"No, silly girls. I only told him that to scare him. But I'm sure going to give him some pain to remember me by. We're all getting fired now anyway. That is, if we survive that thing trying to kill us. My turn."

"Will you barb him, Dayzee?"

"Oh, I sure will, Mare. He's getting my heat too."

Dayzee took slow, deep breaths and lowered herself down all the way.

"You did it too, Dayzee!" said Marilyn.

"Give him the barbs," said Sophia.

When the Boss screamed into the pillow, and Dayzee tipped her head back, the twins turned to each other and smiled.

"Now, the heat!" said Marilyn.

"Oh yeah, girls. Here it comes. So, so hot . . ."

Just as the Boss bit the pillow and screamed into it, a pounding on the door to the garage froze all of them in place.

Chapter 13 – Speaking of Behinds

"Oh, God," said Dayzee. "That must be Bruno. We forgot all about him."

"Why doesn't he just walk in?" said Sophia. "I'll go see what his problem is. You two keep yourselves busy."

"You're going like that?"

"Oh. I'm naked. Sure, it's just Bruno. Be back in a second."

"You like making him crazy, don't you?"

"I sure do, Dayzee."

Sophia left for the back door, and Dayzee climbed down from the Boss's lap.

"Well, that kind of spoiled the mood some."

"Give Sissy a minute, and you can pick right up where you left off. See? It hasn't spoiled *his* mood."

"I like your positive attitude, Mare. His attitude too."

Their heads turned at the loud crash, the screams, the cussing from Bruno, and Sophia running back toward the couch.

"It's those things! The garage is full of them!"

"What was all that noise?"

"One of them got in the house, Dayzee. It'll be here soon. What are we going to do?"

"Well, where's Bruno? We need him to show off his strength, like in the alley. He could—"

"No, he can't! He's fighting them in the garage. He said they won't die. He can beat them up, but he can't kill them."

One of the dead bodies began slow steps around the corner and came toward the couch. Three naked women huddled close to the unconscious man still tied up, and they all saw that this thing had eyes that were focused right on them.

"I kind of wish I had some clothes on," said Marilyn.

"Because the dead guy's checking you out?"

"Yes, Sissy. It's just a bit creepy."

They all took a step back.

"But you look so good naked, Sis. I think you should stay naked all the time because—"

"Even for a dead guy? I'm not sure I—

"Now is not the time, girls! I know . . . let's lure that thing out into the backyard."

"Sure, and then what?"

"I don't know, Fia. We'll figure something out."

All three rose to their heels and began careful steps backward toward the sliding glass doors.

"We'd have an easier getaway without these heels, Dayzee."

"True, Fia. Always better to look good, though."

"You do look good, Dayzee. Sis too."

"Oh, what about the Boss?" said Marilyn. "Should we untie him at least?"

"Heck with him," said Dayzee. "They're his fault anyway, remember?"

Before sliding the door open, they watched the walking dead body pass by their Boss on the couch and keep coming toward them.

"See? Told you. They're not after him."

"Hey, can you get that door open already?" said Sophia.

"It's stuck. I can't open it," said Dayzee.

"Try harder. Hurry!" said Marilyn.

"Oh my God," said Sophia. "Look at her muscles, Sis."

"Is that from the gym?" said Marilyn.

"No, girls, it's all from the fountain. It's like magic."

Dayzee finally got the glass door to slide, and they all hurried out onto the patio and took rapid, short steps in their heels toward the pool.

"It'll be here in a second, Dayzee. What's the plan?"

"I don't know, Fia. We need Bruno, but he's too busy with his own problems."

They stood naked on their heels with their backs to the pool, and only the landscape lighting gave them a view of the dark shape ambling toward them.

"Dayzee," said Marilyn, "think of something!"

"Oh, I have no idea what—"

"Hey, ladies! Here I come!"

Bruno came running across the grass with a head in each hand.

"What a welcome sight you are!" said Marilyn.

"Just like an Earth guy," said Sophia. "Always looking to get some head."

"They do like two better, Sissy."

"They sure do. Remember that time you and I—"

"Girls! Stop a second! You killed them, Bruno?" said Dayzee. "That worked?"

When he got closer, they saw in the dim light that the heads he held by their hair were snapping and trying to bite him.

"No, I think it just pissed them off. The bodies from these two are still stumbling around too."

"Yeah, here they come," said Dayzee as she pointed toward the garage. "Wonderful."

Ten bodies, two without heads, staggered toward them. Bruno threw each head like a football back at them, and one of them hit a headless corpse in its gut, which caused gas to escape loudly.

"Sheesh."

"That's actually pretty funny," said Marilyn. "I mean, where else could this even happen?"

"Gotta love Beverly Hills, Sis."

"Hey," said Bruno, "what happened to the Boss?"

"Oh, him," said Dayzee. "He's tied to the couch. Can you go back in and get him?"

"Why is he tied to the couch? Did you use him for bait or something?"

"Bruno, we got him to admit that it's his fault that thing came to kill us. Why he didn't just fire us, I don't know. But he's the one. He admitted it."

"So, if he would have fired you, then—"

"Yeah, exactly. But no . . . he told the Guild to end the project. See all those monsters coming after us? *That's* how the Guild ends its projects."

"And, Bruno, if you don't mind," said Sophia, "pull his pants back up before you carry him out here."

"Why are his pants down?"

"It's a long story," said Sophia.

"Longer than we expected, huh, Sissy? I mean, he was really—"

"Girls, not now! Bruno, we'll keep away from this one coming out of the house, and when that corpse gang gets close enough, we'll run over and meet you at the limo. We need to get out of here!"

"Okay, Dayzee, we can do that. But the Boss's pants are down?"

"It was a really long story," said Sophia.

"But we handled that long story, didn't we, Sissy?"

"And we would have again because that potion really did a number on—"

"You two, give it a rest! Bruno, you know what to do. See you at the car."

Bruno began a careful walk back toward the house, and when he got close enough, he gave the dead guy a sharp slap. A loud crack rang out in the otherwise quiet backyard, and its head leaned down on one shoulder.

"Hey, Bruno! Grab our clothes too!"

"Sure thing, Dayzee."

"I know this is a weird time to think about it, with that corpse getting so close and a bunch more coming at us from the garage, but look at us," said Sophia. "We're all naked except for our high heels, and we're hanging out by the pool on a beautiful evening in Beverly Hills. Without the dead guys, this would be a rocking party."

"It would make a fantastic photo shoot, Sissy. Let's plan to get naked like this as soon as we get that photographer. We could—"

"We have to move, girls. That thing is almost here. Let's just circle around the pool, alright?"

"Sure, Dayzee," said Marilyn. "I'm glad they're kind of slow because I can't really run in these heels."

"Yeah, but they sure make you bounce around when you do, Sis."

"Yes, I'd have to hold them still while I ran."

"Even hotter. We'll save that for the videos, alright?"

"Come on, both of you. We need to dodge that wrecked man thing until Bruno can find our clothes, then find the Boss, pull his pants back up, untie him, then pick him up, then carry him to the garage, then—"

"Geez, Dayzee. Maybe we should have asked him to mix some drinks while he was in there too?"

"That's funny, Sissy. But you know, I bet he could have. He's pretty amazing."

"Look, girls, the lights just flashed. I bet that's his signal. Let's hurry around the hot tub and swing around the pool to the garage."

Before taking a step, they all stared across the pool at their pursuer, who froze and waited, sunken eyes moving from one to the other.

"Uh-oh," said Marilyn. "He's waiting for us to make our move. What do we do?"

"If we can get him to chase us around one side, we can run in the other direction," said Dayzee.

"Nope, I think I can scare him away," said Sophia, and she stooped down and reached into the pool. She flicked a handful of water at him, and he twitched when the drops hit him.

"Hey, he doesn't like that, Sissy. Just like a cat. Splash him some more."

"You know it."

She reached in again with one hand, threw more water at him, then reached in with both hands.

"Careful, Sissy."

"Oh, there's nothing to—ah!"

Sophia fell in and disappeared beneath the surface. Marilyn screamed, and Dayzee said, "Sophia, get out of there. He's coming around!"

Sophia's head popped up, and she pulled her wet hair back over her shoulders. She turned to see the body stumbling around the pool to their left, closing in on them.

"Get out of there, Sissy! Hurry!"

Sophia walked as quickly as she could toward the right end of the pool, and when she began walking up the steps, Dayzee and Marilyn each grabbed a hand and pulled her up.

"Hurry, Fia," said Dayzee. "We have to go!"

When Sophia had reached the top, they all looked to see the dead man almost upon them. They turned and hurried toward the garage.

"Sissy, you're all wet!"

"I sure didn't plan that. Sorry that I almost got us all killed by that thing."

"We're fine now," said Dayzee. "Let's just dodge that gang coming across the lawn. Oh, and we have to see about drying you off somehow."

"I say we leave her wet," Marilyn said with a giggle.

"You'd like that, wouldn't you, Sis?"

"Who wouldn't?"

*　　*　　*

The slow-moving horde never caught them, even though one briefly got a hold of a screaming Marilyn's hair, and all three rushed into the limo in the garage.

"Lock the doors, girls, at least until Bruno comes out here."

They all waited, trying to catch their breath, and Marilyn shrieked when the car lurched to one side. They all turned to see one of the headless guys climbing up onto the trunk.

"See how angry they get when they don't get head?"

"Sis, you're really on a roll. He probably wouldn't care who he got a head from, would he?"

"Look, girls, here comes Bruno. Unlock his door. Oh, and the back door too. He has to toss that lame Boss of ours in too."

Marilyn kicked open her door, and Bruno dumped their unconscious Boss on her lap. He slammed the door shut, and she locked it. After climbing in behind the wheel and closing the door, he fired up the engine. The car shook again as another thing climbed up on the roof.

"Hey, um, Bruno," said Dayzee. "Got time for one tiny favor?"

He looked in the mirror at the dead guy climbing up toward the roof of the car.

"Sure, Dayzee. It's not like there's much going on. What can I do for you?"

"Sarcasm?"

"A little, yeah."

Dayzee reached up and turned the mirror lower, and when Bruno saw Sophia not just naked but soaking wet, too, he got a big grin.

"That poor girl could use a beach towel. Be a sweetheart, and get one out of the house, alright? There's a linen closet right inside the door."

"Wait. You're serious?"

"Yeah, of course. She's starting to shiver. Come on . . . it'll only take a sec."

Bruno exhaled a deep breath and swung his door open, striking a dead guy that was standing near and sending it stumbling backward. He stepped out, slammed the door shut, gave the dead body a mighty kick, then raced into the house. In seconds, he was back out with a plush towel. Dayzee unlocked his door, and he got back in.

"You're a real honey," Dayzee said as she took the towel from him and tossed it over her shoulder.

"Oh, wow. Thanks, Bruno," said Sophia.

"Here, let me help you," said Marilyn, and she took the towel and began drying her sister.

Bruno turned to watch with a giant grin.

"That's quite a sight, huh, Bruno?"

"Yeah, Dayzee. Damn."

"Um . . . we're surrounded by rotting corpses that want to kill us. How about if we go for a drive?"

"Oh, yeah. Sure, Dayzee. Of course. First, what is with these dead bodies acting like that? If the Boss knows all about this thing the Guild sent, can't he call it off?"

"I don't think he's in any mood to help us. We used our barbs, Bruno. Well, the twins did anyway. I just got started with mine, and I was about to really heat him up too."

"Really? That's pretty cruel. That's supposed to hurt real bad."

"You've never felt it?"

"God, no. Don't want to."

"Are you sure? Maybe just a little bit after this is all behind us?"

Marilyn said, "Speaking of behinds . . . Sissy, lean over a bit. Perfect!"

Bruno kept staring with his jaw hanging down.

"Really speaking of behinds," said Sophia, "look behind us."

The remaining bodies had closed in on the car and stood there watching them.

"What are they doing? Are they trying to figure out some diabolical plan to get us?"

"They can't be that smart, Mare. Especially the ones without heads."

"That's not the heads they think with, Dayzee," said Sophia.

"Another good one, Sissy!"

"Bruno, just hit the gas and plow through. We'll clean it up some other time."

"Sure, Dayzee, but where are we going?"

"Away from here is all I know. We need to lead them away from the house, so make sure you don't close the gates on the way out."

"Got it, Dayzee. Here we go."

The rear tires squealed against the garage floor, and the limo rocketed out, sending body parts in every direction.

"Oh, I didn't even think of what the car would look like," said Dayzee. "We shouldn't drive around in a limo covered in blood and arms and things."

"Relax," said Sophia. "It's still Beverly Hills."

"You're right about that, Sissy."

"Let's just back out far enough to see how many of them are still walking around, alright, Bruno?"

"Sure thing, Dayzee."

He backed out only enough that he could take the circular drive, and they waited there. One body staggered out. Then another. Both had their own heads. Then, another came out carrying a head.

"Maybe I need a drink, but that's funny," said Sophia.

"Maybe it's funny because you're naked and wet, Sissy."

"Good time to have a drink."

"Another good photo: you having a drink while I dry you off all over."

"We all need a drink, girls. Okay, so it looks like approximately one, two, three—"

"That's funny, too, Dayzee," said Marilyn. "Counting people 'approximately!'"

"Like I was saying, almost three of them, and I guess they're not really people anymore. The rest are just scrap that we'll have to clean up later."

"So, where to, Dayzee?" said Bruno.

"Those things are walking really slow. I think we have about an hour before they get to us at the Prism."

"We're going back to the Prism? That sounds good—I want another Popsicle."

"Fia, you—"

"I want to play some more pool."

Dayzee turned around and saw both twins grinning back at her. Marilyn kept drying her sister.

"Um . . . Mare. I think she's dry now. Why don't you two get dressed?"

"Oh. I think you're right," Marilyn said with a giggle. "I just want to make sure. Okay, we can get dressed, but I really do want some more fun with the pool table."

"I know you two are kidding."

They kept grinning.

"You're serious?"

"I want to try strawberry next time."

"I liked the feel of my skin rubbing on the felt on the table. I liked being surrounded by eager pool sticks all pointed at me too."

"Good one, Sis."

"Don't you two ever get tired? Think of all that has happened today."

"Maybe it's the fountain of youth?"

"You're probably right, Mare. That must be it. Alright . . . to the Prism, James."

Bruno sighed deeply and turned to look at Dayzee.

"I mean, Bruno. To the Prism, Bruno, but just for a quick drink and to figure out what we're going to do about all of this."

"And some pool. That's a fun game!"

"And a Popsicle. Strawberry this time."

Chapter 14 – A Human Woman

"Is he awake back there?"

"No, Dayzee, and I don't think he's waking up anytime soon," said Sophia. "We really gave it to him, didn't we?"

"Yeah, we did. Good, I'm in no hurry to ever talk to him again anyway."

"What are we going to do with him?" said Marilyn. "What's he going to do when he does finally wake up?"

"Well, for sure, we can kiss our jobs goodbye. We'll be on our own here from now on."

"Are we going to be okay, Dayzee? If nothing else, we need to keep taking that potion, don't we?"

"Yeah, Mare, but that won't be a problem. We can find all we need for that. If we don't, the crap nutrition here will slowly kill us."

"Bruno, it looks like you're in trouble too."

"Hey, ladies, I didn't do anything to the Boss."

"No, but you sure didn't stop us, and we could always tell him you *did* mess with him after he zonked out."

"Lady Sophia, you wouldn't. You can't."

"I bet he would have, Sissy, if he wasn't busy trying to kill dead guys."

"No way, Miss Marilyn. Killing dead guys is more my thing. You won't tell him that story, will you?"

"Don't take that chance, tough guy. You're stuck with us now."

He turned to look at Dayzee, who gave him a wink and a smile. He sighed and looked back out through the windshield at the dead bodies getting closer to the limo.

"How about just driving for now? We'll figure it all out at the Prism."

He put the car in gear, turned it to the left to take the circular drive, and they left through the open gate. He switched on the wipers, which streaked blood and dragged small sticky chunks around.

"I saw an arm roll off of the hood, Dayzee," said Sophia. "See? The car's cleaning itself up."

"Should we drive through a car wash?" said Marilyn.

"That's actually not a bad idea," said Dayzee, "but we don't have time. Besides, all the body parts stuff would clog up their brushes and drains and things."

"Sheesh," said Sophia.

*　*　*

"See? We were meant to come back here and regroup. We even got the same parking place."

"Sure, Dayzee," said Sophia, "getting a parking space proves it. How much time do you think we have before those things catch up with us?"

"Oh, Fia, we should have at least an hour. They're not a very lively bunch."

"We are," said Marilyn. "I'm ready for another party!"

"Let's just get inside. Bruno, you don't mind carrying the Boss, do you?"

"Not a problem. It'll look kind of odd, though. Three hot women and me carrying what looks like a dead guy."

"You're new here, but you'll catch on. It's like the blood and guts on the limo. No one will care. Everyone's on their phone or checking their look in the shop windows. We'll be fine."

Out on the sidewalk, they began the walk under the flickering streetlamps toward the bar.

*　　*　　*

"Where's Mack?" said Dayzee.

The tall young woman brushed back her long, straight brown hair. She gave Dayzee a smile and rested her hands on her hips, drawing attention to her tight blouse and tighter jeans.

"He had to run out for a while. I'm Kenzie. What can I get you?"

They'd lined themselves up along the bar. Bruno had stashed the Boss on the floor beside him, and he was propped up against the bar and snoring.

"We have a lot of crazy things to figure out. What drink do you recommend?"

"I'd say whiskey, then. That always helps. I'll make them doubles too."

She took a few steps to their right, turned, and reached for a bottle from the top shelf and began pouring.

"I miss Mack," said Marilyn. "He's hot."

"She's kind of hot, too, Sis. Didn't you notice?"

"Yes, she sure is, Sissy, but I can't stop thinking about using my barbs again. That was unbelievable."

"Yep, you do need a man for that. Even a human one will work— for as long as they last. But don't forget about all the heat you can whip up too."

"Oh, yes, you're right. I could burn anyone or anything. Hey, maybe I'll roast this barstool when we're ready to leave."

"Oh, you could, Sis. I wonder if I could melt a whiskey bottle by holding it in my hand? I bet Kenzie would find us an empty one, especially because we're sure going to empty the one we're drinking, and—"

"You better not let her see any of that, Sissy. You know how that affects humans—she'd be drawn to it. You'd hypnotize her."

"You're right about that."

"Besides, you couldn't do anything like that with a human female, not like a male."

159

"No, not like a male, Sis. You're right about that too."

Marilyn leaned over the bar to look past Dayzee at her sister, who was still watching Kenzie.

"Wait a minute," she said, and her sister turned toward her.

"Have you ever . . . with someone like . . . I mean—"

"Here's your drinks, ladies and one gentleman. I'll start a tab."

"Thanks, Kenzie," said Dayzee. "The whiskey will help. Don't go too far."

"Promise. I won't."

Kenzie stepped away to help Prism patrons off to their left.

"I know what our first topic should be, Dayzee: what to do with the Boss."

Bruno said, "I could put a beer bottle in his hand, and we could just leave him here."

"That's pretty funny, Bruno."

"Thanks, Miss Marilyn."

"Nope, we're sending him back," said Dayzee. "I need to get some of this whiskey in me, and then we'll drag him over to the big guy in the big hat."

"How's that going to help?" Sophia said while still looking to her left. "Do you know how to open the portal?"

"No, Fia, but I've seen it happen enough. I have a theory. I think— hey, Fia, are you with us?"

Sophia snapped her head to her right to look at Dayzee.

"Yep. I'm right here."

"Alright, I think the Boss and everyone else at that level has some kind of implants that—"

"The Boss got a boob job? I didn't notice that when Sissy was scratching him all up. I want to see!"

She started to rise from her stool, and Dayzee grabbed her arm.

"Mare, just settle down. Not that kind of implants. Like a microchip or something. If we get him close enough, I think that portal will just suck him in."

"If we gave him another hit of that potion, maybe *we* could all—"

"No, Fia. Haven't we done enough to him?"

"We could ask him, Dayzee," said Sophia with a big grin before she downed the last of her drink. "Ooh, and we could tie him up again."

"You girls . . . you're too much."

"We could ask *him* if he thinks we're too much. Bet he doesn't."

"Alright, just stop. I'm serious. We need to get him across the room, and I bet he'll disappear."

Bruno clinked his empty beer bottle down and said, "Ladies, allow me. I am here to serve you, remember?"

"Like in the pool," said Marilyn.

"Maybe in the pool again later," said Sophia.

"That reminds me of the pool table," Marilyn said as she looked over at it.

The light above the table was on, and two sticks and most of the balls lay on the felt, but no one was playing.

"You're out of luck," said Dayzee. "At least for the kind of game you want to play."

"I wonder if that Popsicle wagon is still out back?" said Sophia.

"I swear, you two. Look, we have to figure this all out. Bruno, go ahead and dump him by the statue. We can place bets on how fast we think he'll be gone."

"Dayzee, what's going to happen when he gets back home? He's going to be so pissed."

"Really, Mare? You think so? You're such a sweet kid. No, we'll haunt his dreams, even with all the pain that we gave him. Earthmen, I bet, would be the same way: you could hurt them real bad, but as long as you show them a good time and don't totally kill them, they'll always come back for more."

"I'm not sure I could stop myself from killing them."

"Me too, Sis. There's nothing like it."

"As soon as I get a chance, Sissy, I'm going to—"

"No. No, you're not. Bruno, we almost forgot about the Boss. Can you drag him over there?"

"Sure, Dayzee. Happy to."

Bruno slid off of his barstool, picked the Boss up, and held him high above his head while walking toward the statue. He set him down gently, and the sleeping man began to lean to one side. So, Bruno propped him up better and left him. He turned to see all three smiling at him and shaking their heads.

When he turned and looked behind him, all he saw was the statue.

"Way to take out the trash, Bruno," said Sophia.

"That was easy enough. Alright, ladies, what's next?"

"Okay, we need to—"

"Another round, gang?"

"Sure, Kenzie. Set us up," said Dayzee.

She soon set their drinks in front of them, looked at Sophia, and said, "If there's anything else you need, just let me know."

"We will. Thanks, Kenzie."

"Love your hair."

"Thanks."

"Anything at all, just call me over."

Dayzee watched her walk away then continued.

"Here's the thing: the Boss told me—"

"Whatcha got going on there, Sissy?"

Sophia leaned over the bar to see her sister smiling back at her.

"What are you talking about?"

"I think you have an admirer," she said with a grin.

"What? Oh, you mean—"

"Yeah, I mean. Kenzie doesn't know you're really too hot to handle, Sissy."

"She'd never survive it," Sophia said before grinning and taking a swig of her drink. "Besides, I wouldn't have to use all that heat."

"That's true. Just your usual hotness, right?"

"Yep, Sis, that's always enough. I mean, it *would* be enough. You know, if I would ever—"

"That would still be way more hotness than that earthgirl ever—"

"Alright already!" said Dayzee after turning her head back and forth following their conversation. "Let's get back to how we're going to kill that thing."

"The Boss really told you how? And you believe him?"

"Remember how good your barbs felt? Well, *that's* how much it hurt *him*. He couldn't lie at that point."

"Point. Point! Good one, Dayzee," said Marilyn.

"Hey, I didn't even try. I'm almost as funny as you two."

Marilyn and Sophia looked at each other then back at Dayzee.

"Alright, maybe I need some practice yet. Anyway, I believe him. To kill that thing, we—"

"Didn't we already kill some of them?" said Marilyn.

"Think about it. All we did was chase it out of one body and into another. Or, into another dozen bodies."

"That's right—there's a bunch of them now, Dayzee," said Bruno. "I trashed up most of them back at your house, but there's approximately"—he paused to smile at Marilyn—"three of them still moving around."

"He said that it's still only one thing, even if it's in three bodies. If we do it right and kill just one of those things the right way, then all of them will be done."

"You mean, for all this time, all we had to do was finish one of them? We didn't have to go through all that?"

"Yeah, Fia, but it's not so easy to kill one. It's kind of complicated, and we'll need help."

"What kind of help?" said Marilyn.

"We need a woman. A human woman."

Marilyn stared, Sophia's mouth hung open, and Bruno shook his head, grinned, and started on his fresh beer.

Sophia found her voice and said, "What are you talking about? No human woman can do what we can do. Why can't any one of us kill it?"

"It's because she'd have to—"

A loud pound swung in the heavy wooden door, and a head bounced on the floor and rolled to a stop. They all turned to look.

Dayzee said, "Wonderful. Looks like approximately one of them found us."

*   *   *

After turning back to the bar and enjoying their drinks in silence, Bruno set down his bottle and said, "What's the plan?"

"Out back. Let's just get out of here. I haven't figured it all out yet."

They all finished their drinks while looking at the head that had come to rest with its eyes looking in their direction.

"Okay, that's kind of creeping me out," said Marilyn.

"Me too, Sis. Bruno, can you go close its eyes?"

"Fia, we need him for more important things. Besides, we're going outside."

"Sissy, I think it winked at me."

"Of course, Sis. Even the dead guys want you."

Three empty glasses slammed onto the bar, and they all headed out through the back door.

"Oh, look—the Popsicle wagon."

"No, Sissy, if I couldn't take time to have an adventure around the pool table, you sure can't—"

"Girls, we really don't have time for that. Bruno, can you take a peek down the alley and see if it's clear? The easiest thing might be to escape if things get bad."

"Sure, Dayzee."

He ran over and looked around the corner, turned back toward them, and gave them a thumbs-up. While he walked back over, Dayzee led the twins to an empty picnic table under strings of lights between the building and a tall tree.

"What now, Dayzee?"

"I know what we have to do, Mare, but I don't know how to make it all happen."

"What exactly has to happen?"

"Somehow, we have to make one of those things have sex with a live human woman. And while he's, you know, going at it, one of us has to burn the hell out of him."

"Are you sure that's what the Boss said?" said Sophia. "Some human woman will have to go all the way with a possessed dead guy? That's crazy."

"Well, he kind of blacked out before he finished. But he said the human woman has to get the thing's thing turned on. He never said exactly what she had to do after that, though. So, I think she has to do it. She has to let that thing have sex with her."

"Sheesh . . . that's sick," said Sophia. "Who thinks up this stuff? Is there some sicko with a twisted imagination making all this up?"

"Sure sounds like it, Sissy. If he came through that portal right now, boy, I'd—"

"I don't think anyone is making up how this all works. I've heard stories about experiments they were doing back home. I bet whatever this thing is that they sent to kill us came from whatever they were doing. They couldn't control how it would work. We should be thankful that it can be killed at all."

"If we ever go back, which we probably never will," said Sophia, "I'm going to find who made that—"

"We'll worry about that later, Fia. Okay, the Boss didn't have time to explain the reasons why, but I know enough about portals and potions and all that stuff to figure it out."

"Good, because we don't have a clue."

"You girls keep planning things out. I'll watch the door. The body for that head can't be too far away," said Bruno.

"Yeah, it's not like the head could get here on its own, you know."

"Wait. Think about it, Sissy. Maybe someone walking or driving started messing with the dead guy and took his head. Then, he saw it was too gross, or maybe he got tired of it trying to bite him, so he tossed it toward the Prism. You heard it hit the door, right? Maybe the body part of it isn't even close to us yet?"

"Mare, I think you're on to something. Good, maybe we have some time."

"Go on, though, Dayzee. Tell us how that bizarre way of killing the dead thing makes sense."

"Okay, Fia. This is what I think: even though those guys are dead, they're not completely dead. Can you guess which part of them is still alive?"

"Approximately alive?" Sophia said with a grin.

"Yeah, you could say that. Which part?"

"Oh, you don't mean—"

"Yeah, Mare, it really does have a life of its own. Something to do with rigor mortis, maybe? Anyway, that's still ready for action, but we have to get a response out of it. Lure it out of hiding. And that will take a human woman."

"Really . . . you mean one of us couldn't do it?"

"Not while he's dead like that. Only a human woman can do it."

"Oh, I'm starting to see," said Sophia. "She has to awaken that last living part of the dead guy, then while it's out in the open, we—"

"Funny, Sissy! 'Out in the open!'"

"Then, one of us kills the sort-of-brought-back-to-life dead guy thing."

"Exactly, Fia."

"This is sick," said Bruno.

Sophia turned her head to him, gave him a smirk, and said, "Have another beer."

Chapter 15 – That Limo Ride

"Another beer isn't going to make any of this right."

"Maybe not, Bruno, but you'll have one anyway, won't you?" said Dayzee.

"Is that an order?" he said with a grin.

"Yeah, it sure is. I'll just call—"

"I'll call her over," said Sophia, and she waved toward Kenzie across the yard. Kenzie waved back with a smile then continued to take the other table's order.

Marilyn elbowed her as they sat at the picnic table.

"You call her, and she'll come," she said with a giggle.

"Good one, Sis, and I can't say you're wrong. Really, I'm just having fun, that's all."

"I know that, Sissy. You're just playing around to amuse me."

"Are you amused?"

"Yes, I sure am. I think you should flirt with her too. You know . . . just for fun."

"The things I do for my sister . . ."

"So, you think you can convince her to come to Dayzee's with us?"

"Hey, Sis, I'm an actress, remember? I can handle it."

"You might end up having to handle *her*," Marilyn said with a big grin. "Or you just might end up with your end up!"

"Wouldn't be the first time, Sis."

"Or the last, Sissy."

"I don't think it'll have to go that far."

"But if it does? Then what?"

"Well, like I said, I'm an actress, so—"

"Or you could share a Popsicle with her, Sissy. That could turn into something fun. Maybe you wouldn't be acting by then?"

"Oh, you'd really like that, wouldn't you?"

"I sure would, Sissy. See? This is why we need that damn photographer to—"

"We really don't have time for that fun stuff, girls. We need to finish that thing off, and then we need to clean up around my house."

"Oh yeah, we really did leave a mess," said Bruno. "When's garbage day? Tomorrow?"

"Yeah. We'll just bag it all up and set it on the curb."

"The humans that gather garbage, they won't—"

"No, they won't care. Not in Beverly Hills."

"Okay, Dayzee . . . easy enough. Lady Sophia, I'm glad you already called the server over. I have a feeling the more I drink, the easier what we have to do will be."

"Drinks all around," said Sophia before she stood and waved to Kenzie as she exited the bar.

Kenzie smiled, held up one finger, and slipped back inside.

"Here's what we're going to do. Sophia, this really is the best option we have."

All eyes stared at Dayzee.

While looking across the table at Sophia, she said, "Kenzie's human. She's a human female."

"Yep, quite an attractive one, too, but—"

"We're going to use Kenzie."

"Oh, no . . . you can't! She seems pretty nice. What you're talking about is a nasty, mean thing to do to an innocent young girl that—"

"Just how do you know she's so innocent, Sissy?"

"Huh. I guess I don't."

"So, you're okay with it, then?" said Dayzee.

Sophia stared a second or two before answering.

"We're not going to kill her, right?"

"No. There's no way we'll let that thing kill her."

"But she'll have to . . . I mean, some dead guy is really going to—"

"I don't know if it has to go that far, Fia. I think we'll just take it step-by-step. How does that sound? She'll have to get him agitated and horny, then one of us will burn him right through his heart. If that doesn't kill the thing, your sweet Kenzie will have to try harder. You see? Step by step."

"Ugh . . . this is gross. Okay, fine. I'd rather take a chance on this crazy scheme than play it safe."

"Will Sissy have to undress her? You know . . . for the dead guy?"

"Oh, Sis, that's crazy to—"

"I'm afraid so, girls. I mean, the guy's dead. It might take a lot to get him riled up."

"Sissy, you'll get her naked, won't you? Come on . . . it's our only hope."

"Alright, fine. She's our girl, then. It's sure going to mess her up, though."

"It's really the only way. Mare, you're in, right?"

"Yes, I sure am. I don't have a crush on her."

"Sis, I do *not* have a—"

"I'm just teasing, Sissy. Where are we going to do this, Dayzee? Don't tell me back here behind the Prism. I know we can get away with a lot in the Hills, but that? I hardly think so!"

"How about back at your house, Dayzee?" said Bruno. "At least we'll have privacy."

"Yep, we'll just put the burnt mess in some plastic bags at the curb," Sophia said with a smirk.

Marilyn laughed and said, "After it all cools down."

"Right, Sis. We can't leave smoking body parts at the curb."

"Are you sure nobody will notice all that in the trash?" said Marilyn.

"Such a sweet kid," Dayzee said while grinning and shaking her head. "It's Beverly Hills, remember?"

"But won't all the parts still be wiggling and twitching?"

"Yeah, Mare, probably. It's fine. It takes a lot to surprise anyone around here."

"Alright," said Sophia, "here she comes, Sis."

"I have your drinks, ladies and one gentleman."

She went around the table setting drinks in front of Dayzee, Marilyn, and Bruno. She lingered just a moment behind Sophia, and she leaned over enough that her hair fell from behind her shoulders and softly brushed across Sophia's cheek.

"And here's something just for you too."

Sophia turned to see Kenzie close by and looking her in the eye.

"If you need anything else . . ."

"I know who to call."

They shared a smile before Kenzie stood up straight and began her walk back to the bar's rear door.

Sophia turned to watch and said, "She handles those heels like a pro."

"Yes, Sissy, and they're pretty high. Red's a good color. This is going to be easy. She'll do anything for you."

"Oh, I don't know about that."

"I do," said Dayzee. "We won't need Bruno to drag her to the limo. You're all the bait we'll need."

Marilyn elbowed her twin sister again, and they both laughed.

"This plan is really coming together," said Dayzee.

"I'm not even making a joke out of that, Sissy, but I sure could! Hmm . . . or maybe it's not a joke at all!"

"Sis, that's not even—"

"I want to watch. Promise me that you'll let—"

"Alright, girls, just stop. A toast. You too, Bruno."

They all toasted and took a drink under the soft lights as a warm breeze picked up.

*　　*　　*

"I still don't hear any screaming," said Dayzee. "The body hasn't caught up with the head yet."

"That's probably better," said Bruno. "It might be kind of alarming for people when the thing walks into the bar."

"Looking for head."

"Funny, Sissy. Like every other guy in there, huh?"

"Sure, Sis, unless you're stripped and bent over the pool table."

"You are so right, Sissy. They'll want a lot more than—"

"So, Bruno," said Dayzee, "you're suggesting we pick it up on the road somewhere between home and here?"

"It's not moving fast. We know that much. I'll pull up, pop the trunk, and shove it in."

"And back at the house, we just need to find a place to do what we have to do."

"Yep, Dayzee," said Sophia. "How many rooms are in that mansion of yours anyway?"

"God, I don't even know. Too many, I think. But we'll have to pick one."

Sophia said, "If we're going to do this right, it means I have to lure Kenzie back for some fun."

"No Popsicles, though, Sissy."

Sophia sighed and said, "Nope, not this time anyway. See, Sis? I'm getting into character."

"Yes, very convincingly too."

Sophia gave her sister a grin and said, "Okay, it has to be a bedroom. Oh, and here's an idea that I just had: we can do it so she never even knows what's going on. Hey, this could really work."

"What are you talking about?"

"Dayzee, I'll try to talk her into wearing a blindfold. If it all works out, she'll be turning that dead thing on, and—"

"That thing might not be the only one, Sissy."

"—and she'll never know it," Sophia said while smiling and nodding to her sister. "This could work."

"But she'll hear us, Fia. How can we do all that and not have her hear it?"

"Well, it's not like the headless guy is going to say anything."

"No, that's true, but there will still be noise because—"

"Hey, put headphones on her, Sissy. I bet she'd like that. I think I would too. Like the next time I'm pinned to the pool table—I'd never hear anything. It would all be a surprise. And the blindfold, too, because—"

"Focus, Mare. Alright, that's a good idea—you can put some headphones on her too. But what about the smell when one of us burns that thing?"

"Hmm . . . I don't know about that. That would be impossible to—"

"Bacon," said Bruno. "She'll know the rest of us are downstairs. Just tell her we're hungry after drinking, and we're frying bacon. She doesn't know I'm a vegan."

"You're an absolute genius, Bruno," said Dayzee. "Yes, that could work!"

*   *   *

"There's no point in waiting, and besides, it's almost last call. Time for you to call Kenzie, Fia. Call your darling female human friend over, and let's get going on this."

"Is this really the only way, Dayzee?" said Sophia.

"Maybe not, but we don't have time to figure anything else out. How many more bodies are going to start trying to kill us? Sure, Bruno slaughtered a bunch of them, but what's next? Twenty of them? A hundred?"

"Oh, Dayzee, could that really happen?"

"I don't know, Mare. I only know I don't want to find out. I want to wrap this up tonight—I'd like to have a restful weekend before starting my next film Monday morning."

"After all this, Dayzee?" said Bruno. "Don't you ever get tired?"

"I have a little secret that keeps me going. These girls do too."

"Maybe I should try that because I'm finally getting tired."

"No, Bruno, you wouldn't want to do what we do."

"Maybe he would, Dayzee," Sophia said with a chuckle.

"Yes, how do you know, Dayzee?"

"Mare, Fia, trust me . . . he just needs some sleep."

"Well, I'm curious now," said Bruno.

Marilyn and Sophia shared a look and a giggle, and Dayzee shook her head with a grin.

"Okay, maybe some other time. Fia, let's get started. Kenzie's probably getting off about now anyway."

"Maybe pretty soon, too, Sissy."

"No, Sis, we really do have to stay focused. You want to stay alive to shoot some pool someday soon, don't you?"

"I sure do. I never knew that game could be so fun."

"Okay, then."

She stood and waved for Kenzie to come over. She had no tray or drinks, only a small purse in her hand. A light jacket draped over her arm.

"It's quitting time, but I can still get you whatever you need," she said with a smile.

"About that. The Prism is closing, but we're not quite done yet. This pretty lady,"—she pointed at Dayzee—"has a sweet mansion in the Flats, and we're going back for another drink. Why don't you ride with us?"

"Well, I don't know. I have a second job early tomorrow, and—"

Sophia touched her arm that held the jacket and looked into her eyes. Kenzie stared for a few seconds before nodding several times and smiling.

"Okay. You know, I think I'd like that."

"I bet Sissy just used some heat, Dayzee," Marilyn whispered in Dayzee's ear.

"Oh, you think?"

"What are you two whispering about?" said Sophia.

"Nothing," said Dayzee. "Don't mind us."

"Alright, Kenzie, how about if I make sure you like it there?"

"Can't say no to that," she said with a big grin.

"Heat. It's like hypnosis," said Marilyn.

Sophia turned and gave her sister a look.

After looking back into Kenzie's eyes, Sophia said, "Bring around the limo, James."

"It's not—"

"I know, I know. Kenzie and I are ready for that limo ride. Aren't we, Kenzie?"

"Oh, I'm more than ready."

* * *

They gave Bruno a few minutes, then walked through the alley to the sidewalk, where they found the limo idling. Bruno jumped out and held the front door for Dayzee. Then, he opened the rear for Sophia, then Kenzie, then Marilyn. He closed the door, walked back around, and sat behind the wheel.

"I've never been in a limo before. This is nice!"

"It sure is cozy," said Marilyn, whose shoulder and hips were up against Kenzie's right side. Sophia was pressed against her left side.

"Dayzee's home can be pretty cozy too. If you find just the right spot," said Sophia.

"I bet you will, Sissy."

A loud crack rang out and shook the car as a bullet shattered Bruno's window on its path past Dayzee and through her window too.

"God, not this again," said Dayzee.

"Do you want me to hunt that guy down, Dayzee?" said Bruno. "I could put an end to this right now."

"No, that's alright. He's a terrible shot, so it's more annoying than anything."

"Someone's shooting at us?" said Kenzie. "What the hell is—"

"Oh, it's okay," said Marilyn as she grabbed Kenzie's thigh.

"It really is," said Sophia before she began rubbing Kenzie's other thigh. "It won't spoil our fun. Home, James."

"Lady Sophia, you know my—"

"Yep, I know, Bruno. Let's get out of here, alright?"

Bruno put the car in gear and began idling west, back toward the Flats. Everyone except Kenzie looked intently all around the car as they rolled down Sunset. The bloody limo without front windows never turned a head, and Bruno turned the car left on Dayzee's street, where he continued to cruise slowly.

"Did you all see that head that someone threw into the Prism?" said Kenzie.

"Yeah," said Dayzee, "those kids and their Halloween pranks. What will they think of next?"

"That," said Sophia as she leaned forward and pointed to the sidewalk ahead of them and on the right.

A headless body was staggering by itself, moving toward the Prism. Its arms were out in front, and its hands were snapping open and shut.

"Looks like it's heading for the Prism," said Sophia.

"'Heading.' Another funny one, Sissy."

"But that looks so real."

"It sure does, Kenzie, and we think we know who that is, don't we, Bruno?" said Dayzee.

"Uh . . . yeah. Yeah, we do."

Dayzee turned around to face the backseat.

"He's a real clown, that one. He waits all year for Halloween, gets shit-faced drunk, and wanders around like that hoping he'll scare someone. No one ever cares."

"He's really not even scary," said Marilyn. "He's just drunk."

"He's going to hurt himself if we don't help him out," said Sophia.

"That's right, girls. Bruno, why don't we take him home and let him sober up before he gets into any real trouble?"

"As you wish, Dayzee."

Bruno pulled alongside the walking dead body and put the limo in park. He hit the trunk button, climbed out, and walked up to the thing, which had stopped and turned toward the limo.

Dayzee turned around again and said, "So, Kenzie, have you been in the Hills long?"

"No, not too long. I just moved out here a few months ago. I'm an actress."

"Aren't we all?"

While they were chatting, Marilyn and Sophia watched Bruno grab the thing from behind and pull it back over his shoulder, where its arms and legs waved around. When it tipped, a bunch of gooey slop fell out and slid down his back, causing him to yell, "Oh, shit!"

Before Kenzie could turn to look, Sophia reached up for her cheek and turned her to face her.

"What was that all about?" she said while looking at Sophia.

"Eh . . . it's just Bruno clowning around. You have beautiful eyes."

Their faces were so close that their noses almost rubbed together. Light from the lampposts lining the street barely filtered into the backseat.

"It's so dark. I don't know how you can see them."

"Damn it!" Bruno said.

Kenzie tried to turn again, but Sophia kept holding her cheek.

"Oh, I can see. I like what I see being so close."

They both smiled and tipped their heads slightly. The car bounced from Bruno slamming the body into the trunk.

"What was that?" she said softly with her lips almost touching Sophia's. "Your friend really is in the trunk?"

"Yep, probably. It's a short ride to Dayzee's mansion. He'll be fine."

Kenzie closed her eyes and leaned closer, her lips just brushing against Sophia's. Then, Marilyn gave Kenzie's head a gentle push, and her lips landed on her sister's. Marilyn held her there, and five seconds later, Bruno climbed in and slammed the door. Kenzie turned and faced forward again with a smile, and Sophia leaned over to glare at her sister, who smiled and gave her a thumbs-up.

"Okay, Dayzee, that friend of ours is safe and sound now. And he sure was drunk—he barfed all over me."

"We'll get you cleaned up, Bruno. The limo, too, but no swimming for you until you scrub that mess off of you, alright?"

"Sure, Dayzee. Of course."

"Oh, wow, you have a pool too?"

"Yeah, Kenzie, I have just about everything. There are rooms I haven't even been in. Probably no one has. You'll like it there."

Sophia held Kenzie's thigh and said, "You will, Kenzie. I'll give you a personal tour."

"I think I like it already."

Chapter 16 – That Poor Earthgirl

"I can't believe there were two more guys dressed up the same way walking down your street."

"It's Halloween, Kenzie . . . all the crazies are out," said Dayzee.

Bruno steered the limo through the entrance gate and up the driveway under the bright moonlight. Dayzee took out her phone, hit a couple of buttons, and both gates closed.

"We don't need any more guests, do we?" she said.

"Nope, just this one," Sophia said and patted Kenzie's leg.

Kenzie turned to smile at Sophia, and Marilyn reached up for Kenzie's head again. But Kenzie turned to look through the windshield, and Marilyn snapped her hand back to her lap.

"Oh my God, what a big house. It's beautiful!"

"Thanks, Kenzie. I think the one in France is bigger, but this one is still nice. Bruno, maybe we should leave the limo out tonight?"

"Oh yeah, that's a good idea."

He pulled it up near the garage and switched off the engine. Other than the sporadic thumping coming from inside the trunk, the night was still.

"Let's get inside, girls, and let Bruno help out our drunk friend."

"I'll try to sober him up and send him on his way, Dayzee."

"Perfect. And Bruno, can you take a look around the yard too? Just a routine security thing. Alright, Bruno?"

"Yeah, Dayzee. Go on ahead. I'll catch up with you soon."

* * *

As they traveled the flagstone walk to the house, past shrubs and flower beds interspersed with soft landscape lights, Dayzee said, "I'm not sure I've ever gone in through the front door before. Yay, a new experience."

"We've had a day just full of those," said Marilyn. "and the night isn't over, is it, Sissy?"

"I think it's cute how you two call each other Sis and Sissy."

"We're really close," said Marilyn. "Being twins probably has something to do with it."

"Oh, I thought you looked a lot alike. Except for the hair anyway."

"How else would you tell us apart?" said Sophia.

"Yes, like in a dark room, Kenzie. Who would ever know?" said Marilyn. "Hey, maybe we should test—"

Sophia gave Marilyn's behind a quick smack.

"Hey, I just mean, you know, if that ever happened, Sissy."

Dayzee unlocked the front door, and they all walked in.

"Oh, this is unbelievable," said Kenzie. "It's beautiful and so big!"

"Thanks. It really does have more rooms than I can count."

"Speaking of rooms," said Sophia after turning to Kenzie, "why don't you run upstairs and pick out a room? They're all suites too."

"Well, I wouldn't want to take Dayzee's—"

"Her suite is the last one down the hall to the left. Go on and take any other. It'll be like hide-and-seek. I'll come hunting for you in a couple of minutes, alright?"

"Sure. Don't take too long, though, okay?"

She gave Sophia a quick kiss and began up the stairs. Dayzee and Marilyn started for the kitchen, and Marilyn turned to see her sister watching Kenzie climbing the stairs.

Marilyn stopped and said, "She does look good in those tight jeans, doesn't she?"

"Oh, I don't know. I guess, maybe. I just wanted to make sure she didn't fall. Those are some pretty high heels she's wearing."

"Uh-huh. Sure. She just kissed you, Sissy."

"You got her started, Sis, back in the limo."

"Yes, that was fun. Too bad Bruno broke it up. If he didn't come back so quick, you'd still be kissing."

"I can play my part if I have to, Sis."

"I know, Sissy. You did good at getting her here. We just have to bring that thing up there and finish it."

"I really hate doing that to her."

"We have a good plan, Fia," said Dayzee. "It'll be like you said: she'll never know, at least if we do it right."

"How long before Bruno can drag that thing up there?"

"Probably not long. He's not really going to walk all around the estate, so he'll probably get in here pretty quick."

"Come on, Sissy, come with us to the kitchen for a minute. I'm starving."

"Um . . . you two go on ahead. Maybe I'll just go up and check on Kenzie."

"Check on her, huh? Oh, Sissy, be careful—anything can happen on Halloween."

"No, Sis, it's not like that. I need to get things ready, remember? With the blindfold and all that?"

"Oh, that's right, Mare. She'll need some time for that. Let's put on some music and get something to eat. I can't believe the sun will be up soon."

"It's been a crazy day, Dayzee. Okay, Sissy, you're on your own. When she has the headphones on, give us some kind of signal, okay? We'll bring that thing up there and get this over with."

"Sounds good. But when I call you, get up there quick, alright?"

"Why, Sissy? Afraid of what you might do? I mean, only because it's Halloween," she said with a big smile.

"I'm not afraid at all, Sis, and if I get in any trouble, I can burn her up like nothing."

"No, no, you can't, Sissy—you'll burn down Dayzee's house!"

"Oh, you're right. Don't worry, Sis, she's nothing I can't handle."

Sophia turned and began climbing the stairs. They watched her hips shifting from side to side in her tight black skirt.

"You know we should have a photographer for what's going to happen up there, don't you, Dayzee?"

"You can't be serious. Getting a headless dead guy all excited, and then—"

"No, Dayzee. Before that. I might even sneak up there and take a peek."

"If you do snoop on them, don't you dare join them. I'll need your help with the dead guy."

"No promises, Dayzee. I get so itchy. Besides, it's Halloween, and I deserve some fun too!"

*   *   *

Sophia's heels clicked on the hallway's tile floor as she went from room to room, opening the doors and looking inside. Three times she saw only an untouched bed and switched off lamps on the nightstands. When she opened the fourth door, she saw that the lamps glowed softly, and Kenzie reclined beneath the bedspread against a stack of pillows.

"Uh-oh, you found me."

"I told you I'd hunt you down. How do you like the room?"

"The room is perfect. There were some men's shirts in the closet. I hope Dayzee doesn't mind, but I borrowed one."

She rolled down the blanket to show her men's white dress shirt buttoned up high.

"I like dressing in men's clothes sometimes. You like?"

Sophia stared for a few seconds, then found her voice again. "Yeah. That's hot, Kenzie."

She walked closer and stood near the bed. Kenzie popped several of the top buttons and made sure the shirt was opened enough to offer a good view.

"Can you still tell that I'm a girl?" she said as she stretched the shirt straight down. She wore nothing under it, and the thin, tight material showed two prominent details.

"Oh, well, yeah, that's obvious."

"Maybe you should get more comfortable too, Fifi? Can I call you Fifi?"

"Yeah, of course. Call me Fifi, if you want, and you're right—I believe I should get more comfortable. Soon."

Kenzie folded her blanket down farther and kicked it away to show her bare legs.

"You're sure no one is going to come up here and disturb us?"

"Not unless I call them."

"And why would you do that, Fifi?"

Sophia studied Kenzie's long, slender legs all the way up to the white shirt that had bunched up high on her thighs. The popped buttons revealed the curves of her breasts, and her excitement was obvious. Sophia took another step closer to the bed.

"Well, I, um . . ."—she stared at Kenzie's breasts—"I'm starting to wonder why I'd ever do that too."

*   *   *

"Who's pounding on the front door? Could that be Bruno?" said Dayzee.

She and Marilyn rushed to the door, and when Dayzee opened it, they saw Bruno standing on a dead guy's neck and holding another by its throat. Beyond him, six or seven more were approaching. They all had heads attached.

"Bruno, what the—"

"They got through the gate, Dayzee. Nothing to worry about, but I wanted to let you know this is going to take a few minutes."

"You're sure you have it under control?"

The dead guy under Bruno's boots tried rolling from side to side, and the one in his iron grip flailed and moved its mouth, but it couldn't make a sound.

"Yeah, this is nothing. I got this."

"Good. Hurry, though, alright? Fia is already up there getting Kenzie ready. We need to get one of these things up there too."

"It doesn't have to be the one in the trunk? Alright, that helps."

He stomped on the throat beneath his boot and shook the other by its neck, dragging its boots across the walk.

"I'll destroy all but one of these and bring it in. How does that sound?"

"Perfect. Just hurry, alright?"

"Sure thing, Dayzee."

After Dayzee had closed the door, Marilyn said, "Maybe there's no rush, Dayzee. Sissy has been up there a while already. Maybe she's not in any hurry?"

"Oh, you think?"

"Oh, I don't know. But she's always bragging about being such a good actress, and—"

"She really is, Mare. You know that."

"Yes, I know, but this is kind of fun. It might not be easy for her, but she'll have to play that part, whether she wants to or not. We can make her wait awhile."

*　*　*

"That's a nice blouse, Fifi. Maybe you should take it off for me? I can't wait to see what you're hiding in there."

"Well, I mean . . . sure, that's a really good idea."

Sophia began to slowly unbutton her blouse, and she watched as Kenzie began to unbutton her shirt.

"I kind of like wearing this men's shirt. Does it look good on me?"

"Oh, yeah. Better than whoever it belonged to, I'm sure."

"Maybe you'll like it better when I toss it on the floor?"

Sophia stopped unbuttoning and watched as Kenzie popped another button between her breasts.

"Oh, yeah, I think that might be the best place for it."

* * *

Back in the kitchen, Dayzee said, "Are you sure we should do that to your sister? Yes, she's a good actress, but it was only to set Kenzie up for the plan to kill the dead guy thing."

"I don't know, Dayzee. I think she kind of likes Kenzie."

"You think? Really? I think she was just messing with you."

"I don't know, but I'm sure she gets at least as itchy as me. Anyway, Bruno will be in soon, and you know what? Maybe we shouldn't wait for her to call us."

"I think you might be wrong about that, Mare. It was her plan, remember? She said to wait until she called us. By now, she might be forcing poor Kenzie into wearing a blindfold and headphones. She seemed like nothing but a sweet kid."

"I thought so too. Sissy is probably taking complete control of her and getting her ready."

"You mean the blindfold and headphones?"

"Yes, probably. Sissy really likes to take charge. Okay, even if Bruno comes in soon, he'll just have to hold that thing until we hear from Sissy."

Dayzee nodded and said, "You're right. Fia can handle that girl."

* * *

"You look good in heels that high."

"You think? I always wear them pretty high."

"To show off your legs?"

Sophia laughed and said, "Yeah, I guess so."

"You should. They're really nice. Really sexy."

"Thanks. Yours look really good too."

"I work out. I run too. Really good muscle tone. You'll have to let me know what you think."

Sophia glanced down at Kenzie's bare legs stretched straight out on the bed.

"I . . . um . . . sure. They sure look toned. Hey, you know what would be fun? If you wore a blindfold. How does that sound?"

Kenzie stared with a grin and shook her head.

"No way, Fifi. I'm not missing anything."

"But it could be fun because—"

Kenzie laughed more and said, "There's no way in hell. I can't wait to see you with nothing on. Oh, maybe just those heels. Keep those on for me, pretty girl."

"Um . . . alright."

*　　*　　*

They heard the front door open and slam shut, and seconds later, Bruno came in by himself.

"Bruno, what happened? You were supposed to bring one of them in here."

"Oh, Dayzee, I forgot all about that. I got carried away crushing in heads and snapping arms and legs, and I just forgot. I'll have to get the one in the trunk."

"Alright, we still have that one. I bet we have a real mess out there, huh?"

"Oh, yeah. I didn't take the time to clean anything up. Are we ready to go up there?"

Dayzee and Marilyn looked at each other and shrugged.

"We're supposed to wait until we hear from Fia. Remember the plan?"

"Yeah, sure I do. What's taking her so long?"

"Well, these things don't always go like clockwork, Bruno," said Marilyn. "I'm sure she's got things under control. Let's just wait."

* * *

"Hmm, I'm about to beat you," Kenzie said as she opened the second to last button. Sophia froze and stared at her as she pulled her shirt open wide, showing her bare breasts.

"Not bad, huh?"

"No, they're gorgeous. They really are."

Sophia continued to gaze at her breasts.

"I bet yours are too. What's taking so long? Come on, show me those boobies already!"

Sophia finished unbuttoning and pulled her blouse wide open, showing Kenzie the lacy black bra she wore.

"Oh yeah, there's a bra too. Well, that won't take long, will it?"

"Um . . . no, probably not. Sometimes, the clasp gets stuck, though, and—"

"Don't make me get up and rip it off of you."

"Oh, you wouldn't."

"Watch and see. One way or another, Fifi, that bra is coming off."

"Well, I—"

"I am so loving this show."

* * *

"Are you going to get tired from fighting those dead things, Bruno?"

"No, I don't ever get too tired. But there's another thing, something I should have mentioned earlier. I just didn't think all of this would take this long."

"What's that?"

"There's a time limit for me staying here, Dayzee, and that's not like clockwork either, Miss Marilyn. I think I have some time left, but I can't be sure."

"What will happen? You'll get weak or something?"

"No, it's worse than that. Have you ever heard of a mobile portal? No? I have one built into me. When my time is up . . . poof! I'm gone."

"What? No, you can't go," said Marilyn. "We'll miss you, and besides, we need your help to kill this thing."

"She's right, Bruno. You simply can't go."

"I won't have a choice. It's a contract thing. Anyway, after we've killed that thing, you won't need me anymore."

"What if we do need you?" said Marilyn. "For . . . I don't know . . . other stuff. Swimming pool stuff?"

"You won't. You girls will be fine."

"How soon can you come back?"

"I don't know. They have to test me to see how messed up I am from being on Earth. I wasn't conditioned like the rest of you before they sent me."

"Well, then," said Dayzee, "why don't you find someone else to send back to help us?"

"Alright, I can try to do that. But remember, the Guild was trying to kill all of you. I'll have to sneak someone back to you. Stay close to the portal, and I'll see who I can find."

"Sit at the bar with a drink, Bruno? Yeah, I can sure do that. Maybe we should get upstairs right now and finish this. How close do you think you are to poofing out of here?"

"It feels like I have some time yet."

"Why don't you get that headless guy out of the trunk?"

"Sure thing, Dayzee."

Bruno turned and left for the front door.

"You think Sissy is okay? Maybe we should go check on her?"

"No, she's fine. Let's wait for Bruno. There's no harm in waiting to hear from her."

"Sure is quiet up there, Dayzee," said Marilyn.

"Well, maybe it's taking her some time to blindfold and headphone that girl."

"That girl doesn't have a chance with Sissy. She can be overpowering sometimes."

*   *   *

"I'm waiting."

Sophia stood at the side of the bed with her blouse opened, and she began pulling it back over her shoulders. She tossed it aside and began working at the clasp between her breasts.

"It really is kind of stubborn sometimes, Kenzie."

"The suspense is killing me. Hurry up."

Sophia laughed and said, "Okay, I'm working on it. Give me a sec."

"I'm about to climb off this bed and undress you myself."

She continued to struggle with opening it and said, "Hey, after I take this off, how about if you try on that blindfold for me?"

Kenzie only shook her head and stared at Sophia's breasts behind the black lace.

"No way, Fifi. I want to see every delicious bit of you, and I'm going to if I have to tear your clothes off myself!"

* * *

Bruno returned, holding the headless dead guy's arms behind him and walking him into the kitchen.

"Alright, Dayzee. One headless guy, ready to go."

"Good. Thanks, Bruno."

"It's been too long, Dayzee. Maybe she's in trouble?"

"You're right, Mare. It has been a while, but maybe she's just having too much fun? Did you ever think of that?"

"Even if she is, that's still not fair. We all need to kill that thing. Sissy can have whatever thrills she wants on her own time. I say we go up there right now."

"I think she's right, Dayzee," said Bruno. "Let's get this thing up there and finish it."

Dayzee thought a moment then said, "Okay, but let's promise not to say anything about what we might see up there, alright?"

"Fine by me, Dayzee."

"I guess," said Marilyn. "Maybe I'll take a photo with my phone, though."

"You'd do that?"

"She'd take one of me."

"No, Mare—don't even think of it."

Dayzee led the way with Marilyn close behind. Bruno carried the kicking and waving headless guy up after them.

*   *   *

Kenzie sat up and swung her legs off of the bed.

"You're taking too long. Come here."

"I'm trying. It's just—"

"No back talk, Fifi. Come here. Now."

Sophia took a step closer, and Kenzie reached out to take her right hand.

"Give me your other hand."

She took Sophia's left hand, too, and she held them tightly.

"That's good. Bet you didn't know how strong I was. I told you I worked out."

"Yeah, well, you're—"

Kenzie pulled Sophia to one side and flopped her onto the bed. She stood, grabbed her ankles, and swung her legs up onto the sheets so that Sophia lay on her back in the middle of the bed with her head resting on the pillows.

"God, you're not kidding! You threw me around like a doll!"

"Hmm . . . you kind of are a doll. My doll now."

Kenzie quickly climbed up and knelt above Sophia with one knee on each side pressed against her hips.

"You can't stop me, and I think you like it."

"Well, I don't know, I mean—"

"Tell me. Tell me you like that you can't stop me."

"Sure. Alright,"—she looked into Kenzie's eyes—"I like that I can't stop you."

"Mm . . . I knew it."

Kenzie smiled and reached down for the bra clasp between Sophia's breasts, and Sophia grabbed both of her wrists.

"Oh, don't get shy on me now. If you won't take it off, I will."

Sophia moved Kenzie's hands away and released her. She smiled and reached for the clasp.

"Well, I do like showing off. How about if I give you a peek, then we get that blindfold on you? It'll be fun, I promise."

"Oh, okay. If it's so important to you. Go ahead and give me a good look."

Sophia unhooked the bra and pulled it to each side, and Kenzie gasped.

"Oh my, they're just perfect. Wow."

"Okay, you've had a look, now—"

"Changed my mind. I'll wear your silly little blindfold for you, but I want to see more first. How about taking that all the way off?"

"Um . . . sure, why not?"

Sophia slid the straps down over her shoulders, pulled it out from under her, and tossed it across the room.

"Oh, now that's just lovely. I feel like I'm hypnotized. I want you to finish unbuttoning my shirt for me," she said as she moved in closer and sat on Sophia's lap.

Sophia hesitated.

"Do it. Undress me, Fifi."

"Okay, sure, then we'll get that blindfold on you."

"Hmm . . . maybe. Come on. Undress me, pretty girl."

Sophia reached up for the collar of Kenzie's shirt, and when Kenzie straightened her arms down, Sophia slid it over her shoulders, and it dropped behind her across Sophia's legs.

While grinning down at Sophia, Kenzie pulled her hands free, grabbed the shirt, and tossed it to the floor.

"Still thinking about calling your friends?"

Sophia only stared and shook her head as Kenzie rose back up onto her knees.

"Now, the skirt. Let's slip that off of you."

"And then, the blindfold?"

"If I do let you put that on me, that'll be the only thing I'm wearing."

"It'll make you even hotter," said Sophia without smiling.

"Sure. Come on," she said and grabbed the top band of Sophia's skirt. Within seconds, it was down around her ankles, and she kicked it off of the bed.

"Oh, now that's a sight. Really cute panties. So hot."

"You have no idea, Kenzie."

"No way you'd think of calling your friends now."

Kenzie sat back down on Sophia's lap, and Sophia looked her over and said, "What friends?"

"Good answer," she said. "By the way, I've decided I'm not wearing a blindfold. Too many sweet things to see."

"But—"

Kenzie touched a finger to Sophia's red lips and said, "Shh, Fifi."

* * *

After looking into the three closest bedrooms, they finally got to one with its door closed.

"Shh . . ." said Dayzee. "Hear that?"

"No, I don't hear anything."

"Exactly, Mare. Whatever's going on in there, they sure are being quiet about it. I think we should hold up a while."

"But she might be in some kind of trouble, Dayzee. We should go in."

"Yeah, but maybe it's the kind of trouble she likes."

"Oh, I knew it. I mean, she sure is a good actress. She's probably acting like she likes whatever is going on."

"Don't forget—we need to have that human girl blindfolded and headphoned, right?"

"Yes, I remember. I'm sure Sissy has that girl doing whatever she tells her."

"I think you're right about that. That poor earthgirl is doing just what your sister orders."

"Yes, she most certainly is. Let's just wait until Sissy calls us."

*　*　*

"Let's try something, just for fun."

She grabbed Sophia's arms and laid them down slightly away from her body. Before Sophia could protest, Kenzie had moved her knees up, and her shins pinned Sophia's arms to the bed.

"Now, you're all mine, and you won't make a sound, will you? You don't want to call for help, do you?"

Sophia shook her head and said, "But I still want you to—"

"Kiss you? Oh, I will definitely start by kissing you, right on those beautiful lips of yours. That's a good place to start."

She placed her hands on the bed on each side of Sophia's head and began leaning in. Sophia closed her eyes and tilted her head back with her lips turned up.

Sophia's eyes snapped wide open when Kenzie moved her hands to her throat. She heard a low growl coming from deep inside Kenzie's throat, and she tried to scream, but the grip around her neck was too tight. She struggled to free her arms and saw that Kenzie's eyes had gone blank.

Without trying, Sophia felt the heat flowing to her hands, the heat that could burn away what was left of Kenzie, but she couldn't lift her arms to touch her in any way. The naked dead thing that used to be Kenzie growled softly and continued to strangle a squirming and straining Sophia in the quiet bedroom.

Chapter 17 – Happy Halloween, Sissy

Marilyn touched her ear against the door and softly said, "Ooh, I think I hear the bed squeaking!"

"Dayzee," said Bruno, "I don't want to hold this thing all night out here while Sophia's scoring in there. Let's finish this before I poof out of here."

"You know, he makes a good point, Mare. Yes, Bruno, we should get in there."

"Oh, Bruno, you're not getting tired, are you, tough guy?"

While Bruno held the kicking and waving headless guy to one side, Marilyn took a step and stood right in front of him. She reached down for the hem of her white dress.

"If you feel like you're missing out, maybe you could, you know, have your own fun for a minute or two."

"Oh, Mare. Really? While he's holding that dead thing?"

"It's Halloween, Dayzee. It's actually kind of a turn-on."

She nudged Marilyn back a step and said, "Come on, Mare, that's just silly. We can all play with Bruno later. Right now, we better get this show going."

"Oh, okay."

She pulled her dress up another couple of inches, showing the man her strong, bare thighs, flat belly, and everything else.

"Later, tough guy. Something to remember me by."

Marilyn smoothed down her dress and opened the door just enough to take a look inside. She put one hand over a big smile and closed the door quietly.

"Oh my, Dayzee. They're both naked and have some weird fantasy thing going on. Kenzie's pretending to choke Sissy. I've never tried anything like that, but if she likes it, I probably would, too, because we're twins, so next chance I get, I'm going to let someone . . . no, I'm going to *make* someone—"

"Mare, no! That earthgirl must have turned into another one of those things! She's a dead thing! We have to go! Now!"

Dayzee shoved the door in, and they all rushed to the foot of the bed. The thing on Sophia never turned, but Sophia's eyes watched them all come in.

"Fia, are you okay for a second or two?" said Dayzee.

Sophia nodded and stared back at them.

"Will it still work, Dayzee? Is Kenzie still human enough? I mean, she still looks good, but—wow, she's in good shape!—but what will this headless guy think?"

"We can only hope, Mare. Bruno, get that thing up on the bed. Hurry!"

Bruno fought with the struggling dead man, and from his powerful grip, a few bones could be heard snapping. Dayzee looked down to see Sophia's glowing hands held up above the sheets.

"Fia, don't burn anything—not until the dead guy is going at it. Remember the plan!"

Sophia still couldn't make a sound as her big blue eyes bulged out.

"Oh, your pretty eyes are popping out! Okay, Mare, let's help your sister."

They hurried to each side of the bed and pulled the thing's arms away from Sophia's throat. While it tried snapping at them, they rocked it to each side, allowing Sophia to pull her arms out from under its knees. She gulped in deep breaths, then slapped dead Kenzie's cheek.

"Aw, Sissy, was that necessary?"

Sophia coughed, took deep breaths, and nodded but didn't speak.

"Mare, help spin Kenzie around. We need her ready for her dead date. Come on . . . we have to do it!"

"That's a good one, Dayzee. 'Dead date!'"

What used to be Kenzie kept reaching for Sophia's neck, but between the three of them, they managed to spin her around and sat her between Sophia's legs. Sophia held both of Kenzie's arms.

"Mare, grab her other leg. We need to pull them apart."

"Wow," said Marilyn, "she sure is flexible."

"You're not kidding, Mare. Hey, how far can she go?"

"Let's find out, Dayzee."

Dayzee and Marilyn yanked Kenzie's legs far apart, and Sophia peeked over the dead girl's shoulder. She found her voice and said, "Damn. Will you look at that? I've never seen anyone's legs so—"

"Alright," said Dayzee, "we just need to hold her until that dead guy senses the bait."

"Dayzee, he doesn't have a head. He can't sense anything."

"You know what I mean. Bruno, can you bring him closer?"

"How long will this take, Dayzee?"

"I have no idea, but the three of us can hold it still. Put him on his knees real close, Bruno."

Bruno worked the dead body up onto its knees between Kenzie's spread legs.

"Okay, I can hold him here until—"

While Dayzee smiled and nodded at Sophia, Marilyn looked to see that the thing's arms waved wildly, and it knelt there all by itself on the bed.

"Oh no, Dayzee! Bruno poofed!"

"Quick, Mare, grab it!"

"What about me?" said Sophia.

"Just hold Kenzie's arms as tight as you can!"

"So, I'm supposed to just lay here with this naked girl between my legs?"

"Oh, I think much more than that would have happened if she hadn't gone all dead like that, Sissy. I think you two were just about to—"

"Mare, stop! We have to hurry!"

Dayzee and Marilyn knelt on each side of the headless dead guy and held him in place. Sophia had her arms wrapped over Kenzie's, who snarled and snapped, turning her head and trying to bite her.

"Now, what?" said Marilyn. "What if nothing happens?"

"Oh God, I don't know. It's not like I've done this before."

"That's pretty funny too," said Sophia.

"Thanks, Fia. Let's give it a minute."

"We don't have to, you know, help him out, do we?"

"Ew . . . no. No way," said Dayzee.

"You look pretty hot like that, Sissy."

"You mean holding a dead naked girl thing, Sis?"

"Yes, exactly. I never would have guessed that a dead girl thing would strip you first and *then* try to kill you."

"Well, it is Halloween, Sis. Looks like anything can happen."

"Yes, I see, and she somehow decided to get herself naked too. That's really something, Sissy, even for Halloween."

"What, you think—"

"You two! Focus!"

"I can't hold this dead chick forever, Dayzee."

"I know, Fia, just—"

"I'd trade with you if I could, Sissy. You know, just to give you a break."

"Oh, is that why? You're really checking her out, aren't you?"

"Well, I know she's dead, but she's still pretty hot. I mean . . . she's damn hot."

"She's biting and trying to choke people, Sis!"

"Okay, but if we tied her down and somehow gagged her so she couldn't bite, what about then?"

"That's crazy, Sis. It's a shame she's dead because she sure was hotter before she died."

"Sissy, did you two . . . I mean, were you about to—"

"Look!" said Dayzee. "He's pulling down his own zipper!"

"How does he even know what's in front of him? He doesn't have a head!"

"No, Mare, but somehow, he knows. Do you think most human men ever use the head that this one's missing anyway?"

"Well, no, especially when there's a naked girl right there between Sissy's legs. Who is somehow also naked, and—"

"Oh my God," said Sophia. "Look. Rigor mortis is right."

"We need to get him closer," said Dayzee. "He's probably going to fight us—"

The dead man stopped struggling, and Kenzie lay still and didn't snarl or snap.

"Aw, that's so sweet—they like each other," said Marilyn. "Let's let him go, Dayzee. I think he knows what he wants to do."

"Wait—get me out from under this chick, okay?"

"No, Fia, we can't," said Dayzee. "Don't you dare mess this up. Just let them get going."

"Oh, you got to be kidding. Hey, I can't stay here while those two things are doing it right on top of me."

"It's the only way," said Dayzee. "Just stay quiet. Hopefully, we'll burn this guy real soon."

"Damn, I hate Earth."

"It's not Earth's fault, Sissy. It's all because Dayzee never ages, and we forgot all about our assignments, and the Boss—"

"Mare, let's both let go."

They released the man's arms, and he fell to his hands and knees. He got in close and lay on top of Kenzie.

"It's working! It's really working!"

Sophia let go of dead Kenzie's arms, they moved up slowly and wrapped around the space where his head should have been, and the dead thing found just the right spot.

"Oh God, I'm feeling every bounce that thing is giving her."

"Happy Halloween, Sissy. I bet it feels good too."

"I hate to admit it, but it kind of does."

"This is the creepiest Halloween ever. I want a photo of this, Sissy."

"Go ahead—I want one too."

Marilyn reached down around her hips, looking for her phone.

"Sorry, Sissy . . . no phone. It's on the kitchen table. I'll just run down there, and—"

"Don't you dare. We don't need a photo that bad."

"But, Sissy, this will never happen again."

"Well," said Sophia, "if we trade these dead people for living people, maybe then."

"Oh, you have the best ideas, Sissy."

"Oh, you girls . . ."

*   *   *

"How long, Dayzee? Can't we burn that thing already?"

"I don't know, Fia. Sure, let's try it. Oh, hold up. You two, wait here. Fia, don't go anywhere."

"That's not so funny, Dayzee," said Marilyn. "Like Sissy could get out from under them even if she wanted to. Which she doesn't."

"I have a fire extinguisher in the closet," said Dayzee. "We're probably going to need it."

Dayzee jumped down from the bed and ran out of the room.

"I see she left your heels on you, Sissy. That's mighty peculiar behavior for a dead girl thing. The one that got naked before it tried to kill you. Peculiar, I say."

Before Sophia could answer, Dayzee rushed back in, and they were ready.

"Mare, would you like the honor?"

"Gladly."

She placed her left palm on the man's back, about where its heart would be, and let it ride along with his steady motions.

"Today, Sis?"

"Okay, okay. Just trying to concentrate, that's all."

"What? What's that supposed to—"

"Okay, I'm stalling. I want to see if what they're doing will, you know, since you can feel it every time, if you'll end up enjoying it so much that—"

"Burn the damn thing, Sis!"

"Okay, okay!"

She sent her heat to her hand, and they all saw the glow. In less than a second, they smelled burning flesh, and Marilyn's hand started to sink in.

"It's starting to glow in front, Sis. You're almost there."

Another second passed, and she'd burned her way completely through. The thing stopped moving and collapsed onto Kenzie and Sophia. The smoldering skin all around the hole through its chest began to flame up, just as Dayzee gave it a good spray from close range, careful to not spray Kenzie or either of the twins.

"Okay, let's drag that thing off of them," said Dayzee. "Mare, grab that arm."

They each grabbed an arm and pulled it to the floor. Dayzee jerked the bedspread off to the side, and Marilyn helped her cover the body next to the bed. They pushed it as far under the bed as they could. When they looked back up, they saw that Kenzie had returned to her natural life. Her hands rested on Sophia's legs.

"Oh, what happened? When did you two get up here?"

She still had Sophia's arms around her, and she reached up to place her hands over Sophia's. She leaned to one side and turned to see Sophia.

"How did my legs get like that?"

"Hey, you're back!" said Sophia.

"What do you mean? Where do you think I went, and how did they get in here?"

"You don't remember anything?"

"No, just that we came up here, and I was just about to—"

"Right . . . then I called my friends. You really don't remember that?"

"No, I don't, and how did I get here like this? I remember that I was—"

"Obviously, she called us by mistake, Kenzie," said Dayzee.

"It's okay. We were just leaving," Marilyn said with a grin, and she and Dayzee turned and began walking toward the door.

"Hey, you don't have to leave," said Sophia. "We were just—"

"If they want to go, who are we to stop them?" Kenzie said before drawing her legs back together.

Sophia tipped Kenzie forward and slipped out from under her on the side of the bed opposite the dead guy. She took Kenzie's hand and coaxed her out of the bed too. Kenzie stood there naked, and Sophia wore only panties and heels and still held Kenzie's hand.

Marilyn gave her sister a big smile and said, "Sorry we bothered you two. See you later, Sissy."

"Bye, Fia. Bye, Kenzie," said Dayzee.

"No, wait. We're getting dressed and coming downstairs."

"Uh-huh. We'll see about that, Sissy."

The door closed.

*　*　*

In the hallway, Marilyn giggled and said, "I bet they don't come downstairs right away. What do you think?"

"I don't know, Mare. Your sister might have to continue the act, you know? So that Kenzie doesn't suspect anything."

"Right. That must be it. Because she *is* a good actress."

Marilyn put her ear to the door and listened for thirty seconds.

"I don't hear anything. How long does it take to get dressed anyway?"

"Maybe Kenzie found the body, Mare?"

"Or maybe they're kissing. That's a photo I'd like. I think I'll take a quick peek, and then we—"

"You girls are really too much. No, Mare. Maybe next time."

Dayzee took one of Marilyn's hands and started walking, dragging her behind. Marilyn forced Dayzee to stop at the end of the hall, and they waited quietly for a minute. She looked at Dayzee and shrugged.

"Sissy sure is a good actress. I can only imagine all the good acting going on in there."

"They might be just talking, Mare, and taking their time getting dressed."

"Sure, Dayzee. That must be it. Let's go get something to eat."

Chapter 18 – Gross Stuff Everywhere

Marilyn opened the refrigerator and said, "What's good in here? What do you have?"

"Oh, Mare, I usually get delivery or go out. Check the freezer. There might be something in there."

She closed the refrigerator door and opened the freezer.

"Well, this looks good. Let's just try some of this."

She took out a box of frozen waffles, looked around for the toaster, then walked over and popped in four of them.

"I'm not even getting tired, Dayzee, and what is it . . . four-o'clock?"

"It's because of that fountain of youth you and your sister just had. Remember that? It seems like a long time ago."

"You just had your own, didn't you? How come you're not as itchy and crazy as Sissy and I?"

"Oh, probably because I've been doing that awhile. It's still a rush, though. Are you enjoying being back?"

"So much has happened in just this one day. It started in Kildare, and wow, all the things that have happened."

"It sure is crazy, Mare. Things were going along pretty well until the Guild sent that thing, whatever it was, to kill us all."

"Oh, and some madman taking shots at you."

"Yeah, Mare, there's that too."

"Do you think the Guild will send another thing to kill us?"

"No. Well, not the same kind of thing anyway. Next time, I bet it'll be worse."

"So, we need to stick together. Sissy and I won't be going back to Kildare anytime soon."

"Speaking of your sister,"—Dayzee looked at her watch—"it's been almost ten minutes."

"Kenzie *is* pretty hot, and if it were me, I'd—"

The toaster snapped up, sending one of the waffles out onto the countertop.

"Oh, breakfast is ready, Dayzee."

Marilyn found two plates, divided up the waffles, and handed one plate to Dayzee.

"They really might be only talking, you know. Oh, you know what? I just thought of something," said Dayzee.

"What?"

"There are bodies all over the place outside. I think your sister is giving us time to figure out how to get Kenzie out of here without her seeing anything."

"You are so right. That's very selfless of my sister to pitch in like that. She probably forced Kenzie back to bed just to help us out."

"You're being sarcastic, right?"

"Yes, I sure am, but I think you're right too—we have to figure this out. We don't have Bruno to help either."

"So, if we don't see those two for a long time, you won't make any snide comments to her? You'll just assume that she only wanted to help us out of this mess?"

"Sure, Dayzee. I won't say a thing."

Dayzee tipped her head and stared at her. Marilyn smiled.

"But I sure will be imagining all kinds things going on up there. Do you want to hear my guess? Well, they're both naked, except for Sissy still wearing her heels, and Sissy probably made Kenzie put her heels back on, too, because that's what I'd do, then they probably—"

"That's alright, Marilyn. We can talk about that some other time."

Dayzee looked at her watch again and said, "Wow, it's been more than ten minutes now. We should figure out—"

"Figure out what, Dayzee?" Sophia said from the stairs.

She was completely dressed and walked into the kitchen.

"I like how you have that extra stairway. Very handy."

"I'm not sure, but there might even be another one around somewhere. Speaking of handy, how's your friend?"

"Oh, her. Kenzie practically collapsed right after you closed the door. Maybe it was something about being dead for a while?"

"She collapsed, and it still took you ten minutes to get dressed, Sissy?"

"Think about it, Sis. I couldn't leave her in that bedroom, could I? With the headless dead guy thing crammed under the bed?"

Marilyn looked at the floor, shook her head, and said, "No, I don't suppose so."

"Dayzee, I put her in a different bedroom. I hope that's okay."

"It's fine, Fia."

"Did you tuck her in real nice? I bet you kissed her goodnight too."

Marilyn waited with a big grin.

Sophia sighed deeply and said, "No, I punched her and hit her with a lamp. Look, I just made sure she was comfortable and got myself dressed."

"Because you're a good actress. That's all that was, Sissy?"

"We had a plan, remember, Sis? And it worked, so maybe before you start—"

"Okay, you two, none of that matters right now. I'm glad you're here, Fia, because we'll need your help. We have a real mess on our hands."

"In the yard, actually," said Marilyn. "Not exactly on our hands."

"Yeah, all over the yard. There are body parts everywhere," said Dayzee.

"I think Kenzie'll be out for a while. I'm not tired at all. Can we drag all the parts somewhere? Maybe into the garage?"

"Oh, about the garage, Fia," said Dayzee. "I think there are still a few of those things in there. Maybe we should just leave them alone for now."

"Aren't they dead now, Dayzee?" said Marilyn. "When I killed that thing, that should have stopped all of them. It sure brought Sissy's girlfriend back to life."

"She's not my girlfriend."

"Okay, one night stand, although I didn't see either of you standing."

"Just stop, Sis. She's not my girlfriend."

She paused to gaze at Marilyn, then a smile spread across her face.

"She sure is hot, though."

"She really is. Dead or alive, Sissy," Marilyn said with a big smile.

"You girls, I never should have told you anything about the fountain of youth. You're both way more agitated than you already were."

"I do get awful itchy," said Marilyn.

"Me too, Dayzee. Awful."

"Yeah, I can tell. At least we all have plenty of energy. You're right, Mare. Whatever is in the garage is probably just dead again. We should be able to load all the rest of the pieces in there too."

"Then what? Put them all out with the trash?" said Sophia. "Even for Beverly Hills, that's probably too much."

"Why don't we worry about that after we clean up the yard, alright?"

"Sure, Dayzee. That makes sense. Then what?"

"What time does the Prism open?"

"Oh, I'm not sure," said Sophia.

"Go wake up sleeping beauty. She would know, and while you're up there with her, you could—"

"I could what?"

"Why, ask her what time the Prism opens. What else?"

"How about if you come up with me? If you want to kiss her to wake her up, that's up to you."

"I never said that, Sissy. I trust you," she said with a big grin.

Sophia just shook her head and looked at her sister.

"Go ahead, Fia. Mare and I will get started out in the yard. Just ask her what time it opens. If she's groggy, remind her that it's Saturday, too, then come down and give us a hand."

"Yes, give us a hand with the hands," said Marilyn. "And arms. Oh, there are legs too. All kinds of parts."

"You're funny, Sis. Okay, I'll join you two in a few minutes."

Sophia turned and hurried up the steps.

"She sure looks eager to get back up there, Dayzee."

"Oh, Mare, I think maybe you would be too."

"I really am pretty itchy."

"Do you want to join her?"

Marilyn only stared up the stairs quietly.

"We'll find something to help you out soon. Alright, she'll be back in a few minutes. We should get started."

"What about the waffles?"

"Oh, I forgot all about those. Let's heat them back up and finish eating, then we'll head out and deal with the mess."

"We'll head out and handle the heads?"

"That's a pretty good one, Mare."

*   *   *

Sophia quietly opened the bedroom door and crept to the bedside. There was just enough light for her to see Kenzie covered with blankets up to her chin and fast asleep. She shook her arm gently but got no reaction. She tried again, and still Kenzie didn't wake up.

She dropped down and knelt beside the bed and hesitated only a second or two before she leaned over and kissed the sleeping girl's cheek. Before she could back away, Kenzie's eyes opened.

"Oh, it's you. What happened? How did I get here?"

"You must have had too much to drink. You passed out, and we thought we should just let you sleep."

"Thanks. I'm still tired. Um, Sophia . . . did you just kiss me?"

"What? No, I was just going to whisper in your ear to try to wake you up."

"You can kiss me if you want."

Sophia stared into her eyes for several seconds before saying, "Um . . . I think I better just let you sleep. I only wanted to ask what time the Prism opens."

"Kiss me, and I'll tell you."

"No, I need to get going. We have to—"

Kenzie shifted closer and gave Sophia a quick peck on her lips.

"There, that wasn't so bad, was it?"

"Uh . . . no, that wasn't bad at all. Okay, so what time does it open?"

"Believe it or not, they start serving breakfast at seven o'clock on weekends. I could probably get you in earlier than that, like while they're setting up for the day. Why?"

"We just need to get back there as soon as we can. Go ahead and sleep. You have a couple of hours yet."

"You can kiss me again."

Sophia hesitated just out of Kenzie's reach. She shook her head and stood.

"Better yet, Fifi, get under these blankets with me. I'm not wearing anything at all."

Sophia gazed down at her form outlined by the bedspread, sighed, then looked back into her eyes.

"Raincheck. Get some sleep."

She turned, walked out, and closed the door behind her.

*   *   *

"First, let's take a peek in the garage. We need to make sure all the dead guys are dead again."

"Good thinking, Dayzee. You first."

"You're one of the Kildare Killers, aren't you, Mare? You should be able to handle them."

"You know I only killed that one guy, and that was an accident. Oh, but I did want to kill the Boss with my barbs. I can't wait to see what it feels like to go all the way with that."

"Later. Come on, let's go see what's going on in the garage."

207

Dayzee led the way to the door, switched on the light, and pried the door open a few inches. She scanned all around in the four-car garage and didn't see any of the bodies moving.

"It looks good, Mare. It's a mess, but they're all dead. Let's head back out through the front door."

"My sister sure is taking her time, isn't she? Just like her to snuggle in with a barmaid while we're doing all the dirty work."

"More like 'bloody' work, Mare. I don't know about your sister. I know what the fountain does to me, and it kinda makes me crazy. I'm game for just about anything after that."

"That's how I feel. Hey, why don't you and I go up there too? We could all—"

"Stop, Mare. Don't tempt me. The sun is almost up, and we have a yard full of body parts. Let's clean that up, with or without your sister's help. Then, if she still isn't back downstairs, I'll race you up the stairs. How does that sound?"

"It's a deal. I'm going to strip everything off along the way."

"Fine, I will too. Can we get going now?"

"I like this plan. Sure, let's take care of business."

Dayzee swung open the front door, and they stepped out onto the low porch.

"Oh God, Dayzee. Bruno really ripped them apart. It's not just arms and legs and heads. There's guts and all kinds of gross stuff everywhere!"

"God, what a mess. I don't have a wheelbarrow, and there's no shovel around either. I don't even have a bucket. The yard crew takes care of everything."

"Yard crew, huh? Call them."

"Mare, I don't think we could trust those guys to keep all of this secret. There's probably only one guy out of the whole bunch that I would trust that much."

"Okay, so call just him, then."

"You know, maybe I should. And you know what else? He's actually kind of hot. I think you'd like him."

"I like him already. What's his name?"

"Carlos."

Dayzee took her phone out of her back pocket, hit a few buttons, and held it up to her ear.

"Carlos, it's Dayzee. Sorry to wake you. I know it's early, but I could use your help with something special. Can you come over right away?"

Marilyn waited and watched.

"Well, for one thing, we have a real mess all over the yard. We'd need you to bring shovels and buckets and thick plastic bags. Can you do that?"

Dayzee listened for a few seconds. Marilyn blurted out, "We need you!"

"Oh, that. That's Marilyn, a good friend of mine. She'll be helping, too, and she's really hot."

More silence.

"Let's just say she's at least as hot as me. How does that sound? We need you here quick."

Marilyn reached for the phone, and Dayzee leaned away and took a few steps back.

"Send him a photo, Dayzee!"

Marilyn turned, smiled back over her shoulder, and lifted her right heel. Dayzee snapped a photo and sent it before holding her phone back to her ear.

"Yeah, that's her. She's something, isn't she?"

Dayzee listened and nodded a few times.

"Good, we'll see you in a few minutes."

She ended the call and said, "He wasn't so sure about coming over until he saw you. What is it about that tight white dress of yours?"

"It sure is tight . . . and short too. It does kind of drive guys crazy."

"I think maybe Kenzie too. Hey, where's your sister? I think you might be right—she might have cozied up with her while we're doing all this work."

The front door swung in and Sophia said, "The only one cozy is Kenzie."

"Hey," said Marilyn, "that could be your cute name for her: Cozy Kenzie!"

"You know, Sis, that's really pretty good."

"We could start a gang called 'Cozy Kenzie and the Kildare Killers!'"

Dayzee said, "Hey, what about me? I like 'Dayzee Dazzle and the Kildare Killers' better. Don't you?"

"That does sound better, Sis. And we're just going to dump Kenzie back at the Prism anyway. She's not going to be some permanent fixture."

"Yeah, you're right, Sissy. She's not part of our gang, no matter how cozy she is. Was she pretty cozy up there?"

"She looked really cozy, Sis. She wanted me to get in there with her too."

"I bet you were about to, but you remembered us down here cleaning up all the dead guys. Isn't that right?"

"Yeah, Sis, I sure was. Ever since we did that fountain thing, I can hardly control myself."

"Me too—I almost ran up there myself. I still might run up there. I feel like getting cozy too!"

"It's true, girls. The fountain does that to you. Try to ignore those urges. You'll calm back down soon."

Sophia looked past them at the yard partially illuminated by the security lights.

"Sheesh. What a mess. What are we going to do?"

"Help is on the way, Fia. His name is Carlos, and he should be here any minute."

"Carlos, huh? How does he look? Is he—"

"I get him first, Sissy. You've been having all kinds of fun with a girl that was alive, then dead, then alive again. And somehow, she found a way to get naked after she died, remember that? I still haven't figured that one out."

"Hey, Sis, who can figure out a dead chick? Right now, I want to meet Carlos."

"What about me? I want Carlos too."

"I didn't have all that much fun with her up there anyway. I was just acting, remember?"

"Sure, Sissy. Uh-huh. I just bet. It sure looked like—"

"Girls! Just stop, okay? Look, I see headlights coming."

Dayzee took her phone back out, hit a few numbers, and the entrance gate swung in. A red pickup truck drove through, and the driver waved as he turned onto the circular drive and stopped near the porch. A shirtless, muscular young man stepped out.

"I came as fast as I could."

The twins looked at each other, and Sophia said, "Well, that's not ideal."

"We still have our potion, Sissy."

Chapter 19 – What Might Happen

Sophia and Marilyn rushed over and stood on either side of Carlos. Each grabbed an arm and began walking him toward the porch.

"I'm Sophia. This is my twin sister, Marilyn."

"Twins, huh? Even with the different hair? How does that work?"

"There has to be some way to tell us apart, don't you think?" said Sophia.

"Unless we're all in a dark room," said Marilyn. "You might think there's two of me!"

She began squeezing his bulging biceps. "Ooh, you're strong. Sissy, Carlos sure is fit."

"We'd sure know it was him in that dark room, Sis."

"I bet he's really fit everywhere. Maybe the cleanup can wait, and we should—"

"Girls, let Carlos go, alright?" said Dayzee. "We really do have work to do. After that, well, that's up to you."

They reached the bottom of the two porch steps.

"Hey, Dayzee, I got here as quick as I could."

He turned to look back over the grounds.

"Yuck. What the heck happened?"

"Oh, um, I think there was a gang fight out on the street, and somehow, I'd left the gate open, and—"

"But there's just pieces of them," said Carlos. "What the hell?"

"It was a huge fight," said Marilyn. "They had swords and machetes and things like that."

"And then, a pack of mountain lions rushed in too," said Sophia. "The guys that were still alive, they got torn up pretty good, as you can see."

"Basically, they're all dead. More than dead. They're all in pieces," said Dayzee.

"But . . . where are the swords and stuff? And where are all those lions?"

All three looked up at Dayzee and waited for an answer. Marilyn bit her lip, and Sophia tipped her head to one side. Dayzee's lips quivered like she was mumbling, but she didn't make a sound. Her eyes darted to each side quickly.

"Um . . . I remember seeing one of the lions pick up a sword and run out through the gate. I think they all kind of followed her lead. Maybe it was like a souvenir or something?"

"That makes sense," Marilyn said as Carlos turned to look at her. "I read that lions are like that."

"I heard they like shiny things," said Sophia, and Carlos turned toward her. "Bloody things too. They probably couldn't resist."

Carlos looked again at Marilyn, then back at Sophia. He turned and looked up at Dayzee, who only shrugged.

"Hey, it's Beverly Hills, Carlos. Should anything surprise you?"

Carlos laughed and said, "Look, I don't care what happened. I'm just here to help. I'll do whatever you all need me to do."

"Ooh, I like the sound of that," Marilyn said in her best cooing voice.

"We can sure find that dark room, Carlos," said Sophia. "Sis and I will take turns, and you'll have to guess."

"After," said Dayzee. "The sun will be up soon. Did you bring some slop buckets, Carlos?"

"I brought everything I need."

He looked down along Marilyn's dress, all the way along her bare legs, down to her white high heels. He turned and started with Sophia's black heels, then he looked up along her bare legs to the bottom hem of her short skirt, and he ended by looking into her eyes as she smiled at him.

"We're not really dressed for this, are we, Carlos?"

"No, Sophia, you sure ain't. Why don't the three of you go inside and have some breakfast? I got this."

"Don't tire yourself out too much, okay?" said Marilyn. "Save some energy for us."

"This won't take long, Marilyn. I'll bag it all up and hose things down."

"Now, that sounds like a plan. I like the thought of you hosing us—I mean 'things'—down."

Carlos looked up at Dayzee with a big grin.

"Yeah, Carlos. Save some for me too. Just like last week."

"Oh, you already—"

"Of course, Fia. What do you think the tips are like around here?"

Sophia leaned over and looked at her sister.

"She's smart, Sis."

She leaned in to kiss Carlos's cheek, and so did Marilyn.

"Okay, girls, let the man work. The sun's coming up."

*   *   *

Sophia and Marilyn climbed the steps, they began the walk toward the door with Dayzee close behind, and Carlos went for his buckets and shovels in the truck bed. Just as Sophia reached for the doorknob, the door began to swing in, and Kenzie stood there in a white bathrobe rubbing her eyes.

"Good morning," she said with a tired smile as she dragged the back of her hand across her eyes.

"Oh, sleepy girl, what are you doing up already?" said Sophia.

"I thought I heard noises out here, so I came downstairs. No one was around, so I thought I'd take a look out here. So, what's going on out there?"

Sophia stepped in as close as she could until she and Kenzie were eye to eye. She reached for her waist and shuffled her back and away from the door.

"Oh, nothing. Just the yard guy. He sure showed up early today," Sophia said with a laugh. "Imagine that."

"My cousin needs a good yard guy. I should go talk to him, and maybe he—"

Sophia squeezed her lips into Kenzie's, and she never finished. She held her close while Marilyn and Dayzee hurried in and slammed the door shut.

"Oh, well good morning to you," said Kenzie. "Not so shy anymore, huh?"

She reached up with both hands and brushed Sophia's hair back over her shoulders, leaving her hands holding her head gently.

"No, that was just . . . I mean—"

Kenzie kissed her again, and Sophia let go of her.

"Mm-hmm. Sure, Fifi. I thought I smelled some breakfast too. What's cooking?"

"'Fifi?'" Marilyn said softly.

"Oh, just frozen waffles," said Sophia. "There's tons of them. Come on . . . I'll heat some up for you."

"How do you like this old house so far?" said Dayzee. "Not so bad, huh?"

"This place is amazing. I bet even your kitchen is unbelievable."

"Well, let's go see."

Dayzee led the way with Kenzie by her side, and Sophia and Marilyn followed close behind. Marilyn elbowed her sister and pointed at Kenzie's hips swaying and her long legs stepping gracefully beneath the short robe.

"That's a nice robe," said Marilyn. "Fits you just right."

"Oh, I just found this in the closet and threw it on. You don't mind, do you, Dayzee?"

"Not at all. It really does look good on you. Help yourself to anything you find here, alright?"

Kenzie turned to smile at Sophia, then Marilyn, then she smiled at Dayzee too.

"You know, Dayzee, I've never really noticed until now. You're absolutely stunning."

"Thanks, Kenzie. I just take care of myself and keep busy. I'm on set Monday morning to start my latest film."

"Oh, now this all makes sense. The house, the limo, the beautiful friends. You're a real movie star."

They'd made it to the kitchen, and Dayzee sat at the table with Kenzie. Sophia leaned against the counter, and Marilyn dug around in the freezer.

"It's a crazy life, but I love it. You know what, though? I like just hanging around at the Prism too. This is all fun, but it's not what matters."

Kenzie smiled and said, "I like your style, Dayzee, but how did you get that name, 'Dazzle?'"

Dayzee shook her head with a grin and said, "Trade secret. I can give you a hint, though—it has something to do with my eyes."

"You do have nice eyes. But 'dazzle?' Do they really dazzle?"

"Um . . . if the lighting is right. You have to see them at just the right time, I guess."

* * *

"Sissy, I have an idea."

Marilyn had brought the waffle box over to the toaster and stood near her sister.

"Just for fun, let's give some of our potion to Kenzie. I can't imagine what might happen."

"Sis, hasn't she been through enough? What we need to do is get her back to the Prism, nothing more."

"Oh, I see. You have your fun, kissing her and who knows what else, and then when I—"

"We didn't do anything, Sis. Really. How about if we just feed her, keep her busy for a few hours while Carlos cleans up out there, and then—"

"Sissy, that's what I'm talking about—keeping her busy."

"What . . . all of us?"

Marilyn nodded quickly with a big grin.

"Oh, Dayzee is right—you're just too much sometimes."

"The potion will probably make her even wilder, don't you think? You can take her upstairs—I'm just sure she'd follow behind you like an obedient pet—and after a while, Dayzee and I will come up and join you. What do you say?"

"Really? You mean, all of us?"

"She likes us all. You can see that. And be honest—she looks good in that tiny robe, doesn't she?"

Sophia turned and gave Kenzie a glance.

"Yeah, she sure does. You know what, though? I think she's kind of got a thing for Dayzee now. Look at them."

They both looked over at the table and saw that Dayzee and Kenzie seemed to have forgotten about anyone else being there. They laughed and talked softly while looking into each other's eyes.

*   *   *

"Well, even when they're not dazzling, they're still quite beautiful."

"Thanks, Kenzie. So are yours."

"What a life you lead. It sounds like every possible dream come true."

"Oh, I don't know about that. Yeah, I have a lot of stuff, but there's something I don't have."

"Like what? I can't imagine."

"My mission here was to—"

"You're on some kind of mission?"

"No, bad choice of words. I mean that my goal was to find someone special, someone to spend my life with, you know? It turns out that scoring films and buying mansions is so much easier."

"Maybe Marilyn and Sophia can help out. They probably know—"

"Oh, no . . . don't even mention it, alright? My life is about having fun and rock and roll and parties. I'm not about to get all serious with them."

"Your secret is safe with me, Dayzee."

* * *

"You jealous, Sissy?"

"Maybe a little."

"I would be too. Hey, heck with them—we'll have Carlos all to ourselves. And you know what? We really should slip Kenzie some potion. It'll serve her right for dumping you."

"Sis, no one dumped anyone. Fine, I'll get the waffles, and you mix up some potion for her orange juice."

"I like this plan!" said Marilyn.

"You know what would make it even better?" said Sophia. "Let's you and me get into robes, too, and when Carlos comes in for his pay or to say goodbye or whatever yard guys do, we'll be waiting for him. We'll pounce on him like those imaginary mountain lions."

"He won't stand a chance, Sissy. I don't know if Dayzee wants Kenzie or not, but she might, because she just did that fountain thing, so she's probably crazy for anything right now too."

"Let's give Kenzie her breakfast, then you and I can slip on our robes and come back down. Plan?"

"Plan."

* * *

Upstairs in one of the huge, walk-in closets, the twins found two more robes. Amid lots of giggling and compliments to each other, they wiggled out of their clothes and soon stood looking in the mirror wearing matching white robes.

"We look pretty damn hot, Sissy."

"We really do. Heck with Kenzie. I'm aiming for Carlos. How about you?"

"Me too. I want that hard-working yard guy. I'm going to use just a little bit of heat on him."

"Not enough to kill him, right? I mean, he is helping us out."

"No, I won't kill him. But a little heat makes it so much better. You know that, Sissy."

"Yep, it sure does, but no barbs, right?"

Marilyn hesitated before answering, and while still looking at their reflection, she tipped her head onto her sister's shoulder.

"Oh, okay. Soon, though. We need to find some human male that doesn't deserve to live another day. There's got to be some like that around, don't you think?"

"Oh yeah, this place is crawling with them. It's Beverly Hills. I'll get one, too, and we'll both barb them. Let's go and see what that potion did."

"To your girlfriend?"

"No, she's not, but we can still call her Cozy Kenzie, alright?"

"Sure, Sissy."

*   *   *

Just as Sophia and Marilyn got to the bottom of the stairs near the kitchen, the front door swung open, and Carlos walked in. He still wore no shirt, but he appeared to have washed himself clean because no blood could be seen, and water trickled down all over his skin.

The twins giggled and walked to meet him halfway. He stood grinning and dripping and looking from one to the other.

"We really appreciate all your help, Carlos," said Marilyn as she touched his arm softly.

"How can we ever thank you for all that hard work?" Sophia said as she held him by his other arm.

"Well, I'm happy to help. I got everything bagged up, and the yard looks good again. Damn mountain lions."

"They do make a mess," said Sophia.

"You're the best, Carlos. My Sissy and I want to find some way to repay you. Maybe we could—"

Kenzie pushed them both to the side and stood in front of Carlos.

"Hi, I'm Kenzie. Who are you?"

"I'm Carlos. I'm the yard guy here, and I just—"

"Well, you are just some kind of special amazing, aren't you?"

She put both her palms on his bare wet chest and gazed into his eyes. Sophia shook her head, and Marilyn shrugged as they looked at each other.

"Aw, I don't know how special. I mean, I got things cleaned up, and—"

"That's special! That's really special! So . . . you must be a special kind of guy!"

Behind Kenzie's back, Sophia whispered, "The potion?"

Marilyn shrugged again and frowned.

"It wasn't all that much work. I just—"

"Show me! Show me, okay? I want to see! Can we see it together? Can you show me? Right now?"

"Um, sure," he said and tried to turn toward the front door. "Just take a look out—"

"No. No, no, no. Upstairs. Show me from upstairs? Can you? Will you? Let's go. Let's go! Come on, come on, come on!"

She grabbed his hand and tugged him toward the stairs. Dayzee had followed and stood with the twins, and they all watched as Kenzie practically dragged the grinning yard man up the steps.

"Well, that's quite a sight, girls."

"Our robes are short too," said Marilyn.

"Don't pout, Sis."

Within seconds, Kenzie and Carlos were out of sight. They all stared at the empty staircase until they heard a bedroom door slam shut.

"What the . . ."

"Dayzee, I think that was my fault," said Marilyn.

"You didn't."

"Yes, I did. I gave her some potion. It wasn't much, and I was just curious what might happen. I thought maybe she'd go crazy for all of us."

"Well, Sis, she did kind of go crazy."

"She sure did, Fia, just not for any of us. Hey, what's with the robes, you two?"

"Oh, well, um . . . we kind of wanted to have some fun with Carlos. We thought this would make us irresistible."

"You kind of are, girls. If we weren't such good friends . . ."

"Oh, Dayzee, really?" said Sophia.

"Never mind that. This is good. We have things under control."

"Except for that headless guy, the one who'd be smiling if he could, stuffed under the bed?"

"Oh yeah, except for that. Don't worry about that. I have a guy that can take care of that."

"How would you know someone like that?"

"Oh, you're such a sweet kid, Mare. Let's just say that this isn't the first time."

"Really? A headless guy that—"

"No, Fia, that's a first. It's just that not every guy can keep up with me. So, I've had to figure things out before, that's all."

"So, what do we do?" said Marilyn.

"I'm looking forward to finally having a decent breakfast. After those two are done up there, it should be about time to hit the Prism."

"Yes, and we can leave Kenzie where we found her. Sorry she dumped you, Sissy."

"Enough. She didn't dump me."

"Girls, she dumped all of us."

Chapter 20 – Still Looked Like Kenzie

"I'm starving, Dayzee. I wish your house was stocked up a little."

"Oh, Mare, I'm hardly ever here. We'll get a good breakfast at the Prism soon."

"It's almost six-thirty," said Sophia. "Kenzie said she could probably get us in about now."

"I don't think they're done up there, Sissy. I shouldn't have given her that potion. Maybe she killed him."

"That sure is possible, Mare. I hope you learned your lesson."

"I've learned a lot of lessons, Dayzee. Like, don't let headless dead guys in through the gates. Don't wear a tiny little robe and be sure you're going to get the lawn guy. Don't let your sister bring home barmaids because—"

"Alright, Sis. Let's just figure out how to get things moving here. We have to get back to the portal, don't we, Dayzee?"

"Yeah, we need to be there in case Bruno finds a way to send someone through to help us."

"Can we just leave them up there?"

"No, Mare, we'll need to go break up that little party of theirs. Um, are you two going to wear those robes all day?"

"We could," said Sophia. "That would turn some heads back at the Prism, even at breakfast."

"Oh, and Sissy, I'd like to shoot some pool dressed like this. Think how easy it would be for them."

"This early?"

"Oh, you're right. We can go back later wearing our robes."

"Really, you two. Let's go upstairs, you two can get dressed, and then *all* of us will go see what Kenzie is up to."

"What if she killed Carlos? Did you see how much energy she had?"

"I sure did, Sis. She really did have tons of energy. As soon as that juice kicked in, that damn Carlos walked in."

Dayzee said, "I saw her getting worked up sitting at the table. She looked over, and he was the first thing she saw when it clicked."

"What if he would have stayed outside a while longer?" Sophia said. "I mean, my robe is short, too, and—"

"Your robe is really short, Sissy. She would have picked you."

"Thanks, Sis. Nice of you to say."

"Let's go, girls."

*　*　*

Sophia and Marilyn walked together up the stairs, and Dayzee followed.

"I got to tell you, girls, that's quite a sight from down here."

"Oh, thanks, Dayzee," said Marilyn. "This robe is even shorter than the dresses I wear."

"Yeah, I know, but don't you usually wear something under the dresses?"

"Define 'usually,'" Marilyn said and giggled.

"She usually does, Dayzee. I'm the one that usually doesn't."

"That's what I thought. You're not the least bit shy about walking around like that?"

"Huh. I wish you had a camera," Sophia said as she turned back and gave Dayzee a wink.

At the top of the stairs, Dayzee said, "Okay, go get some clothes on. I'll wait outside their door."

The twins disappeared into a bedroom and made a quick change in the closet. Within minutes, they were back in the hallway beside Dayzee.

"It sure is quiet in there."

"It sure is, Sis. Let's just do it," she said and turned the doorknob.

She peeked in then pushed the door all the way open. They saw Kenzie and Carlos asleep in each other's arms and snug under the blankets.

"Aw, that's kind of sweet," said Marilyn. "They weren't just wild animals—they like each other."

"Best of all, I think Carlos is still alive," said Dayzee. "I had my doubts."

"Hey, can we have him take that other body out of the house?" said Sophia.

"I don't think so," said Dayzee. "What would we say? A couple of mountain lions dragged him up here and ate his head?"

"Oh, you're right. You better just call your dead guy removal guy."

"Should we wake them up?" said Marilyn.

"We have to. We need to take her and get ourselves to the Prism. Who wants to wake her?"

"I'm still feeling kind of itchy," said Sophia. "I'm tempted to chase you two out of here and wake them up myself."

"If she won't do it, I will," said Marilyn. "Oh, I think I'd slip that robe back on first. No. Off would be better."

"Hey, Sis, maybe we should both wake them up? Dayzee, you could go hang out at the Prism and call us if anything happens. We could find out if Carlos has any strength left."

"Yes, and you could see if Kenzie's potion is still giving her that weird buzz."

"So, what are you thinking, Sis? We both get on our robes, then we—"

"Girls, no. You two wait here, and I'll wake up Kenzie."

Dayzee walked over to the side of the bed and gently shook Kenzie's arm. She opened her eyes and smiled, then rubbed her face and brushed her hair back.

"Hi, Dayzee. I don't know what came over me."

"Carlos came over you. He's damn hot, isn't he?"

"Yeah, but not *that* hot. I kind of lost my mind for a while."

"Do you feel better now? We need to get back to the Prism."

Kenzie folded down the covers and slipped out of the bed. Dayzee was waiting with the men's white shirt, and Kenzie put it on.

"Alright, just get dressed, Kenzie, and we'll get going."

"Sure, let's go. What about Carlos?"

"Oh, just let him sleep. You really wore him out, huh?"

"Of course, I did."

She turned toward the door and saw only Marilyn still watching. Sophia had stepped around and out of sight.

"Okay, just give me a minute, and I'll be ready to go."

Dayzee walked back out into the hall and closed the door behind her.

"Finally, I think we're back on track. It's been one hell of a night, girls."

"I'm ready. How about you, Sissy?"

Sophia kicked at the carpeting and didn't answer.

"Sissy?"

"Oh, um . . . yeah, I'm ready. But who's going to drive us? Bruno's gone, remember?"

"I can drive, Fia. Or maybe we can talk Kenzie into it. Either way, we need to get going."

The door opened, and Kenzie came out.

"All finished in there, Kenzie?" said Dayzee.

"Uh-huh. There's not much left of him. I'm kind of worn out, too, but I still feel kind of crazy."

"You'll be fine. Let's hit the road," said Dayzee, and she and Marilyn began the walk toward the stairway.

"Not much left of him, you said?" said Sophia.

"Yeah. I was out of control," Kenzie said, then turned to glance down the hall and saw that Dayzee and Marilyn had started down the stairs. Then, she turned back to Sophia.

"I do feel pretty amped up, and there's still plenty left of him. We didn't do anything. Nothing at all."

"Oh, you have to be kidding."

"I was losing my mind when I dragged him up here. Once we were in bed, all I felt was tired."

"He sure looked tired too."

"He's pretending. Like I told him to."

"So, what happened?"

"I got a great deal for my cousin—Carlos is going to do his lawn real cheap!"

"That's it? All you two did was talk?"

"I swear . . . that's all."

"So . . . I could go in there, and he'd give me his best performance?"

Sophia turned the doorknob and pushed the door in an inch. She gazed at Kenzie and waited.

"I guess you could."

Kenzie looked at the floor, turned, and took a few steps before stopping and turning back to Sophia.

"But I wish you wouldn't. I'm just sure you could do better, Fifi."

Sophia smiled and pulled the door closed, and they both hurried to join Dayzee and Marilyn.

*　*　*

"Kenzie, we all voted," said Dayzee. "You have the immense honor of chauffeuring us back to the Prism."

"I'd love to. I've never driven a limo, but how hard could it be?"

They all filed out, and Dayzee pulled the front door shut.

"You have a beautiful property here, Dayzee. It's so clean and tidy. It looks perfect."

"Thanks, Kenzie. We have Carlos to thank for that. I guess maybe you've already thanked him enough for all of us, though?"

"Oh, you know it, Dayzee," she said with a laugh before she turned to Sophia to give her a wink.

Sophia laughed and said, "She sure did, Dayzee. Did you see Carlos? She wiped him out."

"Good. He got paid and then some."

They all opened their doors and climbed in, with Dayzee up front, the twins in back, and Kenzie behind the wheel. She found the key already in it, so she cranked the engine and started it up.

"Oh, I didn't notice you had two gates, Dayzee. Nice."

"You should be able to get around the yard guy's truck. Go ahead and take the circle."

Dayzee tapped her phone a couple of times, and the exit gate swung in. Kenzie backed away from the garage, turned into the circular drive, and waited.

"How are all of you wide awake? I need to jump-start my day. Hang on."

She held the wheel with both hands and floored the gas pedal. Tires screamed, and the long car fishtailed before it began speeding around the curve, leaving twin trails of smoke from the tires.

"Slow down!" said Dayzee. "You'll never stop in time!"

"Who's stopping?"

The limo raced through the gate, and as soon as the front end touched the street, Kenzie turned the wheel to the right and hit the gas. The car's rear slid across the road, spraying gravel from the spinning tires, and leveled out to head northeast toward the Prism. She laughed once and let off the gas, allowing the car to slow down.

"That was cool," said Marilyn. "Bruno never would have done that just for fun."

"Maybe not, Sis, but he was fun in other ways. Remember the pool?"

"Do I ever. I miss that. Maybe he'll come back for us, Dayzee?"

"I don't think he can," said Dayzee. "He said it was a contract thing. I just hope he can send someone to help us."

"Help you with what?" said Kenzie.

"Oh, um, we pissed off some people, and it's possible they'll come after us. Remember the gunshot? Bruno was our bodyguard, but he's gone now."

"That's why you need to get back to the Prism?"

"Yeah, Kenzie, that's where we'll meet. We just don't know when."

"Fine by me. We'll be there in about thirty seconds."

"The way you're driving," said Marilyn.

"Hey, I slowed down. Am I too fast, Fifi?"

Sophia only smiled, and her sister elbowed her, giggled, and whispered, "Fifi!"

*   *   *

Seconds later, Kenzie parked the limo along the curb across the street, and they all got out.

"I'm really hungry now," said Marilyn. "You said they serve breakfast?"

"Yes, they sure do, Marilyn. Come on."

She led them around back and used a key to get in.

"They're not open yet, but the cook is probably getting things ready. He'll set you up."

*   *   *

Seated at the bar, all four soon had plates of hot breakfast in front of them. Kenzie sat at the far left, then Sophia, then Dayzee, then Marilyn. Three sets of eyes looked only to the right between bites of eggs, bacon, toast, potatoes, and hotcakes. Rarely did they look down for their coffee mugs. Instead, they groped around gingerly until locating and raising them for a sip.

Across the room, the tall statue wearing a wide-brimmed hat looked back silently.

"Oh, do you see that, girls?" said Dayzee.

"No, what, Dayzee?"

"Behind the statue guy. On the floor."

"It's the head that winked at me!" said Marilyn.

"Only in the Hills," Sophia said with a smirk.

"When I get a house like Dayzee's, I'm getting a statue just like that one, except maybe one with a smile."

"Do *not* call our friend, Sis, and bug him for cash for a silly statue."

"Fine. How long will we have to wait, Dayzee?" said Marilyn.

"Who knows? Bruno didn't even promise that he'd send someone else."

"At least this food is absolutely delightful," said Sophia. "Why am I so hungry? Is that from the fountain too?"

"Probably," Dayzee said without turning to look at Sophia. "It kind of buzzes us up in all kinds of ways."

Marilyn took her last bite and set her fork down. A few seconds later, she finished her coffee and set the mug on the bar.

"I'm getting bored. There's no one to play pool with."

"Do you even know how to play pool, Sis?"

"I sure don't. I guess I should have said, 'play on the pool table with,' huh?"

"That sounds right. That was kind of fun for me, too, except for Bruno strangling me. But I liked seeing you getting into all kinds of trouble. That was something."

"I know, Sissy. And what about you? Remember that Popsicle thing you like so much? Maybe you could—"

"Popsicle thing, Fifi? What's that all about?"

A loud whoosh came from the statue, which didn't move a muscle . . . didn't even blink. A light breeze hit them all, puffing their hair to their left, and they kept staring and waiting.

"It's windy in the Prism?" said Kenzie.

"Was that it?" said Sophia.

"I don't see anyone," said Marilyn.

"Girls, Bruno wasn't what we expected, remember? Maybe someone came through that's hard to see?"

"We have an invisible man watching out for us? Is that possible, Dayzee?"

"Oh, Sis, now you're just being silly. There's no such thing as—"

"Sophia," said a deeper voice from Sophia's left.

The three of them turned and froze at the sight. Kenzie still looked like Kenzie, only a bit taller on the barstool. Facial features began to change in subtle ways, becoming more harsh and not the delicate, feminine look from before. Sophia looked away from Kenzie's eyes and saw the tight t-shirt stretching out from growing muscles, and before long, the thin cloth began to split around the shoulders and under the arms from the growing back. She gasped at seeing that Kenzie's breasts had shrunk down to nothing, too, and were replaced by thick chest muscles. She looked farther down and saw Kenzie's slender legs thickening up and threatening to rip the jeans. Then, the jeans did rip down each thigh, showing Kenzie's smooth skin.

"Kenzie?" said Sophia. "What happened to you?"

"Kenzie will return when my mission is complete. I am here to help you three. Bruno sent me."

"You're not Kenzie? Is Kenzie okay?"

"Kenzie is fine."

"Who are you?" said Dayzee.

"I bring no name with me, only a resolve to complete my assignment."

Sophia turned to look at Dayzee then at her sister. Dayzee shrugged, and Marilyn only shook her head, so Sophia turned back to Kenzie.

"Okay. Sure. *What* are you, then?"

"I am a Model One-Eighty Displacement Operative. I am skilled in all security and defense methods."

Sophia reached down for Kenzie's arm and squeezed the bulging bicep, then turned when Dayzee spoke.

"I've heard of One-Eighties," said Dayzee. "I didn't think any more of them existed. I can't imagine how Bruno found one."

"Well," said Sophia, "this one seems to be getting stronger every second."

She turned back to Kenzie.

"Can we still call you Kenzie?"

Before Kenzie could answer, Marilyn said, "Hey, make it 'Kozy Kenzie,' okay? And 'Kozy' is with a 'K.'"

"How about it?" said Sophia. "Can we call you Kozy Kenzie?"

"That is an acceptable name."

"Maybe just 'Kozy' would be better," said Dayzee.

"Yes. That is fine also."

Marilyn whispered from down the bar, "Sissy, ask Kenzie—I mean Kozy—if she's still a girl," and giggled before Dayzee shushed her.

"Um . . . Kozy?"

"Yes?"

"Are you still . . . um . . . a girl?"

"A female of the human species? Not in any way. I have assumed the biology of a male for the duration of my stay on this planet."

Sophia glanced down again at Kozy's chest flexing beneath the thin t-shirt cloth. She smiled and shook her head.

"Oh, I see. You still have Kenzie's hair, and I see her nail polish is still there. Other than that stuff, you're a guy?"

"Yes. In every measurable way."

Sophia stared, and Dayzee leaned forward to stare, and Marilyn lay across the bar and stared.

"What? Wait . . . what do you mean?"

"It is the nature of a One-Eighty to change the sex of our mission vessel. This vessel was female, you said, and named Kenzie. My arrival here is only possible by a complete switching of the host."

"Why?" said Marilyn. "How does that happen?"

"It is a result of displacing the original life for the arrival of a new one."

"Oh, now I get it," said Dayzee. "One-Eighty. As in one-hundred-and-eighty degrees."

"Yes, you are correct. Does it matter?" said Kozy. "I am here to protect you. It is what I am able to do that matters."

"Yeah, 'what you can do'—that's what I'm thinking," Sophia said and turned to look at her sister.

"I'm thinking about it, too, Sissy."

"Girls, try to remember that we could be in some serious trouble soon."

"We remember, Dayzee."

She turned back around.

"You sure look like you could save us."

"I have extensive capabilities in all functions."

"My kind of—oh, I don't really know!" said Marilyn. "Guy, I guess?"

"And you're a One-Eighty?" said Sophia.

"Yes."

Sophia turned to Dayzee and her sister and said, "Ooh, this is going to be fun, but why Kenzie?"

"That's your fault," said Dayzee. "Both of you. You gave her that potion, remember? Maybe that had something to do with it."

"Oh yeah," said Sophia, "she did get kind of strange from that."

"Sissy, check to make sure because Kenzie didn't have a . . . you know. I'll bet you knew that for sure because she somehow took her clothes off after she died, and then you—"

"Yeah, Sis, I did know for sure. She definitely didn't have one, but it was all for the plan, remember?"

"Sure, Sissy. You did all that for the plan. What an actress!"

Sophia turned back around and said, "I hate to even ask, but—"

His strong hand grabbed her wrist so quickly that no one saw it move, and Sophia's hand was pulled over and pressed between Kozy's legs.

"Oh, Sis. It's true. Kozy has one now!"

"Sissy, is it . . . I mean, I want it to be . . . is it—"

"Yeah, like you can't even imagine!"

When her wrist was released, Sophia didn't pull her hand back. Instead, she got a better grip and leaned in close. By the time Kozy's lips met hers, she already had her other hand on Kozy's chest.

They kissed for only a second before Sophia pulled away. Then, she leaned back in, and after twenty seconds, Marilyn said, "Hey, we want a turn too."

"We really do, Fia."

Sophia pulled away from the kiss and said, "I think there's enough for all of us."

"I am here solely to help you. Are you in danger?"

"Even worse," said Marilyn. "We're horny!"

Chapter 21 – Let's Rock and Roll

While Sophia still looked Kozy up and down with a big grin, Dayzee turned to Marilyn.

"I guess we're done with the portal for a while, huh, Mare? Maybe we should go back to the house. I'd like to take a dip in the pool and get started on a relaxing weekend already."

"Yes, we might as well leave. Breakfast was good, but what's going to come after us next, Dayzee?"

"Let's hope the Guild gives up and doesn't send anything. Maybe they'll just give up on this planet and leave us here."

Marilyn raised her mug for a coffee refill and said, "Is that likely?"

"Who knows? But if that's true, they probably fixed the portal so that we can't go back. We might be stuck here."

"There are worse places to be marooned, Dayzee. We can just carry on as Dayzee Dazzle and the Kildare Killers. We'll still have lots of fun."

"What about Kozy?" Sophia said without turning around. "Is Kozy part of the gang now too?"

"Oh, sure, but for how long?" said Dayzee. "Remember Bruno and how he got poofed out of here?"

"Good point. Okay," said Marilyn, "we need to find out how long Kenzie will be Kozy, and I hope Kenzie will be Kozy long enough to stop whatever is going to try to kill us, then Kozy can be Kenzie again."

"There's a tongue twister in there somewhere," said Dayzee, "You enjoyed that. I know you did."

Dayzee turned around to see Sophia about to try another kiss with the One-Eighty they'd named Kozy, who had just transformed the barmaid named Kenzie.

"Yeah, and your sister's about to do some tongue twisting herself."

A rattling behind them caused Dayzee and Marilyn to spin around. On the pool table, two cue sticks were vibrating and starting to rattle against each other. The business end of one jumped up, then clattered back down. Then, it lifted up again. A second later, the heavy end snapped up into the air. It floated horizontally, pointing toward them at the bar.

"Uh-oh," said Marilyn. "That creepy thing is looking right at me. Dayzee, maybe we should—"

Marilyn felt Kozy's strong hand holding the back of her head and pressing her face into hot, solid chest muscles.

"Ooh, nice to meet you too!" she said while looking up and not trying to back away. "Really nice, Kozy."

His hand relaxed, allowing Marilyn to lean back only enough to look toward the pool table. She saw the tip of the cue tight in Kozy's other hand and only inches from her heart, and the heavy end shook up and down and back and forth.

"God, how did—"

Kozy seemed to vanish, and the pool stick clattered on the bar's wood floor. Kozy straddled one of Dayzee's thighs, facing her, and held the other stick just an inch from Dayzee's neck. The one on the floor rolled once more and came to a stop.

"My God," said Dayzee.

"That thing almost got you, Dayzee," said Sophia.

"Oh, that? Yeah, *that* piece of wood almost got me. So what? It's the other one I'm talking about."

She looked down and saw Kozy excited and pressing into her leg through his stretched jeans. She grabbed his hips with both hands, looked up quickly, then grinned and looked back down.

"Someone's about to rip some more denim."

"That is an expected reaction," said Kozy. "Danger has that effect."

Kozy dropped the second cue stick to the floor.

"You mean," said Marilyn, "when stuff like that happens"—she pointed at the cue sticks on the floor—"then *that*"—she pointed at Kozy's noticeable bulge—"happens too?"

Kozy looked back at Marilyn without any change of expression.

"Yes. One-Eighties are naturally like that. Attributes we have assumed are stimulated by danger. We become more aggressive to neutralize any threat, and the host body responds."

"The more danger . . . the more spectacular it gets?"

"Yes, it is an unavoidable symptom."

"Well, no one here would ever want to avoid that," said Sophia. "Danger can be a fun thing now."

"Well, it's nice to have you around, Kozy," said Dayzee. "What happens when there's absolutely no danger at all? Like, not even a chance?"

Kozy tried to take a step away from Dayzee, but she continued to hold him.

"Your adversary has arrived on this planet. You will never be without danger until it has been eliminated."

"I'm just saying what if, alright? Suppose everything was safe as could be?"

"Then, I will remain in a relaxed and ready state, able to spring into action—"

"Kozy said 'spring!'" said Marilyn.

"—at a moment's notice."

"Like, if you were tucked into a quiet bedroom with someone," said Sophia, "you couldn't just spring up all on your own?"

"Only if there is noticeable danger."

"What about all those muscles?" said Dayzee after looking up into his eyes.

"Yes, those are a constant feature. I am not familiar with Earth, but they might also expand as the danger increases."

"They won't go back to natural Kenzie size?" said Sophia.

"No, they will stay as they are. Or larger. I hope that is acceptable. We One-Eighties tend to exaggerate all natural characteristics. And we . . ."

"You what?" said Dayzee.

"If we spend enough time on a mission like this, we become . . . programmed."

"Huh?" said Sophia. "What does that mean?"

"It means that we identify with the attributes and functions of the host species."

Sophia shook her head with a frown and said, "I still don't—"

"They get horny, too, Sissy!" said Marilyn. "Danger or no danger, it'll be Krazy Kozy soon!"

"Well, that bulge sure isn't disappearing," said Dayzee. "And those muscles. God, they're just . . . I mean, what a—"

"There is generally always a measurable amount of danger. I am trained to observe it and respond."

"Girls," said Dayzee with a chuckle, "do you still miss Bruno?"

"Not at all," said Sophia. "I liked him just fine, but this? Kozy is more than—"

In a flash, Kozy stood in red high heels pinning each cue stick to the floor, where they rattled and bent up several times. Dayzee and the twins watched his leg muscles expanding, splitting the jeans more, and something else right in the middle threatened the tight fabric too.

"I'm rooting for more danger," said Marilyn.

"Those heels have to go," said Dayzee.

"No kidding," Sophia said while shaking her head and grinning.

Finally, the cue sticks seemed to die and lie still. The skin of Kozy's legs, seen through the rips, had a sheen from the effort, and they all kept staring at the muscular legs and more.

"You saved us again," said Marilyn. "You're our hero!"

"Alright, that's all real exciting, but what the hell are we dealing with?" said Dayzee. "What the hell is going on this time?"

"I have seen this before," said Kozy. "It is a force that can animate things and make them kill."

"What kinds of things? Not just other bodies, you mean? We've just dealt with the dead body thing."

"It is too soon for certainty, but I think it can bring to life things made of large indigenous Earth plants. Perhaps the entire plants themselves. Anything with wood."

"Just like you!" said Marilyn before giggling.

"That's pretty funny, Sis."

"Or it could morph. It will probably morph."

"Into what?" said Dayzee. "God, I'm not starting that new film just yet. No way."

"It might choose to animate other things. Perhaps larger things."

"Like a limo?"

"Yes, Dayzee. Larger, even."

"As if this thing isn't scary enough. Okay, Kozy, let's hope it doesn't figure out anything like that."

"Yes, we can hope."

"Girls . . . and Kozy . . . why don't we all go back to the house?"

"I will go wherever you need me."

Kozy stepped off of the resting cue sticks, and within a couple of seconds, they shook once and stopped. Kozy froze with one leg up, a red shoe ready to stomp. Instantly, the Prism's front door swung open, ripping apart its locks. A sudden breeze rushed out, dragging a few cocktail napkins from the nearest table, and the door slammed shut.

"It has left this structure."

"Good," said Marilyn. "It gave up on us. Kozy is just too good of a protector. Really hot too."

"It has not conceded. It is likely preparing a trap for all of you."

"Oh, I know where it's going," said Dayzee. "It's going back to my house."

"I believe that is likely," said Kozy.

"Just wonderful. Well, girls, and Kozy, there's no sense in waiting. Let's head for home. Maybe we'll get lucky and that killer thing will take a break."

"I hope it doesn't take a break," said Sophia. "I'm ready for a lot more danger."

"I'm with Sissy," said Marilyn. "One danger after another."

Kozy kicked the sticks back toward the table and came to stand in front of Dayzee. Marilyn grabbed one arm, and Sophia held the other. Both squeezed and rubbed his tight arm muscles. Dayzee reached up with both hands and rubbed the new stubble on his cheeks.

"So, Fia," said Dayzee, "you don't miss Bruno, do you?"

"Nope. Not even a bit. How about you, Sis?"

"I absolutely love Kozy, but I do miss Bruno some."

"Sure doesn't look like it," Sophia said with a smirk.

"You know that I have strong feelings, Sissy. I'm only human."

"No. No, you're not, Sis. That's one line you really can't use."

"Okay, but I still have feelings. I'm ready to go back to Dayzee's mansion and have fun with Kozy."

"Yep. Me too, Sis, even though that new assassin is waiting for us."

"We've sure had some thrills so far, haven't we?"

"Oh yeah," said Sophia, "and there were a lot of kills too."

"Well, girls—*and* Kozy—what do you expect from Beverly Hills?" said Dayzee. "Let's rock and roll!"

Enjoy the Story?

Thank you for reading! Please consider leaving a review and/or a rating at your favorite bookseller or with your favorite book club. Help your fellow readers meet Dayzee Dazzle!

For more about Edward Allen Karr and his books, visit:

www.LakesideLetters.com

What's Next for Dayzee Dazzle?
Find out in
Dayzee Dazzle and her Manic Mansion
Thrills N Kills in the Hills Book Two

Dayzee and her best friends, the beautiful twins Marilyn and Sophia, managed to destroy the assassin sent by the Guild to kill all of them. Of course, the Guild still wants to terminate them, so they sent something else . . . something more devious. It fled from their favorite bar, the Prism, after arriving through the portal near the giant statue guy. Its startling but unsuccessful attempts to kill them were thwarted by Kozy, the barmaid formerly known as Kenzie, who has become their muscular and devoted protector. Where did the killer go? How will it try to erase them and any evidence of their true origin? From the title of Book Two, it looks like it's waiting for them at Dayzee's mansion in the Beverly Hills Flats.

About the Author

Edward Allen Karr was born, raised, and continues to reside in Ohio, USA. His adult life has followed a meandering path, ranging from working an automotive assembly line to designing space flight hardware. And through all of it, he's seen that life is a captivating and ultimately unexplainable endeavor. His writing seeks to add a splash of wonder to a world already awash in it.

* * *

For more information, please visit:

www.LakesideLetters.com

Have You Met Lin Finity?

She's the powerful star of her own series titled the Fringes Of Infinity. In the beginning, she's forced to learn how to control the unstoppable, magical power she earned at age fifteen. After killing her abusive uncle with her deadly new ability, she locked it away inside herself. Now, she's in her forties, and it's back. She calls it *Mayhem*. And it's done waiting.

Book One and the Novella are free in e-book format. Just visit https://www.LakesideLetters.com

Lin Finity And her Mayhem Rising
Lin Finity in Holding On

www.ingramcontent.com/pod-product-compliance
Lightning Source LLC
Chambersburg PA
CBHW021247200726
48288CB00015B/2569